THE BONE ORCHARD

The Bone Orchard

Joseph Trigoboff

A Blue Star Press Book

Walker & Co.
New York

Best Books for Public Libraries

First published in the United States of America in 1990
by Walker Publishing Company, Inc.
Published simultaneously in Canada by Thomas Allen & Son
Canada, Limited, Markham, Ontario

Library of Congress Cataloging-in-Publication Data
Joseph Trigoboff
The Bone Orchard / Joseph Trigoboff
ISBN 0-8027-5758-8
I. Title.
PS3570.R46B6 1990
813'.54—dc20   89-25028
CIP

Printed in the United States of America
2 4 6 8 10 9 7 5 3 1

To Kimberlee, of course.

A special thanks to Janet Hutchings, my editor, and Kevin McShane of Fifi Oscard, my agent.

THE BONE ORCHARD

$\bigtriangledown$

One

"I HATE THIS CITY. I have a dream about leaving here, but with my luck I'd end up in some idyllic New England town and my first day at the coroner's office there'd be two ax murders. But even if they were both chopped up like liver they'd have to look better than this guy. He's got to have more holes in him than the Yankee infield."

Detective Yablonsky looked, not entirely unsympathetically, at the corpus delicti. The body lay sprawled on the bed. The black mask that had hid its brilliantly handsome face was now resting alongside it. Withers had placed the mask there. The hands behind the back were still tied, a piece of black cord dangling and looped loosely around the deceased's wrists like a noose.

The killer had stuffed a gag inside the victim's mouth—a silk handkerchief, rolled into a gray little ball. Yablonsky could plainly see the shiny letter P. He knew it stood for Pierre Cardin. Death by design.

"He had good taste," Withers continued. Yablonsky wasn't sure whether Withers was talking about the victim or his killer. Withers, liaison man from the Medical Examiner's office for the past nine years, was able to empathize with everyone, murderer as well as victim. "Maybe one of

1

this poor shmuck's neighbors lowered the TV during a commercial and heard the screaming. The walls of these renovated apartments are so damned thin you can hear your neighbors arguing two buildings away. Pay attention, Yablonsky. The guy we're after is familiar with renovated yuppie apartments. Whoever killed this kid stuffed a gag in his mouth when usually a mask is enough to muffle screams. Therefore I'd say the killer lived in Manhattan."

Yablonsky wished he had Withers's unfeigned insouciance when faced with violent death. A detective for the past five years, Yablonsky had reached that point in his career where the display of disarrayed corpses no longer made him look sick in front of reporters and other detectives. As always when faced with violent death, he reached for a cigarette. It was the only time he smoked. He forced himself to reach into the victim's mouth and extract the handkerchief.

Withers was already bright-eyed with anticipation. "Our first clue." Although it was Withers's job to meet each detective at the scene of each murder and wait with the body until the stiffmobile from the Medical Examiner's office finally arrived, he considered himself something of a detective as well as a corpse valet. Whenever he was called to the scene of a murder he would cheerfully offer up his own conclusions to Yablonsky and the other detectives. Yablonsky was used to it. However, there were so many murders in Manhattan, and the ratio of cleared to uncleared cases was so meager, that he usually accepted help and advice from anyone. The thing about being a detective was that, unlike a cop, you seldom stopped a victim from being murdered. You were supposed to stare at corpses. Then you tried to catch the perpetrator. As a detective for the precinct that included jurisdiction over the United Nations, you could be used to fulfill a different function as well. Often, you didn't even try to solve a case, since diplomats could not be prosecuted. The reporter who interviewed him last week about the murder of a twelve-year-old girl, a case that Yablonsky knew he had little chance of solving, had claimed that the quality of detective work had lately been deteriorating. Yablonsky had answered back that the force was only trying to keep up with the times. His comment had not been printed.

The face of their most recent corpse could have been designed by Calvin Klein or Halston, Yablonsky reflected. Blond hair that fell about his forehead in ringlets; the kind of hair that never needed to be combed. Cleft chin. Jutting jaw. A face beloved by many mirrors.

Withers's voice was full of admiration as his eyes rested on a lower portion of the corpse's anatomy. "Now I know why they call them stiffs."

Yablonsky's eyes followed Withers's. The corpse valet was right. Even in death the piece of artillery between the victim's legs bulged out of the G-string. Until he had had the bad luck to meet the perpetrator and become the deceased, this guy must have had quite a fan club.

Yablonsky decided that the apartment was affluent looking, rather than affluent. Reproductions of Rothko and Stella had fallen to the carpet, the shattered glass shards from the frames mixing with blood and looking like brightly colored costume jewelry. Near the rear of the studio apartment was a set of Henredon cane chairs. One was upended and lay with its four legs resting against the burl-finished wall. The other chair was on its side, half of it sticking out from under a marble-topped dining table.

There was track lighting and a gaudy chandelier with glass that had been molded to resemble a Man in the Moon holding a spoon and tooting: a tribute to the now-defunct

Studio 54, a leftover from another era. The light on top of the chandelier tossed off different colors as it spun. Near the bathroom was a lamp shaped like a traffic signal, blinking its green and red warning. Levolor blinds blocked the afternoon sun.

Beside the bed on the carpeted floor was an enormous stereo, with stacks of albums beside it. Four huge speakers stood in different corners of the room. The kid must have been a dreamer, Yablonsky decided. All he had to do was bring his hand down from the bed, flick a dial, and he'd hear music.

Withers picked up a few albums and looked them over. It was obvious by his expression that he did not like the victim's taste. "Donna Summer. The Village People," he muttered. The man from the Medical Examiner's office looked unhappy, trying to solve a mystery that to him was more important than the murder. "Why was this kid still into disco?"

Yablonsky looked at the body and sighed. He might be incapable of stopping murder, but he was still capable of coming up with a solution. After all, he was a detective. "Maybe things were better for him then."

He thought of his tinny little non-quadraphonic Kenwood back home in his small apartment as he gazed sadly at the four massive speakers; for a moment he considered lifting them. Who'd be the wiser? The boy was now in disco heaven. From there the blast of the speakers would be dim indeed. On the other hand, the speakers would benefit Yablonsky immensely on earth. However, his superiors in the department did not share his humanitarian sentiments, so as usual he would have to control the corrupting impulses that occasionally tempted him. His own sporadic dishonest inclinations did not bother him anymore. He had watched the corruptibility gene functioning infallibly in his precinct for five years.

The rug on the floor was not the shag usually found in studio apartments like this, but Berber, wall-to-wall. Wall-to-wall carpeting was now a sign of wealth to Yablonsky. After his divorce and as a result of the settlement, his newly-made ex-wife had been able to furnish her two-bedroom home with two-inch-thick Kaufmann shag, wall-to-wall. Yablonsky had made all the appropriate compliments when, after their divorce became final, she had invited him over for a viewing.

Blood had soaked into the carpet. When Yablonsky had received the call from Studnick, the day watch, that sent him to this apartment on East 44th Street, Withers had met him at the doorway. In New York you had to run an obstacle course before you were allowed to reach the victim's side and begin your investigation. The super had refused to open the door, insisting they break it down, the way it was done on *Miami Vice.* Yablonsky, patiently explained that there was no need for excess violence and dramatics; this city already supplied enough. "At least you can enter with your gun," said the super. "I don't carry a gun," Yablonsky answered.

As a detective he had never needed one. Then finally, having earned the right to enter the apartment, even though he had tried to prepare himself, there was the initial shock and disbelief. Withers had recovered first. "The red matches the carpet nicely, doesn't it?" he'd asked.

Now Withers led him over to the walk-in closet and they peeked inside discreetly. Intruding into victim's apartments, viewing them disembodied and naked was everyday stuff; looking at their clothes, a violation of their privacy. Grasping the sliding door, Withers pushed. Inside were row upon row of neatly pressed suits, their labels displayed proudly like trophies. Hickey Freeman. Bill Blass. Three G. Perhaps after the deed, the killer didn't have the time or strength to lift them. Perhaps he didn't like designer clothes. Perhaps he already owned enough of them.

Withers glanced inquiringly at Yablonsky.

"They're not our size."

They moved away from the closet. Dozens of hardcover books were scattered throughout the room. Withers picked up one, leafed through it quickly, and tossed it on the floor. Yablonsky noticed that he didn't bother to look at the title.

"Hey Al," he said. "We got our second clue. At least we know he's not illiterate."

Yablonsky smiled. Another case solved by the diligent, caring corpse-sitter from the coroner. Withers always tried to see past Yablonsky's ineffectualness to the bright side of things. In the past year he and Yablonsky had seen seven murdered corpses together, and Yablonsky had managed to clear only two of them. It was not that he was a bad detective. It was just that there were so many corpses, and in a triage situation so little time could be devoted to matching each body with its murderer. As if in response to Yablonsky's helplessness, Withers had shrunk two inches in the past nine months. He had stiff joints and sciatica. He claimed that he was already beginning to resemble the corpses he babysat, whose murders Yablonsky rarely seemed able to solve.

Withers led Yablonsky back to the dead boy. After Yablonsky left, he would be its bodyguard until the photos and evidence gathering were finished. This time he was happy to stay behind at the scene of the crime. As soon as he had noticed that the corpse came with a mask and tied hands he had felt the case would have great media potential.

"Christ, look at the bod on him. He's in better shape dead

than I am alive. Look at those pecs. If the guy was straight he must have been a joy for any woman to behold." Withers shrugged. "I'll find all that out later anyway after forensic completes its examination of the tush." He pointed to the stab wounds that laced the body. "There's enough interior decorating here to keep a couch full of shrinks busy for months constructing theories as to motive. 'The methodical pattern of the stab wounds on the chest could mean that the killer was sexually repressed during adolescence. The deep, slashing wounds to the genital area point to an uneasy relationship with his mother.' And the pattern of those two lines of cocaine that must have spilled onto the carpet from the bed leads me to believe that after foreplay got a bit rough, the killer was trying to scoot with all the toot."

Yablonsky smiled at his "partner." He had expected this from Withers. When it came to analyzing Withers's modus operandi, he was a hell of a detective. His eyes focused on the drug paraphernalia. A necklace that held a tiny golden spoon and pendant lay beside the bed. Near the stash-cache on the carpet, a tiny thin line of cocaine slithered out from a white pile. A sizable white pile.

Draped over one of the four-foot speakers was a pair of jeans. Yablonsky could read the label from where he stood. *Guess?*

He turned to survey the carnage. He knew it wasn't so, but he felt as if the jeans had been deliberately placed there for him to read the label. A taunt that encompassed not only this body, but all his other failures.

The pockets of the jeans contained a silk handkerchief and a thin wallet. There could be a print on the wallet, so Yablonsky opened it carefully. Zero. No money. There was a Master card; Yablonsky noticed that it was plain and not gold. There was a photo of the victim that identified him as a member of the waiters' union. Another card said that *Sean Maysfield* had passed all courses and was now a licensed bartender. He showed it to Withers, who he knew would try to be ironic. Continually trying to be ironic must be the ultimate irony, Yablonsky thought.

"What a great day that must've been for him," Withers said.

The foldover part of the wallet contained a compartment, which Yablonsky opened. A large key ring was inside. He noticed that there were two keys on the ring. A Medeco. For the top lock. A standard type of key for the bottom lock. A key ring that size should have more than two keys. There were no other photos in the wallet. No driver's license. No other means of identification.

"Can I clean up in here now?"

Both men looked up. Rodriguez, the building's super, faced them. He was a thickset, short Puerto Rican with plastered-down hair that covered his ears and smelled faintly of pomade. He kept his sideburns clipped razor sharp. The arms that showed through the T-shirt were heavily muscled. He smiled and nodded at them in a friendly way. A long-handled broom and dustpan were by his side.

Rodriguez' eyes inspected the room. He's taking inventory, Yablonsky said to himself. He remembered. Rodriguez had not registered surprise when he saw the bloody corpse. The super was either disrespectful of the dead or indifferent to death.

"I got to clean up. This place is a mess."

Physically the place was mess, but for Yablonsky the room was full of other things too. When a man is murdered, every emotion he feels leading up to his murder—wet fear, hatred, and disbelief—becomes a distinct odor and mixes with the blood. It stays frozen and discernible in the room, like something solid. That smell of death had attracted Rodriguez, drawing him like a magnet to the apartment door, and then, knowing what was inside without even having to open it, to a phone to call the police. Why had that faint smell of murder only been recognizable to the super and not the rest of the tenants who passed through the hall? When Rodriguez had led them to the apartment earlier, he was eager to present his alibi. He assured them that he had spent the previous night running a floating poker game from a nearby basement. Patrolmen Sanders and Henderson were helping him run it and would back him up. He knows his men, Yablonsky thought. He would check Rodriguez' story with Sanders and Henderson, but sub rosa, of course.

Rodriguez cased the room. Looking for clues? Yablonsky asked himself. Rodriguez had spotted the white substance on the floor. That was no pile of Ajax. "I can start here first," he said.

He picked up the broom and dustpan and started across the room. "That's pertinent evidence," Withers said. "If you're not out of here in one minute I'll go over your nostrils with a spectroscope."

Withers took a step towards Rodriguez, who stood his ground.

Yablonsky raised his hand, and Withers backed off. He empathized with Rodriguez's plight. The powder on the floor was worth more than gold or silver. Scarfing even just some of it would have been better than winning the Lottery.

Yablonsky wanted to give the room another "see." Rodriguez stood in the door frame, watching both of them carefully and looking as if he were ready to send for the marines at the first hint of dishonesty. If he was'nt going to get a free noseful, he'd be damned if the detectives would.

"What do you think?" Withers asked.

"You saw the condition of the locks," Yablonsky said. "Forced entry, doubtful." He forced himself to stare at the wounds, feeling a little sick. He hated murder. The boy looked so young. Probably a seldom-employed actor, out waiting tables between appearances in soap operas.

"What do you think?" Withers repeated.

Yablonsky's eyes moved slowly from the body to the rest of the room, carefully studying it. Withers was just talking out of nervousness. Yablonsky rarely ventured method and motive until he had more time to think. Besides, even if the clues were printed on newspaper, Yablonsky doubted he would actually find the killer. Murders that were committed during domestic arguments or drunken brawls were relatively simple to solve because the murder itself was unpremeditated and therefore done clumsily. It was the high incidence of these kinds of murders that enabled the department to trumpet fairly impressive statistics of its cleared cases to the public. But in fact what Yablonsky and other detectives knew was that if the murderer killed with even the slightest hint of professionalism, he usually got away with it.

"I think it was a sex and drugs thing. Sex and drugs. All the way." Rodriguez's confidence was returning. He took a step closer to them.

Both men turned to look questioningly at the opinionated man. "You sure about that?' Withers asked sarcastically. "Anything we might have missed?"

Help from civilians was never threatening to Yablonsky. "What makes you think that, Carlos?" Was he actually about to get some information that would help him? That would be a change! "You don't look surprised or shocked by any of this."

"I'm not surprised one bit. Not with the kind of life those

boys led."

"You said 'those boys.'" Yablonsky waited patiently.

Rodriguez nodded. "He had a roommate. Up until a month ago anyway."

"Can you give us the name of the boyfriend?" Withers asked.

"I don't know if they was boyfriends," Rodriguez said. "They both seemed pretty macho to me."

"Do you think you might be able to remember the roommate's name?" Yablonsky asked.

"I don't remember names," Rodriguez said. "I only remember rent checks. All the rent checks were signed by *him*." He pointed to the body.

Rodriguez decided he had been helpful enough and slowly backed away. "I thought you wanted to be helpful, Carlos." Yablonsky said.

"I do want to be helpful. You want me to get you a six-pack?"

Both men shook their heads. However, Rodriguez was determined to at least try to maintain good political relations with the precinct. "You give me fifty and I lead you to the biggest cock-fighting ring this side of Cuba."

Yablonsky shook his head again. People were always trying to complicate his life by offering him additional crimes to investigate.

"No thanks, Carlos. What did this boy do for a living? Movies? Commercials?"

Rodriguez laughed. "Both of them were male strippers in an uptown club called O'Farrel's."

Yablonsky and Withers looked at each other, then at the naked body. "At last he died in his working clothes," Withers said.

Rodriguez left. Yablonsky wished he could put clothes on

the boy before the reporters and photographers arrived. The
least the poor shmuck was entitled to was a dignified death
pose.

In a somber mood, Yablonsky examined the slash
wounds. Though the boy had been stabbed, a knife had not
done the killing. He wondered if his hands were tied before
death or after. Was it an impulse murder? Were the cocaine
and the bondage equipment toys that fueled impulses during
a playtime that had gotten out of hand and led to murder?

He moved to examine the small, roll-top desk that was in
the alcove. Piles of letters. He would have to go through his
correspondence. Envelopes with faint postmarks were missing stamps. Yablonsky could picture this stripper feverishly
laying out twelve hundred dollars for a sound system that
would really move the walls back, and then peeling twenty-
five cent stamps off envelopes to economize. The young man
was probably part of one of the many groups in the city that
spent each night partying, popping, or peeling in the clubs
until early morning. Yablonsky considered them to be his
chief clientele. They lived fast but vulnerable lives and
furnished the city with many of its murder victims.

Yablonsky reached for the address book that was alongside the pile of letters. A trick book? He leafed through the
pages. *Mr. and Mrs. Andrew Maysfield. 112 Hendrickson Ave.
Oak Park, Illinois. 10652.* There was an inkstained asterisk.
Then a notation. *Their anniversary. Call Monday.*

Yablonsky showed it to Withers. "You'll have to notify his
parents," Withers said. He allowed himself a sigh. "*Call
Monday.* Some anniversary present."

"He doesn't give the date," Yablonsky said. "It could be
any Monday. He went through the pages carefully. "Friends
and relatives. It's not his trick book. No more asterisks," he
added ironically. The trick books he had seen had always

had notations concerning the personal tastes of their owners' clients. Most of these pages were disillusioningly blank and nonincriminating.

Was there anything in this apartment that could help him? He was about to continue his search when he noticed a young man standing in the doorway. He looked about twenty five . . . well dressed . . . well built . . .

"You his roommate?" Yablonsky was hopeful.

"Of course not," the boy snapped. "Rodriguez just phoned me. I'm the new tenant."

Withers looked puzzled, but Yablonsky immediately understood. In a city where the vacancy rate was less than two percent, people might not be willing to commit murder in order to find a Manhattan apartment, but there was no reason not to profit from one.

The young man looked at the corpse, then back at Yablonsky.

"When can I move in?"

"Not for at least three months. We have to seal the apartment."

"Three months? *Three months?*" He looked at them pleadingly. "Isn't there anything you can do to speed things up? I don't want to have to go back to Queens again."

Yablonsky, who lived in Brooklyn, understood. "I don't blame you."

A new thought must have occurred to the boy, because he looked even more anxious than before. Yablonsky realized that if this kid was twenty-five, then he was only ten years older than him. He was an old thirty-five.

"No one's been here earlier, have they? If I lose another apartment I'll die."

"Like him?" Withers asked.

The young man met his gaze. "Worse."

Yablonsky wanted the interrogation to end on a hopeful note.

"There's always the chance I might find his killer sooner than we expected."

"Always the chance," the young man echoed softly. "I doubt it."

"So do I," Withers said.

"No one was here before," Yablonsky assured him. "Rodriguez might be further down the hall. He's the man with the broom and dustpan."

The young man nodded and in an instant was gone.

There was really nothing more to do until the reports from forensic and the interrogation unit were in. Right now cops were questioning the tenants in the building as to what they saw, or to put it more accurately, what they didn't see. Bag ladies and derelicts who had emigrated from the west side of town to live off the streets of a more expensive neighborhood and store owners who were open late last night and may have noticed anything unusual, were all being questioned. Later on, the names in the address book would be checked. If any of them evolved into suspects, then their whereabouts would be looked into. Yablonsky doubted it, though. They were all out-of-town addresses.

Right now he knew exactly what his own modus operandi was going to be. Murder always brought out gourmet instincts that lurked within him. After satisfying those instincts, on to the precinct where he would hand in his report.

"I'll see you later," he said.

Withers nodded absent-mindedly. He looked preoccupied, already trying to devise quote lines for newspapers.

Yablonsky decided it was better to report to the precinct first. There would be more time that way to savor *tre agnoletti* or *pesce del giorno no. 1. Seafood mariscada* was also a worthy choice. He was too clever to frequent the very best restaurants in Manhattan, where the presence of a detective often brought the long-repressed foibles and guilt of the cognoscente to the surface, depressing them and giving them indigestion. He did his dining at the best of the second-tier New York restaurants, establishments that were content to complacently follow the trail their betters blazed. Imitators and trend followers, but with earnest and trustworthy selections, whose owners did not begrudge Yablonsky his frequent meals on the cuff. Eating good food instead of the usual cop slop was both remuneration for overseeing murder and a compromise between greater corruptions.

Withers waved at him dismissively. "See you at the next one."

Yablonsky was already out the door. Passing through the hall, he noticed Rodriguez talking to the guy who had been in the apartment before. The young man was handing Rodriguez five one-hundred-dollar bills.

"Welcome to my building," Rodriguez said. "I'll call you in three months."

Both of them ignored Yablonsky. Yablonsky thought it best to ignore them, but he felt a real pang of regret as he saw all that money going to Rodriguez. Once again money had ended up in someone else's pocket. Perhaps he was in the wrong business.

$\triangledown$

Two

THE PRECINCT HOUSE ON East 44th Street was a small building sandwiched between the Honorable Mission of the Republic of Mali and the Honorable Mission of the Republic of Mombassa. Compared to these two tall and angular buildings, the precinct house looked like it had been placed there as an afterthought. The Honorable Republics themselves were both dictatorships.

Yablonsky turned the corner, pushing on toward the precinct house. He had always believed that the political authorities who ordered the construction of precinct headquarters unconsciously wanted them built to resemble whatever neighborhood they resided in and supposedly had to protect. A station house constructed on Staten Island vaguely resembled the modern, colonial houses of the Mafia dons it stood near. The outside walls of the most recently built precinct house, off Christopher Street in Greenwich Village, were built smooth and even, as if the architect had unconsciously wanted them to be filled up with pro-gay graffiti and left-wing slogans. The police precincts in the burned out, largely deserted slums of East New York, Brooklyn and the South Bronx had been built into broad, squat squares that resembled forts, outposts that were situated on the wild frontiers of the city.

This precinct house did not look like a prison block. Its floors were not bare, but carpeted. Its restroom toilets did not grip the buttocks harshly or coldly, but with foam rubber. Most precincts had to grovel on their knees before politicians for additional funds. This precinct had had enough extra money to hire its own interior decorator to redesign the locker rooms. Other station houses always complained of noisy pipes and water-pressure problems. This precinct was the only one in the city with its own small gymnasium, complete with two stationary bikes, three Nautilus machines, and two tiny saunas. Like all precincts however, it was incapable of stopping the tidal waves of crime that engulfed the city; it merely tried its best to keep track of them by recording them.

Yablonsky started up the steps, nodding to the half-dozen reporters he was trying to avoid. They crowded around him and he was surrounded. Entrapment, he thought. He realized he would have to play the game.

Bob Anders of the *New York Post* asked, "Any statements to make about the stripper who got clipped last night?"

"A short one," Yablonsky. "The boy was killed sometime last evening. Method of death was stabbing. No suspects as of yet."

"No suspects," from Martina Christopher of the *News*. "Just corpses. The usual."

He turned to her. Her tone of voice sounded as if she were testing out familiar headlines of police incompetence. He had always given her easy access. Maybe she would give him a break. "Must you print that?"

She smiled at him. "No comment."

Bob Bracken, *ABC*. "We hear that the murder duplicated certain aspects of the Vesti slaying. Complete with mask and mutilizations."

An art student named Eigil Vesti had been murdered a few years back. That case had created sensation in a city usually satiated by sensation. That case had been solved, but not by him.

He shook his head, refusing to answer: anything he said could be used against him. They let him pass. He reached the precinct door, opened and closed it. He braced himself and waited, but they remained outside.

The precinct took no notice of his arrival. Murder was not news to cops: they filed their papers, ran their errands, waited to process the perps, dispassionately consoled victims.

Sanctuary.

He walked to the right, towards the detectives' squad room. Cops he passed nodded or waved "hiya's."

Yablonsky saw them all file in dutifully to the patrolmen's squad room. The lack of effectiveness of the police in fighting crime had been perceived by the public and noted by the media and politicians. As a result, anomie had set into the precinct force. Due to the high rate of recidivist criminals and something new, "recidivist victims," the precinct felt itself besieged by both criminals and public alike. If the force's function was no longer one of deterrence, but of simply recording already-committed crimes and murders, maybe there was little point in the police trying to do their jobs at all. The notion that major segments of society could believe that there was no longer any need for cops and detectives pained Yablonsky the most.

This was reputed to be one of the most highly trained and professional precincts in the city. Yet despite all the efforts it made, there were too many criminals to catch. Too many criminals, even when caught, went free. To counter the feeling of helplessness that gripped his precinct, Captain Larry "Noah" Flood came before the police commissioner with a clever proposal that liaison departments between the men and their superiors be established to help maintain police morale.

The commissioner had misheard him at first and thought that what Flood had said was that a department be set up to help maintain police *morals*. He blanched at that, but after Flood explained more fully, he gave enthusiastic approval. He added that if an improvement in morale was spotted by the media, he would see to it that these departments be set up in every precinct.

So Flood had had his bureaucratic victory and the department now had Deputy Coordinator Edwards, who had enough pull with one of the mistresses of a former police commissioner to make sure the job was delegated to him. Deputy Coordinator Edwards believed that he was destined to develop a yen for politics. As entry into the arena, sparking the morale of cops was strictly bottom turf, but it was his new job and he was determined to take it seriously, even if everyone else in the precinct was too discouraged to do so.

Yablonsky stood outside the room, just out of sight, and listened for a moment. Edwards's door was open. As always, his speech was a series of ellipses that were well-thought-out, emotional, and definitive sounding.

"Murders in this precinct have increased almost twofold since last year. The ratio of cleared to uncleared homicides is still the same, unfortunately. Reported assaults upon the street people have climbed eight percent. We suspect the unreported numbers are much higher. Nine people have been raped in the past two months, four women and five men." This precinct contained a large percentage of gays. Yablonsky heard some men snickering.

"In the last quarter we have seen a slight decrease in burglaries, I'm happy to report."

The reason behind this was so obvious Yablonsky was surprised that Edwards didn't see it. He risked a peek inside. Certainly the two dozen cops who sat with their chins dropping tiredly to their chest saw it. There was nothing left to steal. At least, he thought, the morale of whoever did most of the breaking and entering in the neighborhood must be high.

Edwards, by now thoroughly warmed up, at last had reached his main theme: the unity of the precinct in the face of a disunified world. "The increase in crime is a societal phenomena and not restricted to this precinct. According to sociologists there has been a general loosening of the moral fiber that holds society together. The decadence we experience in society"—at that the cops perked up, for many of them had not yet experienced this decadence—"is a result of the video generation of latchkey children. The point is, we should not take the difficulties we have in enforcing these currently lax laws personally.

"Some of you are surrendering to these pressures and committing impulsive, destructive acts. You already know that last week two patrolmen passed out drunk within the precinct building itself in front of a reporter. While we lucked out in that no photographers were present, some of you thought of these patrolmen as celebrities, before their two-week suspensions. Some of you are stealing barbells and weights from the exercise room and some of you are urinating into the whirlpools. There have been complaints from some of our female officers concerning sexual harassment. It seems that a few of you appropriated a drill from Supply and poked holes through the locker room and bathroom walls so that you would be able to invade their privacy. I assure you that these holes have been plugged. I realize you feel that you are a precinct besieged, but this is not the way to *unite*."

Yablonsky had been leaning against the wall alongside the door, perfectly concealed. He straightened. Even though he was a detective he was still expected to attend. But as tempting as it was to stay, it was time to leave. He could anticipate the speech's torrid ending.

Knowing his captain's habits, he was aware that Noah Flood had probably already been apprised of his presence within his precinct house and expected to be reported to forthwith.

He climbed the stairs. The locker room was filled with chatting patrolmen in various stages of undress. Some of them were eating sandwiches they had copped from the bar and grill around the corner on First Avenue. A few were lounging around drinking out of "flutes," coke bottles that were filled with beer. Others were gathered in a semicircle around a small round opening near the rear wall; the wall that separated the women's locker room from the men's. On the floor was a drill.

In the spirit of unity, each took a turn.

Vince Mazarella, desk sergeant, seeing Yablonsky, whispered, "Yabs, it's Ramos. Engaged in a strip search of her own person. Care to undertaken surveillance?"

He was tempted. Ramos was the precinct sexpot and he had not seen a naked woman since his divorce almost two years ago. During the last six months of their marriage, he had not even seen his *wife* naked. Was he in mourning? He was okay looking, but since he'd become single there had been no opportunities for a long-term relationship, and he was too terrified of getting AIDS to enjoy one-night stands.

Despite this involuntary period of celibacy, he was not desperate enough to become one of the boys. It was just a circle jerk without the masturbation.

He shook his head. "Flood must want to see me."

"We already heard about it," Mazarella said. "'Non-appreciative fan splits open stripper, retrieves his balls as souvenirs.'" He went back to what he was watching. "Now this is *real* burlesque."

It was time to see Captain Flood.

Yablonsky walked briskly toward his meeting. Larry "Noah" Flood had been the chief of detectives in the precinct for three years. It was the political pull of his wife, a friend of the mayor and an avid political contributor toward his many campaigns, that had gotten him his assignment. When Flood had first joined the department the detectives thought that his approach toward his job would be like most of the other political appointees they had seen. They expected him to mouth platitudes about law enforcement and assure them that there would be no place for politics in his precinct. He was expected to make the usual contribution to the department's decline by gradually evolving into whatever level of incompetency he discovered his detectives could live with.

Flood surprised them. He told each of them individually, "Of course I got my job through politics, but I assure you that I don't have that much pull. If my wife had had a deeper pocketbook the job of traffic coordinator for Manhattan would have been mine. Now that's a real sinecure."

As captain of this department, he had not been particularly effective in stopping crime, but what Yablonsky liked about him was that he was as polished and smooth in the ways of the world as a gold coin. He was an administrator, not a detective, and had no illusions about trying to be one. He knew his natural functions within the department and backed his detectives to the limit of the boundaries imposed on him by the governing authorities and interest groups. Whatever face he put on for the administration and political staffs that had appointed him, he said privately that idealism that refused to be ameliorated by experience was the greatest crime of all.

Yablonsky knew that Flood liked him. He had confessed to Yablonsky once that one small part of him was not saddened whenever there was an increase in murders because he knew that the increase meant he would inevitably see more of Yablonsky. Yablonsky felt that he would always look out for him. The men sometimes exchanged confidences. One year after Yablonsky's marriage had soured, he had come to Flood to tell him his troubles and Flood had dutifully suggested that he thought Yablonsky's dick was in danger of becoming a vestigial organ. As for Flood's own marriage, because it was one of the few among precinct captains that was not foundering, he claimed, typically, it must be troubled.

He looked up as Yablonsky entered his office, pretending to be surprised to see him. "That asshole's not finished with his speech yet. Why are you here?"

"I've heard the speech before."

Flood nodded. "So have I. Just give me another minute, Al." He turned back to the stack of papers on his right. Yablonsky saw him studying the papers intently, occasionally making short notes to himself in the margins. He crossed things out, started writing again. At last he looked up wearily. "Another gift from our friends at the UN. A delegate from one of the African countries was caught using slugs in the subway turnstile on Lexington and 42nd. Drunk, he assaulted the nearest passerby, a forty-three-year-old woman who suffered a black eye, cuts to the face, and bruises on the arms. The arresting cop was transit, but he knew the rules. I've already been in touch with the Mission. They expect us to respond in the usual way. I think I can get "assault" changed to verbal harassment. If I lie enough, I can whittle the drunkenness charge down to a disorderly. Transit will swear the victim was cut and bruised because she slipped." He paused. "Of course I had to contact Stoller of Central Intelligence and Whitney at Federal to apprise them of this latest wrinkle in diplomatic relations. Meanwhile, the Mission's chief delegate is still carrying drugs into this country by diplomatic pouch." He pointed to the topmost report on the stack of papers on his left. "Domestic news is not that much better. A year ago a twenty-year-old girl is raped by an ex-con who is out on parole. He gives her AIDS. His attorney successfully petitions the court that his client is too ill with AIDS to be sent to jail and he's let go." He shook his head with disbelief. "American justice."

"It's not that bad," cried Yablonsky.

Flood laughed sardonically. "I'll bet you that as bad as you think it is, it's worse." He forced himself to be calm. "Okay, here's what I have for you on the home front." He reached for the sheaf of papers directly in front of him, glanced briefly at each, the handed Yablonsky the preliminary reports of both the Medical Examiner and the patrolman who made the "discovery."

Yablonsky's eyes widened. "So fast?"

Flood nodded. "Ever since the Medical Examiner was dismissed during the last investigation, his replacement's been busting his balls to get these reports to us in half the time of his predecessor. It's almost as if he goes through each corpse, accompanied by a secretary taking shorthand." He looked up at Yablonsky thoughtfully, his voice unaccustomedly gentle. "Of course, department investigations aren't the end of the world."

Yablonsky read through each report, mentally noting the salient points:

From the office of the Chief Medical Examiner. Submitted by W. Blochner, Acting Chief.

Yablonsky noticed the title, Acting Chief. A salient point.

Murder victim is a caucasian male, approximately twenty-five years old. Weight - 165. Height - 5'11". Decedent appeared to be in excellent physical condition at time of death. Multiple contusions were found throughout the chest and abdominal regions. Analysis revealed that the wounds were not made by a knife or knives but by a wedge-shaped implement such as a letter opener. Two of the wounds were inflicted while victim was alive. All the others, after death. Victim's hands were tied and a mask placed over his head before death. Time of death: estimated to be between 1:00 A.M. and 3:00 A.M. on April 6.

"Toxicology doesn't even note the amount of drugs in the bloodstream," Yablonsky said. "He must be writing on the run."

"Who has the time these days to devote full attention to just one murder victim? This is a busy city. At least he died while he was high. Sometime between David Letterman and Joe Franklin," Flood added unhappily.

Flood was addicted to late night TV. It was upsetting to him to realize that someone could be murdered while he was watching his favorite program. Yablonsky read the report from Discovery.

At 7:30 in the morning of April 7, Patrolman Jacobs received a radio call from the precinct that he should proceed to 226 East 44th Street, a brownstone walkup. The call to the precinct had been placed by building superintendent Rodriguez, who had reason to believe that a murder was committed in one of his apartments on the third floor.

Patrolman Jacobs was able to discern a faint odor of blood from outside the apartment.

Except for a mask that had been placed over his head, the victim was naked. His hands were tied behind his back. Leather rope. Black leather mask. Cause of death believed to be from multiple stab wounds.

Subsequent investigation revealed that the victim's name was Sean Maysfield. Age twenty-five. Employed at O'Farrel's, an exclusive club on the Upper East Side.

Trace's of cocaine were found in the victim's hair and on the mask. We took fingerprints from the bed frame and stereo. All were victim's. No latents.

Subsequent investigation in the apt. revealed that the door lock had not been broken or forced open, indicating that victim may have known his killer. The window blinds were drawn. We were unable to determine whether it was victim's habit to sleep with drawn window blinds. If we had been able to ascertain that perpetrator had drawn the blinds upon entering the apt., we could have assumed the crime was premeditated.

Large amounts of cocaine were found on the floor. Estimated amount fifteen ounces. Estimated street value: $15,000. We checked the closets, under the rug, and in the bathroom and kitchen but were unable to discover any more cocaine. Small amounts of marijuana were found in the victim's night-table drawer. Upon entering the apt. we turned the stereo off. Therefore we know that it must have been playing during the victim's death. Victim had large collections of records and clothes. Many of the records were autographed. Subsequent interrogations of tenants revealed that the victim often played his records and tapes loudly late into the night.

No one in the building heard any sounds of struggle. Interrogations of storeowners and street people in the neighborhood revealed no unusual occurrences on the night of the murder.

Flood filed his own copies of the reports inside a desk drawer. "The newspaper and network reporters are already calling it *'The Murder of the Man in the Mask.'* They're making it look like a tug of war over some cocaine, combined with a little weenie whacking. Do you think the crime was drug related?"

"No."

"You're the detective. Why not?"

"If the struggle was over the coke, why was so much of it left behind? Maybe whoever killed Sean wanted it to look like a drug hit."

"Do you think entry was forced?"

"I think the killer and victim knew each other."

"Why?"

"Sean was in great physical shape. Who'd be capable of forcing his way in past him? I think he let his killer in, then was taken by surprise."

"He took him by surprise," Flood repeated.

"It could be a woman."

Flood laughed. "Did you see how brutal that homicide was? Women don't kill that way."

Yablonsky smiled. "You're not a modern man, captain."

"You know, the media people have already decided that this case is one of the important ones."

"By important, you mean sensational," Yablonsky said.

Flood shrugged. "The ratio of time we can spend on a case is directly determined by the amount of time the media and therefore the police commissioner devote to it. That's the way it is. Anyway, give the killer his due. It is a sensational homicide."

That was true enough, Yablonsky thought. Anything that had to do with sex was sensational. Right now he was trying to solve half a dozen murders. Adding this to his caseload meant that after four months of work he would probably solve none of them.

"Put everything else you're working on, on hold." He gave Yablonsky a sympathetic look. "That has to be of some help to you."

Yablonsky thought of Dorrie Stevens, age seven, found inside one of the subway tunnels between 42nd and 50th Streets. Her clothes had been torn off, her tiny body almost crushed and twisted beyond recognition. James Ruth, a doorman, had been struck by a hit-and-run driver at the intersection of his luxury building at York Avenue and 61st while attempting to help two tenants out of a taxi. His legs were crushed, permanently crippled. Billie and Mavis Green's bodies were discovered in the back seat of an abandoned Toyota, throats cut. The car had been put up on cinderblocks. Whoever had stripped the car of its tires, engine, transmission, and radio had ignored the bodies, which were in plain sight. Because time was so tight, he supposed that with some creative writing on the part of Discovery, the case could be cleared by making the double murder appear to be a double suicide. The body of Paul Dennis had been found propped up on a gate of one of the auxiliary roads of the 59th Street bridge. The naked body, showing signs of deep hematomas and soft-tissue injuries on the soles of its feet, had plainly been moved. Yablonsky suspected that the Queens precinct had dragged the body west. That way the Manhattan side would have jurisdiction over it. The same policeman who had discovered the Greens was on his way home last week when he had the misfortune to have his Honda swallowed by one of the giant potholes on 55th Street and First Avenue. The tow truck hoisted his car out. While in the act of bending over to gaze disbelievingly at the pothole's size, he found a body lying in one of its crevices. After the department cleared him of running over the victim, it was determined by Discovery that the victim was a white female of approximately sixty-five years, identity unknown.

Yablonsky faced the prospect of four months of work put on hold. Even if he cleared the case, all his unsolved murders would still be waiting for him, unless he begged Flood to shift his caseload to other detectives.

Before he could begin bargaining, Flood said, "Unfortunately, every other detective is as overworked as you." He did not wait for a response. "Actually, when given enough time, you've shown you can be a fairy competent detective. You've just had a run of back luck, that's all."

"I assume I'll be on this one by myself."

Flood dipped into his desk for his briar pipe. When he became overburdened, he would occasionally puff away for a few minutes. As vices went, it was relatively harmless. He lit the pipe. "I assume I won't have to go into why you work by yourself."

Nothing more had to be said. Other detectives were afraid to work with him, despite his abilities. He had been a great plainclothes cop. No one could point a finger of blame at him. Perhaps life with him in plainclothes proved to be too real for the average soul to withstand. Or perhaps Flood was right and it was simply a run of back luck, but strange things seemed to happen to his partners. The decoy cop who was working a prostitutes' stroll with him quit the department after six months to become a real hooker. A cop who worked traffic with him to nail drunken drivers was sober when he cracked up his car. A detective he penetrated a horse theft ring with to search for ringers now spent most of his time at Aqueduct. Then of course, there was what happened to Dwyer . . . Yablonsky knew he *was* a good detective. After all, they had promoted him. It was just that people were a little leery of working with him now. Working alone had made him resourceful.

Flood's eyes narrowed shrewdly. "What I like about you is that you don't necessarily have to solve a case to get results. You're creative. That car-parts theft ring in Murray Hill that no one was able to stop? You were in plainclothes then. Theft of auto parts dropped forty percent once you were assigned there."

None of his great detective skills had come into play in breaking up the car ring. It was just that he was able to use a quality very few modern detectives possessed but he had in abundance: patience. He did not pound the pavement in a fruitless search for clues. He already knew he would never be able to catch them in the act. He simply figured out the places they were most likely to drive the cars to and waited. By hanging around the garages on Eleventh Avenue, he easily spotted the gang that was involved. He knew them. They had all done time for auto theft before, and he knew that the slim chance of serving more time was a meaningless deterrent to them. The ring was broken up because one night he decided to short-circuit their own auto burglar alarms, then drive their cars into the same chop shops which they had used, where their own cars were disassembled and sold for spare parts. They got the message.

"Captain, most of the men in this precinct have cleared more cases than I have. Why choose me?"

"I'm all too aware of your limitations, Yablonsky. But most of my other detectives are too uptight to deal with the types of characters they'll meet during this kind of investigation. You know how to get along with the press. Shit, you can get along with anybody. That's what I need now."

Yablonsky, expecting to be dismissed, was surprised when he wasn't. He watched Flood slowly pour tobacco from another pouch, press it into his pipe, and tap the pipe against his desk. It was a ritual Flood employed when he had bad news for one of his detectives.

Yablonsky straightened in his chair, tried to meet Flood's direct gaze, and failed.

"Internal Affairs has decided to make you the subject of one of its investigations."

Fear gripped his stomach. He forced himself to respond. "An investigation?"

"Into your eating habits. I've warned you before about your gourmet yearnings. Every other cop stuffs sandwiches into his mouth. You spend most of your off-hours in credit-card restaurants as if you're Craig Claiborne. There was bound to be talk."

There was real anguish in Yablonsky's voice. "Is an investigation really necessary?"

"They feel it is. They're sending over one of their shooflies. He'll supposedly keep an eye on you, in between his own free lunches."

Of all the venal acts, in this precinct filled with venality, they had decided to focus on his. Maybe his ex-wife was right. Minor-league corruption was far more dangerous than the major.

"It's all politics," he said bitterly. The problem was, he had never befriended anyone with really deep pockets.

"It's always 'all politics,'" Flood said. "You're lucky I was able to warn you. Change your eating habits for the next couple of weeks, and they'll probably have nothing to pin on you."

He got control of himself. Certainly the owners and maître d's of the restaurants he had *formerly* eaten in would say nothing. They all liked him, despite the occasional nibbles of free food. Every owner who fed him knew he had been placed under Yablonsky's personal protection. A couple of weeks of anorexia, and he might be able to squeak through.

Before there could even be an awkward silence, Flood said, "I was downtown the other day on my way to Police Plaza. You'll never guess who I bumped into. Dwyer. He asked about you."

"Another one of my successes," Yablonsky said bitterly. After two years as a cop, he had been assigned to the UN Security Task Force. Dwyer had been his partner. He had also been his teacher. Yablonsky had felt closer to him than to his wife. He had been a great cop. Now he was chief of security for a bank.

Flood seemed genuinely surprised at Yablonsky's reaction. His voice showed his concern. "I wasn't with you in the precinct at the time. But I heard about it, of course. You were barely a rookie. I would have done the same thing."

"Maybe."

"You saved his ass. I got the impression he was grateful."

Yablonsky saw Dwyer only occasionally now, but still felt close to him. How Dwyer felt about him, he could still not really say. The man did not seem bitter. But grateful? Yablonsky knew better.

He took the reports and left. Through the office window, he saw that Flood was already reaching for another stack of investigative reports.

His own desk was much neater than Flood's, but he felt he usually had just as much work. He shoved the paperwork for his other six cases into the pending section, then looked over the new reports, deciding on priorities.

The first thing he did was place the obligatory call to the boy's parents. The cop who had discovered the body had also found another picture of the boy. Clothed, he looked like he had just graduated from a top-flight eastern college. Before the lure of show business, probably he had.

"Mr. Maysfield?"

He heard a man's voice ask what he wanted.

"This is detective Yablonsky of the Twenty-first Precinct in New York." He always paused before he delivered the by-now familiar line to signal to the person at the other end that he had bad news. "I'm very sorry to have to tell you this, sir. Last night your son was murdered."

There was silence on the other end of the phone. Then the man's voice, unemotional. "I'm sorry my son is dead. What day is today?"

"April seventh."

"Last Easter I told him he'd be killed if he moved to your city."

"Will you arrange for a funeral here, sir? Or should we ship his body back home to you?"

The voice at the other end spoke calmly. "Neither. My son was into drugs and promiscuous sex, Mr. Yablonsky. I expected to hear this kind of news eventually. Now I won't have to count the days on my calendar anymore." There was a long silence. Then the man began to cry. The phone clicked.

The people who benefit the most from his death should bury him, Yablonsky thought. The reporters. He would ship the body back.

There were pool tables in the precinct's lounge, a clock radio, and a projection screen TV, the kind the bars had. Most of the cops were gathered on couches around the TV, jeering at the assembled group of male strippers. A reporter must have gotten hold of some of them and was standing outside of O'Farrel's, interviewing them.

They stood on the street in the mild spring weather, barechested, their outfits completed by tight satin pants and matching blue bowties. "They're wearing formal clothes for the interview," one of the cops yelled out.

Mazarella, back from his surveillance of patrolwoman Ramos, turned to Yablonsky. "Most of the guys are really impotent, aren't they, Al?"

Yablonsky smiled. "Wishful thinking."

The cops laughed. The reporter asked one of them if, being Sean's ex-roommate, he could tell them something about him. The camera focused in. The young man's pectorals filled the screen. "Sean was a gentle person. His dancing made many people happy."

"Nijinsky," Jenkins shouted. The roommate slipped back into line. The reporters continued questioning the others. Strong. Sleek. Atlases, all of them. "They're perfect targets," Mazarella said. He took out his police revolver and pointed it at the screen. He pretended to pull the trigger. "There goes another one."

Yablonsky closed the precinct door and stood outside. The reporters were gone. He began to head toward the nearest restaurant, then stopped himself. It was lucky for him that he remembered in time. He peered at the Sabrette hot-dog stand on the corner. Was this what he had to resign himself to? He surveyed the street, hoping the shoofly was not aware that Yablonsky was watching out for him. He sighed at the unfairness of it all, then started toward his car. He had to be careful. He was now a wanted man.

$\bigtriangledown$

Three

THE EIGHT O'CLOCK SHOW would not begin for another two hours, yet women were already lined up outside O'Farrel's.

Two guys, obviously dancers, given their physiques, walked past the line of women toward the door. Hands reached out to touch their bodies.

"Not yet," one of the guys laughed.

Yablonsky stood alongside the line. The other dancer looked him over curiously, for men were usually not allowed in before twelve o'clock. Yablonsky overheard him say, "God, they're really desperate tonight."

The doormen were dressed in the same outfits they had worn for their TV interviews. They were enormous-looking men, as big as professional wrestlers, and in costume Yablonsky supposed they could pass for them. Like all men in their thirties for whom it was now sufficient merely to stay "in shape," he felt stabs of envy.

He walked toward them, conscious that there were no feminine hands reaching out for his body.

The doormen took one look at him and instantly placed him. "Security enters around the back," one of them said.

Yablonsky laughed and flashed his badge. "I'm from homicide. You don't mind if I ask you a few questions?"

"Ask away."

"Did Sean Maysfield leave with anyone the night he was murdered?"

One of them shook his head. "I couldn't say." The other guy nodded meaningfully at the waiting line. "It gets pretty hectic around here. We don't notice things like that."

Yablonsky would be patient. There was plenty of time to find out the things he needed to know. "Did he ever leave with anyone?"

The other doorman laughed. "He was like all of us. He had an active libido. And plenty of opportunities."

So they did notice things like that. The one who had just spoken looked at Yablonsky anxiously. "We're not murder suspects, are we?"

"No way," Yablonsky said. He looked enviously at the throng of women. He tried to imagine how they would all look naked. "When would you find the time?"

He stepped past them into the club. A number of people, dressed in tuxes and formal evening gowns, worked behind the coat racks. A tray of cocktail franks was on the hat-check counter. Free hors d'oeuvres. Yablonsky lifted a couple. Force of habit. Was the shoofly following him? He'd have to dispose of the evidence quickly.

The gods and goddesses inside the checkroom looked him over curiously. Was he a cop? Or from the press? As he showed them his badge he sensed their disappointment. The press was always accompanied by photographers.

He walked down a corridor. The main room was a whirling blur of black with gleaming stars, throbbing lights, and music. The stage where the men performed was in the center, the main attraction inside this man-made planetarium.

Yablonsky was dazed by it all for a moment. Everything glittered like liquid gold: slick, polished, professional. The bar that was opposite the stage was as tall and thick as the walls of a fortress. Yablonsky recognized it. It had belonged to a club that had refused to admit women and was now defunct. Inside an aquarium behind the bar, multicolored fish swam in and out of jutting reefs. Water music.

The customers were still outside. Yablonsky noticed a dozen men lounging around. Some had taken drinks to the couches that lined the stage and sat around bullshitting like athletes in a locker room before the game. Two of the six men on stage wore tight leather pants and jackets that showed half their chests. Another three were dressed in Hawaiian shirts, sunglasses, and bermuda shorts, with suggestively long cigars jutting out of their mouths. The last dancer was cross-dressed in a platinum wig, a tight crimson dress, and a wraparound fur boa. At the rear of the stage, there was a set of paintings of cloud-strewn hills, movie theaters, palm trees, and a Mercedes. Scenes out of Hollywood.

Leaning against a couch on the lowest level alongside the stage, a woman stood, looking up at the dancers. Yablonsky imagined what the view from there must be like.

"Remember to flash your equipment, boys. The name of the show is Seventy-seven Sunset *Strip*. Those women will want it all."

The men laughed. Since she was the only woman inside the club's main room, Yablonsky figured she had to be in charge.

Yablonsky approached. She looked like she was in her late twenties. Ballet-dancer thin, with long, graceful fingers. "Are you the manager?" he asked.

She glanced up at him. "You're not suitable for dancing here. Try another club."

"I'm from homicide."

She was surprised. "Cops hassle us all the time. You look

too nice to be a detective."

"I'd like to ask you some questions about Sean."

"I really can't believe it. You dress better than most of them, too. Only a year behind the times."

On stage one of the dancers in sunglasses was mouthing a Tom Jones song.

"He lip-syncs during cunnilingus too," she said. She turned back to Yablonsky. "I run a legitimate business. The cops who come here insult my dancers. Make rude remarks. Question their sexuality."

"Only a man pretty confident about his sexuality could wear outfits like that. How long did Sean work here?"'

"A year . . . Every media person who covers this murder does nothing but emphasize its sensational aspects. My dancers are anxious, lieutenant, and so am I. Would you like having your profession denigrated?"

Yablonsky stepped up on the stage, realized what it was, and awkwardly got off. "Sean had a roommate, didn't he?"

She pointed to the stage with her chin. "Paul. He's up there. The one who's dressed like a Santa Monica Boulevard hustler."

The outfit Paul was wearing looked pretty sensational to him. Yablonsky turned back to the manager. "Why'd they split?" He paused. "A lover's quarrel?"

I'm not their den mother, lieutenant. I don't know what they did with their cocks."

"Were they dealing?"

"I don't know what they did with their nostrils either. Ask them . . . What the hell is wrong with women wanting to get together and enjoy themselves?"

"Not a thing. Did Sean ever quarrel with anyone at the club?"

"He was a wonderful boy . Women loved him."

"Did you?"

"I made love to him, lieutenant. A year ago. When he first started here." She smiled at him. "He was naive enough to think that sleeping with the boss would advance his career. Where could his "career" have gone? But I don't exploit these guys. If some of them want to add to their salaries by making money horizontally, that's their business so long as it goes on outside my club."

"I see."

"You know, the media accuses me of creating an atmosphere that could encourage violence against these guys . . . But doesn't a woman have as much right to enjoy herself as a man?"

His wife had asked him the same question before cuckolding him. "Absolutely," he said.

"I work my buttocks off to make a success of this place. I'm here practically twenty-four hours a day. I was here with my bar boys till five in the morning the night Sean was killed."

"I believe you," Yablonsky said. "I'd like to question the others now." He had thought the interrogation was over, but he could see that she was not finished with him. It was the ultimate irony in his life: a possible suspect grilling the investigating detective.

"Be my guest. One more thing, lieutenant. Women enjoy my club, they say I'm a pioneer, but they don't like the sensationalism and publicity. Murder is bad for business. Especially a brutal murder. I hope you catch the guy who snuffed Sean, fast."

"Maybe it was one of those women who killed him," Yablonsky said.

She laughed harshly. "Men commit most of the murders in this world, lieutenant. You're a pretty lousy sex."

By now, he was sure that the dancers knew who he was.

He motioned with his hand. The guys behind the bar came over.

Paul sat on the lip of the stage, the others moved to group protectively around him. Blonds. Brunets. Redheads. Heavily muscled. Some in costumes. The two guys who tended bar barechested wore black leather tights that bulged around the crotch. If what was inside their tights was real, and not stuffed socks or tissue paper, they were eminently qualified for their jobs.

He watched them slip nervous smiles onto their faces as easily as they probably slipped out of their clothes. It was not often he had the chance to make people feel less guilty. "Relax," he said, smiling. "After I finish with my questioning, none of you will be detained. So far, none of you are suspects."

They looked at him in shock and disbelief. One of them stared questioningly at Paul. Paul appeared to be the only one of them who wasn't nervous. Yablonsky made a slight, negative gesture to the boy. He understood. After the detective finished with them, he was expected to stay behind for further questioning. A blond lounging against the stage ramp said, "But lieutenant, one of us could still have killed Sean. Maybe out of anger. Or during a struggle over the cocaine."

"I have the feeling that most of you engage in illegal activities outside this club," Yablonsky said. "It wouldn't make sense for any of you to kill Sean. I doubt any of you would want to be placed under our surveillance."

In the silence that followed, he continued. "If the murder was a sexual killing, none of you would have left the mask behind, because you'd know its presence would immediately connect you to the case. If it was over the cocaine, then why was so much of it left behind in the apartment?" As a detective, Yablonsky had often seen this kind of reaction.

Because people were guilty of so many petty crimes, they were suspicious of a cop who wanted to clear them of a major one. They still believed that at least one of them was capable of murder. Perhaps the strippers were a better judge of human nature than he was.

"Were any of you with Sean the night he was murdered?"

They shook their heads. The detective said, "A cop will be here and take your written statements as to where you were that night, and then check them."

One of them spoke up. His hair was reddish, and his face was covered with pale freckles. He was as heavily muscled as the others, but much shorter, thinner too. Yablonsky could tell by his costume that he tended bar, but did not actually dance. The runt of the litter.

There was a hint of defiance in the runt's eyes. "My name is Bobbi," he said. "Many of us might be engaged in some of those activities you talked about before." He hesitated. "Suppose the only alibi we have is that the person we were with that night was married? It's not considered good ethics here to furnish cops with their names."

Yablonsky gave him a look, then shrugged. "Murder's more important than infidelity. If clearing you of suspicion of murder violates your high code of ethics, tough shit."

The runt's eyes narrowed. He looked like he was about to say something, then thought better of it.

"One more question," Yablonsky said. "Do any of you know someone who might have wanted to kill Sean?"

A chorus of negatively shaking heads. Had Paul given Bobbi a quick glance? Bartenders were the recipients of gossip. He made a mental note to speak to Bobbi later.

After Yablonsky dismissed the others he found himself alone with Paul. The dancer looked at his Rolex. "I'm afraid this will have to be short, lieutenant. I go on stage in an hour." He pointed to his perfectly sculpted face and smiled. "Makeup and costume. But hey, hang around here for a while. The first break I get, I guarantee I'll find the time to talk to you. Hell, I'll *make* the time, that's a promise."

"The problem with that, Paul, is I'm pressed for time."

A sympathetic look. "I know how difficult your work is, lieutenant." Yablonsky watched patiently as the boy's features set. As if he had come to a decision. "Okay. I guess I can cooperate with the police. I know how hard you guys work. Jesus, there's probably more legwork in your job than ours. Ask me anything. I'll answer as honestly as I know how."

That's the problem, Yablonsky thought. "Why did Sean and you become roommates?" He paused. "Did you finally find your Mr. Right?"

"I'm straight as an arrow, lieutenant."

"As an arrow," Yablonsky repeated. It was the first time he had ever interrogated a bodybuilding male stripper. Massive chest, shaved and gleaming with perspiration. Tree-trunk-sized legs and arms. The boy appeared to be supremely confident. Invulnerable. No reason to be afraid. Yablonsky would bring up the missing keys, and why he thought Paul might have reason to be afraid. But later. Right now he wanted other kinds of information.

"How long were you roommates?"

"We met at the club. Moved in about a year ago with each other to save on the rent. I swear that's the truth, lieutenant."

"When did you move out?"

"About a month ago."

"Why?" Again a delicate pause. "Lovers' quarrel?"

"Of course not. You've already guessed that we occasionally bring women home to party with. It was more convenient having separate apartments."

That was plausible. "A large amount of cocaine was discovered in Sean's apartment. Paul, how deeply was he involved in drugs?"

"Jesus, lieutenant. You told us before that you didn't believe Sean's murder was drug related. I'm being honest with you, but you've got to be honest with me."

Yablonsky explained. "Obviously, the person who killed Sean left the drugs there for a reason. Whether Sean was killed because of drugs or not, he had to be involved with some people who were. What were those parties of yours like?"

"We have fun with the women, lieutenant. It may not be good clean fun, but they enjoy themselves. If I told you that on occasion we smoked pot and snorted a few lines, you wouldn't arrest me, would you?"

"I've already assured you I wouldn't."

He looked Yablonsky directly in the eye and smiled. "Then I confess. Sometimes we supplied the cocaine, sometimes they had it. But it was usually only a line or two."

"Who were your sources?"

He shrugged. "We'd get it at parties. Or outside the club. No self-respecting stripper would be caught dead without some. The stuff's like currency, lieutenant, easily circulated. We never bought from just one person. We never had to. You have to admit I'm helping you now."

"Yes, you are," Yablonsky said. "Who do you think killed Sean?"

For a moment Paul looked as if he were deep in thought. "Maybe it was a fan," he said at last. "Many of the women who come here develop attachments to us. Each of them has her own favorites." He nodded decisively. "I think it was a jealous fan."

"Somehow I don't think it was a jealous fan, Paul."

"Okay. But only because I think I can trust you." He leaned forward, as if betraying a treasured confidence. "Don't let the brotherly act here fool you. All the dancers here are extremely competitive with each other and Sean was one of the main attractions. Maybe he was killed because of professional jealousy."

Yablonsky appeared to consider the matter seriously before discarding it. "That's probably not it either, Paul. Try again?"

Paul paused for a minute, rubbing perspiration deep into his cheek. The whole texture of his face changed, became smooth and shiny. "Don't blame me, lieutenant. The only reason I'm throwing out these ideas to you is because you keep insisting that I should be helpful. I don't know who killed Sean."

"I think you do. You're just not ready to tell me yet."

The boy shook his head confidently. "I can't tell you what I don't know." He showed Yablonsky his Rolex again. "They expect me on stage in half an hour. Makeup, lieutenant," he reminded him.

Yablonsky flashed his Timex. "You really look much better without makeup, Paul. Stay just a while longer."

"But I've got to change into another outfit, lieutenant. Otherwise I fuck up the show."

"What you're wearing now is very attractive," Yablonsky said. He didn't want to tell this to Paul, but the interrogation was almost over. Why was this "helpful" hustler being so evasive? Unless you resorted to tactics that were from the Middle Ages, you couldn't force people to tell you what you wanted to know. You had to show them you were willing to be patient with them. Eventually, when they felt it was in their best interest, they would tell him what it was they were concealing.

Yablonsky watched Paul as he pretended to be absorbed for a while by the ceiling's decor. "Are you going to pin Sean's death on me because I'm a stripper?"

Yablonsky's features were impassive. Actually, he had decided that Paul was probably not a suspect the moment he saw him. In Yablonsky's experience, the average person, unlike the professional killer, reacts with shock after he kills. He may have killed out of anger, jealousy, or drunkenness. The victim might be a acquaintance or a stranger. The average person usually reacted in the same way. His shock was not from having killed—not even from being caught. The shock came when, after being asked the usual police questions—*What had gotten into him? Why had he killed?*—he realized that nothing had gotten into him that was not already there before. Paul's reaction and appearance were similar to the others. He did not look like a sufferer from post-murder trauma.

Yablonsky wondered if he should keep the boy in suspense. Give him even more of a reason to rub perspiration into his handsome face. He continued to be silent for a moment, then his conscience got the better of him. "No," he admitted. "I don't think you killed him."

"That's a relief. You know, lieutenant, a guy can make a few mistakes in his life, but still consider himself basically honest."

Yablonsky thought about himself. "I can understand that, Paul."

"I'm glad we agree. I loved Sean. Like a brother," he added quickly. "But he's dead and I've got a life to get back into."

"I admire your inner strength," Yablonsky said. At least the boy had confirmed one of his suspicions. The interrogation wasn't a total loss. "You don't know anyone who might have wanted to kill him?"

"Not a soul. You know I'm on your side, lieutenant."

"I appreciate that, Paul." A delicate pause. "You're not frightened at all, are you?"

The stripper folded his huge arms against his chest. "Why should I be frightened?"

"We think that the person who murdered Sean may have stolen one of his door keys. So he just might have a plan to enter another apartment."

Paul laughed. "No one wants to kill me, lieutenant."

"No reason to be scared?"

The arms that flexed before Yablonsky were massive. Before these powerful instruments, danger must dissipate like dust in a storm. The eyes that stared at him were serene. "I live the kind of life that other men envy, lieutenant. To a woman I'm a fantasy come true. I consider myself a lucky man."

Yablonsky stood. "I might have to question you again."

"I'll be here, lieutenant. Good luck." He waved to him.

Yablonsky gave him a small wave back. "Stay lucky yourself, Paul. That's really a nice outfit."

The boy looked pleased. "I designed it myself. I design all my costumes. You'll have my fullest cooperation. As always."

Before he left, Yablonsky decided to pass by the bar. As Bobbi saw him, he straightened and dropped his elbows to the elegant polished wood. He held out an already-filled glass.

Since the drink was for free, Yablonsky surprised himself by his own answer. "Not while I'm on duty."

The runt kept his composure before Yablonsky's speculative gaze. The detective prodded gently. "You're like the rest of them. You have no idea who killed Sean?"

"I'm just like the rest of them, lieutenant. Only much shorter."

Yablonsky admired the way he avoided the questions. This little hustler might be useful to him later on. He gave Bobbi his card.

"You never can tell when you might need a friend."

He moved back from the bar so Yablonsky could see him plainly. He had no pockets and slipped the card into his jock strap as if he were accepting an offer. The strippers who saw him do it laughed. Yablonsky blushed. It was time to leave. He couldn't really be sure if this kid knew anything. "You can't help me then?"

Another pair of serene eyes. "I've always said I can't, lieutenant." It was the response he expected. He had learned practically nothing in this club that would help his investigation.

Stepping outside, he noticed that the line of women waiting to get into the club had become much longer. The women were laughing, chatting, psyching themselves up for their big night. Limousines were parked four abreast against the curb. Because of the murder, business was *slack*?

They stood and moved as elegantly as mannequins, their practiced eyes swooping to Yablonsky, subjecting him to quick, relentless inspections.

"You look like a sweet man," he heard one of them call out. "I'll give you fifty bucks if you stay the night."

"I'll pay you twenty-five," another yelled. Laughter. More offers.

At the corner he used the phone to call in to Flood. "What did you learn?"

"Not much," Yablonsky admitted.

"It's getting late. File a report. Then go home."

"Can I get a cup of coffee first? I need it."

"Just be sure to pay for it," Flood warned. "You sound tired." Yablonsky heard him change to his dry, amused tone.

"Just what are they concealing from you at this club?"

"Burlesque isn't what it use to be, captain. They revealed nothing."

Four

PAUL DILIGENTLY APPLIED HIS makeup. He didn't consider it effeminate. It was a necessity. It helped him to keep his cool under the hot spotlights.

The other strippers came over. One by one.

Elliot was first. "How's it going?"

He shrugged and continued carefully applying a layer of tanning oil to his chest. He was supposed to perspire and he liked the way the stuff made his muscles glisten.

Elliot was his usual indiscreet self. "I've got two women in their thirties lined up for tonight. Not bad looking, but more than I can handle. Interested?"

He pretended to think about it. Christ, it was true he needed money. The three thousand dollars he had made last month had slipped through his fingers as fast as some of those joy buttons he had expertly helped to lubricate. He had blown it all like a goddamn fool. Now he was on the make again. He had learned that he usually did better when he made his own arrangements. He didn't want to write off the offer entirely, though. You could never be sure how things would turn out. Look at Sean.

He made in face in the mirror. Were his teeth beginning to yellow? He'd have to start using more whitener. "I'll let you know by the end of the second set."

That was more than fair. By the end of the night there should be more offers.

Keith was next. He was dressed in his trademark costume. The cowboy. Pistol always primed and ready. Paul wondered why he had come over. He had already made it clear to Keith that he had no time for him.

"I thought you handled that detective well. You got plans for tonight?"

He didn't want to hurt him more than necessary. After next week, he did not intend to be here to *handle* anyone. The reporter who first interviewed Paul had confided that Sean's hands had been tied together and the mask placed over his head while he was probably still alive. It was time to pull up stakes.

"Sorry. But my mother told me never to speak to strange men." From what he knew about Keith's sex habits, he was a very strange man. Definitely beneath his standards.

He thought Keith took his rejection well. Showtime was in ten minutes. The other guys came over to talk about Sean.

"He was a helluva nice guy," Tom Bryers said.

"He'd give you the shirt off his back," Bob Bryers added. They were identical twins. On stage, dynamite. Very popular after hours.

They all wanted to learn more about Sean. First the reporters. Now a pair of hick strippers. Everybody was trying to be a detective these days. He had been Sean's roommate for a few months, not his father confessor. He wasn't really sure who killed him. He only knew it was best to take no chances.

After a few minutes of the silent treatment the twins left. Most of the other guys had disappeared too. The volume of the rock music increased, signaling the beginning of the show. Shouts and cheers drowned out the music. What anticipation!

A knock on the door. Kathy entered. He kept his features immobile. He had worked for her now for nine months. She was the worst cunt of them all. Her hand went to his shoulders as if in sympathy. In public she observed all the proprieties.

"You must still be very upset about Sean."

Of course he was! But since Sean's death he had become frightened for himself.

"As a dancer, and as a person he may have been irreplaceable . . . but you'll have to fill in for him."

The only thing he planned on filling was the vagina out there that would pay him the most, so he could leave. He was going on the lam.

"Can I depend on you?"

She was seeking reassurance. He gave her a warm smile. "I love dancing. I intend to be at O'Farrel's for a very long time." In three days he would be in Los Angeles. That was the place for him. Center stage. He had grown up in L.A., so he knew his way around.

He looked at his Rolex, hinting, but she was still there. "How long will it take to learn the rest of Sean's choreography."

He decided to hit Wilshire first. Meet all the right people. He glanced again at the bitch. He wanted her to remember this conversation and be shocked by his treachery.

"I already know his steps."

"Okay," she said. Before she left she nodded to the guys who were still there. They all were sure to smile back.

On stage those swirling lights were hot. The guys in the chorus were dressed in ties, tails, and fancy cardboard collars. No pants. Just jockstraps.

He turned and kicked to the music. In one of his hands he held a cane. The scene was out of Fred Astaire's *The Continental*. Whenever he raised his leg in a kick the women caught a glimpse of his equipment. Clever choreography. Since the movie had taken place on a boat, Kathy could improvise a little, fill the stage with suggestive-looking cannons.

As he moved, the women clapped, yelled, hooted. His eyes focused on a young girl, sitting alongside the stage. She motioned for him to turn around. He flashed her a smile. Pivoted. He felt her pry open his jockstrap. Stuff a folded bill into the crevice of his ass. He winked at the chorus guys, spun around, and flashed a "thank you" grin. He wiped sweat from his forehead to show them he was working. Everywhere he looked, hands clamored for him.

"Take it off. All of it."

He did. He twirled his jockstrap through the air as if it were a baton, the brought it down by the lip of the stage. He smiled slightly. He must be spreading heat, all the cunts were filling the cup with money.

"Show your ass."

"Ladies," he yelled and laughed. "You've already seen everything."

After his set he slipped into the chorus line. Usually he showered between sets. There was not time for that tonight, however. He had to accumulate capital fast. The smell of male perspiration was like an aphrodisiac, letting women know what was in store if they had enough cash to buy him for the night.

He stepped off the stage, moved toward the bar. There was Marjorie, twenty-eight and not bad. She was a court reporter, so he enjoyed the irony of taking her to bed. But she was only good for a hundred. She whispered her offer. "I'm horny as hell tonight. One fifty."

That would pay for the plane ticket, but he intended to have a stake when he reached L.A.

"Christ. I'd like to. Only I made a prior commitment."

"Shit, my loss."

"Another time?"

He stood at the bar's end, away from Bobbi, waiting for another bartender to put a drink in his hands.

Donny sidled up to him. "Any prospects?"

"Just checking out the action."

"Me too. See you later."

The speaker systems were muted. Women sat together or alone, ordering drinks. A few men wandered into the club. They were allowed in once the ten o'clock set was over.

His eyes swept the room. The Jeffries. They lived in Teaneck, just across the river. Paul considered them steadies. They came to the club a couple of times of month, usually managing to leave with him. They were good for three hundred.

As he glided through the crowd toward them, a hand reached out. A middle-aged woman, standing by the railing. She looked at him hopefully. "Your dancing made me feel ten years younger."

He was already past her. "Thanks, beautiful. You've made my day."

He moved into the spot next to the Jeffries, and was served a drink. They smiled up at him.

"You're drinking heavily tonight," the guy said. He was in his early thirties. Every time he saw Paul he managed to tell him that he had joined a health club because he too was determined to stay in shape.

Paul leaned closer to them, sharing a moment of intimacy with good friends. "Liquor improves my performance."

The guy put his arm around his wife. "We're already aware

of that. When can you leave?"

"I just did my last set. Anytime you want."

They waited outside for him, in front of the club. In the cab he sat between them. They each held one of his arms. "It's wonderful getting together with close friends," Mrs. Jeffries said. "That's why we come to the club. We like to socialize. We really like you, Paul. As a person."

When they reached his apartment, Paul moved to turn on the floor lamp. He thought that his place really looked sharp, like a movie set. He watched them as they settled on the sofa. They really weren't so bad. Not kinky. Just active. He put a compact disc into the player.

"Which recording?" Mrs. Jeffries asked.

"Holst's 'The Planets.'"

"That's an excellent piece of music to make love to," she said.

"I've got good taste."

"Yes," she said. She waited.

He went to the bar, handled a shot glass. "Would you like anything?"

He watched her straighten slightly, press her legs together. "I'd like you to mix me a strong vermouth."

"And then?"

"I want to put my hands slowly between your legs, strip you down so you're naked at last. And then you can eat me out."

$\triangledown$

Five

AFTER YABLONSKY FILED HIS report, he took Flood's advice and went home.

Because the subways had been so bad lately, people were driving into the city in greater numbers than ever before. The mayor complained, forced new restrictions. Nothing helped.

The traffic near Battery Park Tunnel was a mess. Many cops solved the problem of traffic jams by flashing their lights and running their sirens, scattering the driving public before them. For a moment he was tempted to take out the red globe, but relented. He sighed. There was nothing to do but inch his way forward along with the others. When he had illicit impulses, he usually managed to overcome them. His ex-wife use to complain that his occasional lapses into corruption had no finesse.

It had not helped his ego any when the sergeant she took up with after leaving him prospered. Under her tender tutelage, he made lieutenant, then captain, then finally head of security for Harrah's in Atlantic City, so she got to see Sinatra and Bennett for free.

He reached the Belt Parkway, rolled open the window. Fiddling with the radio, he heard snatches of rock music. The music was as jarring as his murder investigations. He switched to a station that played classical music. He was no longer a rookie cop but a detective, and somehow the quality and age of the music was reassuring.

He exited at the Prospect Park Expressway in Brooklyn, resigning himself to eating his dinners there for the length of the investigation.

Ocean Parkway was crowded with black-garbed Jews heading for synagogues. Groups of Hispanic teenagers crossed the street, bound for discos on the other side of Coney Island Avenue. There were cars in front of La Mer tonight. Husky men whom Yablonsky would not care to tangle with flanked the bride and groom. The groom's suit already bulged with envelopes. Another Mafia wedding.

Sal's Pizzeria was on Avenue X. He drove there. The restaurant was nearly empty, and he was quickly ushered over to a table for two. He sat alone. That was divorce.

Sal waited on him himself. Yablonsky had eaten here when he was a patrolman.

Sal seemed glad to see him. "You haven't eaten here much since moving on to bigger and better things. I'm glad you've come back."

Yablonsky looked over the limited menu. He ordered veal scallopini and a slice of pizza. Both were fair.

Getting up, he left a two-dollar tip and approached the cash register.

Sal, behind the register, made a dismissive gesture.

"Your money's no good here."

"I can't let you do that, Sal."

"It's on me, lieutenant."

"I can't let you do that, Sal."

"Please, lieutenant. You're my guest. I insist."

"I have to pay my own way. It's the law."

Ocean Parkway was no longer crowded. He made a left

onto Avenue Z, and quickly drove the few remaining blocks home.

He lived on the far side of Sheepshead Bay, in a block of houses opposite Randazzo's Clam Bar. He parked, walked past the line of fishing boats, and crossed the wooden bridge. Fisherman scooped buckets of the remains of the day's catch into the water. The gulls had a field day.

As he passed the Zeigler home he saw their two kids sitting on the steps. They were playing a variation of Cops and Robbers. "I'll be the mugger and you be the victim."

"I wanna be the mugger!"

He lived two houses away from the beach, on the bottom floor of a two-family. He turned the key that opened his private door, looking back at the Zeiglers. Even ten-year-old kids knew where the odds lay these days.

On his door was a sticker that said: *We have joined Operation Identification. All valuables on these premises have been marked for ready identification by the New York City Police Department.*

Other people had them on their doors, too. Sheepshead Bay was considered a wealthy neighborhood, and there were burglaries.

All valuables have been marked. A warning from the police department to a thief—yet temptation too; and all in the same sentence. Yablonsky called it advertising.

He entered. He went to the refrigerator, in a mood for a beer. A six-pack of Heineken, two packages of frankfurters. The refrigerator's emptiness gave the lie to a salary that was supposed to be, by civil-service standards, a generous one.

He didn't live badly though. The money he saved by not paying for his dinners had enabled him to buy a VCR, a projection TV, and a video camera.

He went into the living room, sat down on the recliner,

reached for some popcorn, and turned on the VCR to watch the tape of the news. Surprise! There he was, filling the almost lifesize forty-eight-inch screen, stolidly trudging up the precinct steps.

The reporters asked their questions. He gave answers that were vague and therefore would not incriminate him later. It was almost as good a detective movie as the ones on HBO.

Two framed pictures, one of his ex-wife, the other of his childhood gang of friends, stood next to the popcorn on the cocktail table. He and his friends had grown up on the streets of East New York, one of the worst neighborhoods in the city. Two of them had been ordered hit by the Mafia. Three were permanently crippled from gang fights. One had returned from Vietnam with Agent Orange in his lungs and for a while had made an effort to keep in touch with Yablonsky. Then doctors had told him that cancer was eating up his testicles, and he had committed suicide by driving his car off the Rockaway Parkway Bridge.

Some of the guys he had played ball with in high school had grown up to become button men in the Mafia, but he had never had any trouble with them. He had sat out the war by attending college. Maybe that was why he became a cop after the war. He knew why he had become a detective. More prestige. Less violence.

During spring and summer he and the guys used to drift over to Manhattan Beach, across from Sheepshead Bay, to play handball and basketball with the blacks who hung out there.

He had met his wife near the handball court.

She had been watching him demolish Frankie Albanese, only in turn to be demolished by Leroy White.

After the set, Yablonsky handed White a twenty-dollar bill. She spoke up. "You could have used that twenty to take me out tonight."

He drank beer from out of the can, turned on some Earl Klugh. He wanted to drift off to sleep while the record played. . . . His wife had been dissatisfied, sarcastic. He was content to be just a detective, but that's all he was, and he would never be anything more. He would never even be a "great" detective. He knew his work at best was only adequate. The things he had going for him were patience and, when given enough time on a case, a determination to succeed. Still, he doubted he would solve Sean's murder.

He stretched out on the sofa. The moon came in behind the stained glass window above the door, lighting its colors until the glass looked polished. He heard waves from the ocean and the wind flatten the beach sand.

The phone rang, awakening him.

He peered at the luminescent clock, but he couldn't make out the time. His eyes were filmy, and the room was full of dark, indistinct shapes. He decided to keep his eyes shut.

The phone rang again. It must be Arlene! She often called when he had been on TV. She would wish him a perfunctory hello, then begin reciting her husband's accomplishments. Strangely, Yablonsky didn't mind. If she still called, then she still cared for him, despite what she said.

He picked up the phone, waiting patiently to hear her voice.

"Detective Yablonsky?"

"Yes? What time is it?"

"Sergeant Hagan, night watch. It's four in the morning. Sorry to disturb you, detective. There's been another stabbing in an apartment on the East Side. A stripper named Paul Matson is dead."

$\triangledown$

Six

WITHERS WAS GLAD TO see him. He pointed with his chin to Paul's body. "I told you I'd see you soon, detective."

"It's always nice to be proved right," Yablonsky said.

He went over to the sofa bed to check out Paul. All the qualifications for being a homicide victim were there. First of all, Paul was dead; secondly, he had plainly been murdered—you did not have to be a detective to deduce that. His body lay sprawled and bloody on the carpet next to the sofa bed. He was wearing a mask, his hands were behind his back; a leather cord dangled from his wrists.

Withers stood over Paul's body for an even closer look. As he inspected the body and its surroundings, he was his usual jovial self. Yablonsky was glad that at least one of them was in a good mood. "You have to admit it, Yablonsky. This is a creative killer. He killed both victims with slash wounds, but the pattern on each body is different. The stereo's on, like before, but I bet different records were put on this time to mask the screams. There's more cocaine than before, too. He's leaving us his signature, yet showing us he can still give his victims the individual touch. I call that consideration."

Yablonsky did not feel like discussing Withers's assumptions with him. The stereo turntable revolved almost silently. He went to the closet and on a hunch pulled the doors open. Designer suits. Detectives from Discovery, as well as from Toxicology, would go over the apartment after he left and in hours present him with reports. Cops were questioning Paul's neighbors, especially the woman who lived next door and who'd reported hearing screams. Then the all-night groceries and newsstands, shopping-bag people and derelicts. Again the usual pattern of a night had been broken by a killing, but the posse had been sent for and was diligently seeking the murderer.

Withers winked. "Are you going to round up the usual suspects, Humphrey?"

Yablonsky moved closer to the body, bent over, and carefully took the mask off Paul's head. He sighed as he stared at Paul, then began untying his hands. He didn't want to tamper with the victim before the Medical Examiner's people arrived, but he believed in giving his corpses a more dignified death pose when possible. Yablonsky unclenched the fist, and a piece of paper fluttered to the floor. He saw that it had been torn from a newspaper, and that it looked like part of an ad from the personal columns. The rest of the newspaper was lying under the sofa bed. It was called *Let's Get Personal*. Yablonsky had heard of it. It came out biweekly, publishing ads from people who wanted to establish long-term relationships or one-night stands. He assumed that Paul had managed to grab a piece of it while he struggled with his murderer. Why had he held onto it?

Withers sat on the sofa alongside the body to wait patiently for the wheels of the murder bureaucracy to catch up with him. Yablonsky decided to leave. As he left, Withers hit him with his usual parting line, "See you at the next one."

Outside a crowd had already formed in front of the

apartment building. How do they find out so quickly? he wondered. He flashed his badge and got their attention. "The apartment of a murder victim is sealed for three months. No one can take occupancy now," he said.

He watched the mob of prospective tenants curse, complain, and scatter before him. He felt like Wyatt Earp.

When he reached the precinct he negotiated his way silently through the groups of reporters and cameramen. He glanced at his watch. Nine A.M. News of the murder had broken too late for the morning dailies, but would be in the afternoon editions. Flood was waiting for him outside his office, and the two of them had a hurried conference.

"Two strippers murdered. They expect us to call a press conference out there. Can you give me anything concrete?"

"I didn't learn much," confessed Yablonsky.

"Shit. Why are the murderers in this city so much smarter than us cops? We'll have to wing it again."

"I've had a lot of practice at that lately," Yablonsky said.

"So have we all."

They stood on the steps outside the precinct, facing the reporters and cameramen. Hand microphones were thrust in their faces.

"We have not yet apprehended the suspect, but we are in the process of following leads," Flood said.

"You do have a suspect then?"

Flood nudged him. "One of our best men, Detective Yablonsky. As you know, he's been assigned to the case."

Yablonsky was ready. "Definite clues were left at both murder scenes." He paused, deciding to tell them what they wanted to hear. It would divert them from the cases' lack of progress and it would be better for his investigation to have the killer think he bought the sex-drugs motive. "We think that both boys were killed by the same person. Both victims were wearing masks. Large quantities of cocaine were discovered in both apartments."

"A sex-drug ring composed of strippers!" Bob Adler of the *New York Post* said. "'Stripper Clipper Strikes Again!'" He glanced questioningly at Yablonsky, trying out the prospective headline on the detective first.

"It catches the mood, Bob," Yablonsky told him.

Flood stepped forward. "As soon as we have additional news you'll all be notified. There won't be any exclusives this time," he said, eyeing them, already beginning the bargaining process. "You can say that this department remains hopeful that the investigation will be brought to a successful conclusion."

As they reentered the building, Flood turned to whisper to Yablonsky. Pertinent data? the reporters wondered. "I owe you one."

Flood led the way back to his office. His desk was filled with stacks of manila envelopes. He glanced at the topmost report as he seated himself. "More UN stuff. An assistant delegate from Nigeria was being given a ticket by a meter maid. He became verbally abusive, stepped out of his car, and assaulted her. Witnesses say he looked drunk. The assault charge will disappear. Driving While Intoxicated will become Creating a Public Nuisance. A misdemeanor, of course."

Yablonsky nodded sympathetically. "I know how it is. We arrest one of them for rape and he's booked for indecent exposure. In the end, we have to let him go anyway. Diplomatic immunity.

"The curse of our precinct." Flood returned to the pile of envelopes on his desk and handed the top one to Yablonsky. "Blochner prepares them faster every time."

Yablonsky leafed through the reports from the Medical

Examiner and Discovery, noting the details he thought were pertinent. He looked up.

"Sean's and Paul's murders were similar," Flood said. "Their wounds were wedge shaped. Whatever struck them was not a knife. Both apartments were ransacked. Large amounts of drugs were found. They were wearing masks, their hands were tied, and they were dancers in the same club. Are they the first victims of a serial killer?"

Would there be even more murders? It was what the killer, or killers, wanted everyone to think. "I think the same person murdered both these boys. I don't know yet why they were killed."

"Blochner's report states that traces of semen were found on the buttocks. Was this kid killed because of a drug dispute? Or was he just some guy who got perforated in the wrong hole by an angry customer while playing Queen for a Day?"

"Then you're saying Sean was also the victim of a sex killing," Yablonsky stated carefully.

Flood looked irritated. "The victim of a drug hit—or the victim of a weenie whacker? The mortality rate of these kids *should* be high, considering the kinds of things they're involved in," he said.

"If the boys were killed because of drugs, why were their bodies mutilated and left naked?" Yablonsky asked. "Why were masks placed over their heads and their hands tied?"

"So we would think it's a sex killing when they were really killed because of the drugs."

"If it was a drug killing, then why was so much cocaine left behind?" Yablonsky asked. He knew there were other contradictions as well. Whoever had butchered these boys had tried hard to make these resemble typical sex-drug murders. There were the excessive mutilations, the corresponding streaks of blood, the inclusion of the masks and leather. As if no stone had been left unturned in order to make these appear to be sensational murders. The murderer had left his "signature," but it was the work of someone who was profoundly disciplined and orderly, not a psychotic brute.

Flood leaned back in his chair, looking thoughtful. "You're the detective," he said at last, grudgingly. "Can we expect any help from that witness?"

"She wasn't a witness," Yablonsky reminded him. "She lived next door and heard screams. She didn't see anything."

"What did she tell you that we can use?"

"It seems that our boy was into more creative sex-play than Sean. Screams, loud music, love moans, and parties were frequent occurrences. It was only because the screams stopped so suddenly this time that she became suspicious and called the police. She says Paul was not a good neighbor and that she's not sorry he's dead." He paused. "The report says she waited an hour before she called the police. If Paul was being killed, I guess she wanted to make sure the killer had enough time to leave the building. She maintains she was afraid."

"I hope she ends up with a quieter neighbor this time around," Flood said. "Do you think she could identify any of the people who visited Paul's apartment?"

"She assured me she made sure never to see anyone who went inside that place. She only heard them."

"A vicarious life," Flood said. "I doubt her new neighbor will be as exciting as Paul was. After this morning's debut with the media, I'm sure I'll be dining with the police commissioner tonight. Do you have anything for me?"

Once again Flood was asking for assistance. This time he would have to turn him down. He did not want to jeopardize the little he had by having Flood reveal it to the P.C.

"You've discovered another angle on this! Remember, I know how you operate. That's why I gave you this case. Despite this investigation into whether you scarf down food with a spoon or a fork."

The angle he had discovered was as thin as a half-torn ad, Yablonsky thought. He remained silent. He knew Flood. In order to protect the confidentiality of his detectives and thus their freedom to operate effectively, Flood would allow Ben Ward to squeeze him a little.

"Tell me what you can when you think it's best. I've already read the report you've filed. The bartenders. The manager. The dancers. The next-door neighbors. So far, all you've done is *eliminate* suspects."

Yablonsky smiled. "Justice must be served, captain."

"So must the police commissioner." Flood sighed. "If he isn't, they'll be serving my balls to him tonight on a silver platter."

At least he would be eating free of department surveillance. "Enjoy your meal, captain," he said, and left.

Yablonsky walked through the corridor to return to his office. He would go over the reports again. Especially the ones from Discovery. But first, Paul's family would have to be informed.

He spoke into the phone. There was a silence. "I see. You're telling me my son is dead."

Yablonsky spoke quickly. "We don't have any idea who killed Paul, sir, but we're working on it."

"That's all right, detective. I already know who killed him."

Yablonsky controlled a tremor of excitement. "Will you be coming to New York? Or should we ship his body back to you? In either case, we should talk."

"I think not. That is, no to both questions."

"Why not, sir?"

"Because I told him when he left here to go to your goddamn city that either a nigger, spic, or Jew would kill him. Which did it, detective?"

"Whoever killed your son was too clever to leave evidence of his ethnic background, sir."

"Then I choose all of the above," he said, and hung up the phone.

Yablonsky went back to his reports.

It is possible that the weapon in both cases could be a letter opener, but we must emphasize that no conclusions should be drawn from this statement. W. Blochner, Acting Medical Examiner.

Discovery: The white flesh line circling the victim's wrist could have been left by a watch. As no watch was found in the apartment, the killer might have absconded with it. The designer clothes found in Paul Matson's closet were the same name brands as Sean Maysfield's. The albums and tapes were the same types of music. Further proof that the incomes and lifestyles of the victims were similar and that they were possibly murdered for the same reason.

Pressure from the Investigating Committee on Corruption had made Alton's successor type out his reports fast. Evidence from Toxicology and the Medical Examiner's office were now presented as concisely as possible. There was an extreme reluctance to draw conclusions that could later be judged. Method and Motive. Blochner was already beginning to protect himself against future investigations.

Gettis from Discovery presented his information in flowery language that hinted at possible leads, suggested mo-

tives, and bravely listed the clues he felt would help Yablonsky solve the case.

Withers, Flood, Ward, probably even the dancers at O'Farrel's, all fancied themselves detectives; searching for the one
big clue that would solve his case for him. But the clues in
these kinds of murders were usually little things, contradictions that arose between the killer's plan of action and the
actual carrying out of the murder. They were items, or hints,
that most detectives would easily pass.

He wondered about motive. Flood and the media seemed
to be right. Assigning a "sex-drug" type of motive to the
murders made sense. They were business sidelines for the
boys. But, for a price, anyone who was with them those
nights could have had both. So then why kill them?

He looked at the newspaper fragment, feeling he had made
the right decision in withholding it from Discovery and
Flood. The rest of the newspaper was in his desk. Did Paul
grab part of it because he knew there was something there
that would incriminate whoever murdered him? Or was it
another plant by the murderer, like the masks and the drugs,
to mislead him? He sighed, then straightened, and began
rereading the reports for anything he might have missed.

Seven

HE WALKED AROUND TO the rear entrance of O'Farrel's. It was showtime, and he didn't have to be told that the presence of a fully clothed male would be awkward.

He found himself in a closed-off hall kept separate from the rest of the club. Someone's hand came to rest on his shoulder. "Men aren't allowed in the club now." The voice was amused rather than angry. "Where did you think you were going before I stopped you?"

"I'm a detective. Reach into my pocket, remove my shield, and you'll see."

"I'll just bet you'd like me to reach into your pocket. But I don't think what you'd like me to *pull on* is your shield."

"I'm a detective."

"I think that you're a naughty boy who . . ." The grip softened, he allowed Yablonsky to turn around. "Jesus, lieutenant. I didn't recognize you. Sorry. We get guys trying to sneak in here all the time. Some of them like to razz the women. Some of them get off on trying to sniff the dancers' underwear. I hope you won't take this personally."

"I'd like you to direct me to the dancers' dressing room. I intend to question them about the latest murder." He made his eyes hard. "Don't worry, I'll knock before I enter. I wouldn't want to catch any of them in a state of undress."

"But they'll be performing in ten minutes."

"Maybe I'll walk up on stage and question them there."

"No! I'll take you."

He caught them in their dressing room before they were to begin their act. They recognized him. Peered at him anxiously.

He took out a cigarette and lit it. It was the same thing he did when he viewed his corpses. "First, let me assure you that none of you are suspects . . ."

Showtime was in five minutes. He heard the hoots and calls from the women. Sweat began to stand out on the dancers' already well-oiled foreheads. He was telling them yesterday's news.

"As you already know, I requested that from now on two cops be present at your shows, for your protection . . ."

Those crystal-clear eyes on those handsome faces looked worried. They certainly did already know. The cops were plainclothes. Yablonsky had asked the precinct to send two women so as not to make O'Farrel's patrons feel self-conscious, but still! When the strippers made rounds after the sets, trying to establish a little contact, they might be winking or saying charming things to cops who would then entrap them.

"Detective. It's showtime."

"And of course the show must go on." Yablonsky smiled at them. The best time to secure information from people who might not want to give it was when they were harried and perceived you as a nuisance. If you caught them at their leisure, they invariably had the time to mislead you.

Howie, Rudi, all of them in costume: shoulder pads, uniforms, and jockstraps with numbers on them: 9 1/2. 8 3/4. Prices? Measurements? It was not the usual kind of football team.

"Two of you have already been killed. Maybe I should stop the show tonight for your own safety."

"Jesus, lieutenant. We're supposed to be on stage now."

"What a coincidence. I'm supposed to be on duty now, too."

"We're supposed to be out there taking off our *clothes*."

"You look attractive in your football outfit, Rudi. I also like the way you wear your padding . . ."

"Please, lieutenant!"

"From evidence found in Paul's room, we're pretty sure that the night he was murdered he left here with someone. Who?"

A chorus of groans.

"Was the person Paul left with a regular here? Did he leave with more than one person?"

"Kathy. She could probably tell you."

"Last time I was here all she told me was that those kinds of things don't go on in her club."

Howie spoke up. "Ask her. Really, lieutenant. Each of us is too busy trying to make our own contacts to notice who the other guy is with."

As Yablonsky waded through the club room, the dancers kicked their way on stage to tumultuous applause and loud music. He found Kathy sitting alone at the rear of the club, waiting for him. She was wearing a tight pair of jeans; her silk blouse stood out against pale, unflawed skin. She looked like the cover of *Vogue*. He, in his pin-striped, tapered "detective" suit, out to solve a murder, looked like a headline from the *New York Post*, and some of the women began to watch the wrong male.

"I wouldn't mind if you took off your clothes, lieutenant. Actually it might be kind of exciting. The novelty of seeing a normally proportioned naked male."

Yablonsky stared at the men on stage. He had not seen so many naked men in one place since summer camp. Being wanted by so many women must be something. He turned back to her and smiled. "Would I have to wear a number?"

"Yes. Probably."

"Then I'll have to pass on my show business career. Did you see Paul leave the club with anyone last night?"

"His death was an even bigger shock than Sean's. I wish I could say yes lieutenant."

"I wish you could say yes, too."

"Because of these murders there are cops in my club now. I don't like that kind of scrutiny. Neither do my dancers. I wish you would catch the bastard who did this so I can put this all behind me. You understand that people come here to have a good time, but they expect confidentiality. I have to turn a blind eye."

"You understand that I can book you as a material witness in a murder case? You can end up in jail."

She laughed. "Who goes to jail these days?"

That was true enough. He could not really threaten her with much else.

"I've got to think of my club's survival. The place is crowded, but there are empty seats tonight. If another dancer gets himself killed, I may have to close. I did see Paul speaking with a couple by the bar, but I can't tell you that I saw him leave with anyone specifically, lieutenant."

The two men who were behind the bar, serving drinks, were plainly not stripper material. They were smaller than the rest, less muscular. They watched the show as avidly as the patrons, hooting and whistling along with the others, contributing to the atmosphere. Yablonsky remembered one of them from before. Bobbi. He had given the little hustler his card in case he decided to help. There had been no calls.

As Yablonsky moved towards Bobbi, he saw the other guy turn away, and Yablonsky caught a glimpse of a tense face.

Bobbi put a drink on the bar and smiled. "You look thirsty, lieutenant."

"I am. I hope that's a beer."

"Molson's."

Yablonsky drank half of it, left the rest. "Kathy tells me you know who Paul was with the night he was murdered."

"O'Farrel's is full of rumors, lieutenant. The place seethes with unreliable information."

"I wish you would help me, Bobbi."

"I'll help you any way I can."

"Do you know who Paul left with?"

Bobbi's forehead tightened, as if deep in thought, and Yablonsky knew he would be seeing this little hustler again. "I'm trying to recall that awful night. So many drinks to serve. So many sad stories from the women to listen to. No, lieutenant. I don't recall."

"I thought you wanted to be helpful."

"No, lieutenant. What I said was, I'd help you any way I *can.*"

It did not occur to Yablonsky to threaten the boy with a squad room interrogation. There were usually more ways to obtain information than there were excuses not to give it.

"It doesn't bother you that two of your friends are already dead?"

"It bothers me. It's just that I can't do anything about it. Even assuming I saw Paul with people last night, despite what Kathy said I couldn't tell."

"They're just names, Bobbi. They won't know you told me."

Yablonsky's eyes shifted to the other bartender, who was edging closer to him. The boy looked frightened. Yablonsky could see that Bobbi was aware of his fright. He seemed to be calm. "If word got out I supplied you with people's names, my job here would be finished."

"Suppose I pass the word that it was you who gave me the name of Paul's tricks anyway? Either way you'd be out of a job."

"I don't like the way you think, lieutenant. That's dishonest."

"Lieutenant?"

Yablonsky turned. The other bartender said, "Paul was talking with a couple named Jeffries last night. They come into the club about twice a month. They're regulars. They left with Paul. They're from Teaneck, New Jersey." He pivoted toward Bobbi. "You can have me fired, I don't care. There've already been two murders. Isn't that enough for you?"

"Asshole," Bobbi muttered. He smiled at Yablonsky. "From the mouths of babes. I told you I'd help you, lieutenant."

"And with no risk to yourself."

"You aren't angry at me, are you?"

"Of course not. You helped me all you *could*."

Traffic through the Lincoln Tunnel was light. Yablonsky drove past the giant Bergen malls, then off Route 4 onto a country road. The wooded, two-acre estates struck him as being sensuous. The design of the suburban houses, compared to the monotonous towering co-ops and condos of the city, was refreshing. The manicured lawns looked like the well-tended fairways of the exclusive country clubs that would never offer him membership, but which he might be asked to guard.

This time, no one would mistake him for a gardener or insurance salesman. He had called ahead. The Jeffries were expecting a detective. He pulled his car into the circular driveway, in front of the tall pines and pillared colonial. He imagined the amount of money needed for their upkeep.

The Jeffries answered the door together, smiles frozen on their faces. A detective questioning them about two murders! As they slowly led him toward the living room, they looked like they were walking the last mile.

They were a good-looking couple. He was in his late thirties had most of his hair, and a tight, trim little body that had to be the result of at least three racketball sessions a week at the health club. She looked like she was in her mid-thirties, and despite her fear, there was an adventurous gleam in her eye. He could tell by the toys scattered on the floor that they had children. A suburban home, landscaped lawn, socially redeemable lives. And they were swingers?

They invited him to sit on the loveseat opposite them. They sat on the sofa, holding hands.

The man spoke first. "I love my wife deeply, lieutenant. You look at us, you got to say to yourself, 'Here is a contented couple.'"

"I thought it was a contented threesome," Yablonsky said.

Mrs. Jeffries looked at the detective with uncertainty. "We've lived together in this home for fifteen years. We're moral people."

"Though our definition of morality might not be everyone's," the husband added.

"What did this *person* who gave you our names tell you about us? That we're kinky? Swinging *saved* our marriage, lieutenant."

So they had read or heard the stories about the mask and rope. The man gave his wife's hand a squeeze, continued. "Because of swinging we discovered a love for each other that we didn't know we had. But murder? Drugs? We hardly ever did drugs."

"Only a little cocaine occasionally," his wife echoed. "Snorted, never freebased."

"We were with Paul because my wife and he enjoyed each other's bodies, but there was never any perversion. I have no idea what Paul and the other young man who was murdered did with others, but perhaps a jealous lover killed Paul *after* we left. There was never any homosexuality involved in our relationship. I watched Paul and my wife give pleasure to each other. I'm not a fag basher, lieutenant. Those kind of men deserve pity, not scorn."

Traces of semen had been found between Paul's buttocks. Yablonsky watched Jeffries lean back, grip his wife's hand even harder, and smile in a confident, manly way. The Case of the Wayward Semen that had bothered the Medical Examiner's office so much was solved to Yablonsky's satisfaction.

"Just because we swing occasionally and were at Paul's apartment, you'll take us down to the station and book us. That's not prosecution. It's persecution," Mrs. Jeffries said.

"Book you for what?"

They exchanged glances. "On suspicion of murder," she said.

Yablonsky looked surprised. "Why should I book you? You're not suspects."

"We're *not*?"

"For months, Paul took you to his apartment and for months he awakened the next morning. No ma'am, you're not suspects. I'm here to ask you some questions."

Cleared of being murder suspects because they were habitual swingers! Their tension evaporated and they looked at him gratefully. It was reassuring to know they lived in a moral, if somewhat puzzling world.

"What a relief," Jeffries said. "Out from under the gun. People are wrong to criticize the way we live, lieutenant. Swinging's saved more than our marriage this time."

When Yablonsky's sexually bored wife had suggested they try swinging, he had been shocked. "Let's get back down to business. How long were you with Paul last night? Did he speak to anyone on the phone?"

"From around twelve-thirty to two. Not a soul."

"Okay. When you were with him, did you notice a copy of the newspaper *Let's Get Personal*?"

"There was a stack of newspapers and magazines by his bedside," she said. "I didn't notice anything specific. Anything else, lieutenant?"

"When Paul was with you, did he ever discuss any of the women he went out with?"

"That would be impolitic of him, lieutenant. Paul was discreet." She smiled at him. "At least with our names, we hope he was."

"How about the newspapers?" he asked again.

"There were newspapers there." She looked thoughtful. "It would make sense for Paul to keep listings of the personals. Potential customers?" Her brow knitted shrewdly. "If the newspapers were already there, then the killer couldn't have planted it, like he might have done with the mask and the drugs."

Sensing a kindred spirit, he looked at her encouragingly. "Go on."

"Sean and Paul were wearing masks when they were murdered. Since we never saw those things in Paul's apartment, they probably *were* plants, and therefore the drugs and stuff were also put there. To mask why the boys were really murdered." She paused. "I assume you're finished with us, lieutenant. I wish you whatever it is a detective most wants to be wished."

"You did all right," Yablonsky said. "I wish you everything, except monogamy."

$\triangledown$

Eight

IT WAS DRIZZLING. WEST 72nd Street was full of umbrellas. Now that work was finished, the umbrellas emerging from the IRT station, taxis, and buses headed toward the restaurants on Columbus Avenue. Along the way, Yablonsky noticed striped and gray umbrellas stop and shop for pastries at Eclairs. Umbrellas parked in front of the best deli on the Upper West Side, Fine and Schapiros, to ogle hanging rows of salami, platters of sliced Romanian pastrami and corned beef.

Yablonsky knew from his past trips up here that north of Ray's Original Pizza began the longest sustained row of gourmet ice cream parlors, chocolate chip cookie shops, and glassed-in restaurants in the world. Despite the rain the streets remained crowded. The Upper West Side. He watched its inhabitants head in Charivari to shop for clothes whose minimum price was five hundred dollars or enter pet shops where poodles, shar-peis, and akitas were sold for fifteen hundred dollars apiece.

He started his walk uptown. People busily poked through the Korean fruit stands. He passed a store called Fairway and looked in: a floor covered with sawdust trampled on by feet that were encased in hundred-dollar running shoes; every kind of cheese and coffee bean imaginable.

The office of *Let's Get Personal* was located near the "capital" of the upper West Side, Zabar's. The store, which ran for almost a block, was really a collection of smaller shops, each containing different types of gourmet treats. The vendors in front of the store sold used books from under giant umbrellas, and counterfeit designer watches for the poorer among the passersby. Other people shoved petitions in your face and pleaded with you to sign them. He noticed with a pang of regret that cop cars were double parked, the cops inside them munching with impunity on mushroom knishes and spinach quiches. A man stood in front of one of the store's glass windows, playing a zither. Yablonsky walked by, dropping coins into the open case. People dressed in jeans browsed through the book racks outside Shakespeare and Company: every rear end had a designer label attached to it.

On the other side of Broadway, the 84th Street Sixplex was topped by a foundation and skeleton of what would eventually be a luxury residence. The entire area burgeoned with construction. Giant cranes, walled-off walkways, constant drilling. Skyscraper-size condos and co-ops sprouted from the streets like jungle plants.

Yablonsky turned left on 87th and walked to the Red Apple. Outside the supermarket two Hispanic teenagers were handing out brochures with the logo of *Let's Get Personal* to passersby. The office itself was in a loft above the Red Apple. From where he was, Yablonsky could glimpse the splendor and wealth of Broadway. He was on a side street, definitely off the beaten path.

Yablonsky took the offered brochure. *Come to our Classes, Change Your Life*, it said. He folded his umbrella. No elevator. He climbed the stairs.

The loft Yablonsky found himself in had been partitioned into classrooms and corridors. One of the classrooms was empty and in the other one there were about a dozen people, mostly women. They looked through the personal columns, making little checkmarks or crosses next to ads.

A man on top of a ladder held a paintbrush in his hand. Yablonsky's nostrils filled with the odor of turpentine. On the floor were rollers and cans of paint. He looked up. The man had managed to paint the parts of the ceiling that were close to the bare light bulbs. Further away, the paint was still peeling.

The man spoke without looking at him.

"Cheap paint," he said.

The door was open to Denise Levine's office. There was no waiting room, no sofas or coffee tables. A single lampstand stood before the door, piled with past issues of the magazine. She didn't even have a secretary.

She was on a chair, alongside a filing cabinet. She waved. He watched her juggle the latest copies of *Let's Get Personal*, drop them, get off the chair, pause in the middle of the office as if undecided what to do with them, then suddenly rush over to a metal bookshelf, dumping them there. She lunged for another fistful of magazines, compulsively arranging them into a neat pile alongside the others. "God, I'm manic today!" she yelled, grasping her temples and turning to Yablonsky.

She led him to a chair and he watched, mesmerized by her energy, as she rapidly dialed phone numbers. "My life depends on these calls," she explained to him. "Mr. Edelman, the caps on last week's issue were blurred . . . I'm doing the best I can. I practically run this organization by myself. . . . If this issue's not locked in by next week, you will be responsible for my death. How can I pay my bills when the work's so poor? . . . I didn't know I owed three hundred dollars, your bills are blurred, too." Another call. "You can report that our circulation's at an all-time high. We will soon be on the newsstands. Irene, just make sure you get that report in, in case the *real* figures are published." She winked at Yablonsky. "My circulation's three thousand, and fifteen hundred of those are complimentary copies. What an empire!"

"Ms. Levine, if you'd just be kind enough to answer a few questions. I know you're busy. I saw the people in your classroom out there."

"No, it's all right—you told me over the phone you had questions for me. The women in there like to be kept waiting, lieutenant, it gives them more time to compare notes. Spend as much time here as you want." She unhooked the phone. "As you've no doubt gathered, my present budget does not allow for secretaries. Now, my first question to you. What is the connection between *Let's Get Personal* and Paul's death?"

He thought it best not to tell her about the newspaper fragment. "Your magazine was found in Paul's apartment after he was murdered."

She grinned at him. "I guess in Paul's line of business, my magazine was a necessity."

"You knew Sean too?"

She nodded. "We met at a party, about a year ago. I was just launching *Let's Get Personal*. They were *something*, lieutenant."

With Sean and Paul dead, what would women do for pleasure, Yablonsky wondered. She answered his unasked question. "I only knew about them through *hearsay*, lieutenant. I never slept with them."

"I noticed that most of the people in your classroom were women."

"Yeah, women have it rough. There are seven single women for every unmarried guy in New York. If you don't include the gays, the odds are much worse. They come to us after a divorce or the end of a relationship, and they're depressed. We build them back up, teach them how to meet people via the personal columns or on their own. Get them back into the ballgame."

"What kind of women did Paul and Sean go out with, Ms. Levine?"

"Call me Denise, lieutenant, not Ms. We're in the post-feminist era now. They were celebrity fuckers."

Yablonsky's eyes widened. "How do you know?"

"Those boys had cash registers for eyes, lieutenant. They liked to party around celebrities, liked to go out, be seen with them. Like women who go out with male celebrities, they hoped the women they went out with would furnish them with cash, help their careers."

Yablonsky was truly curious. "What did they want to be, Denise?"

"It didn't matter, lieutenant. They weren't making it on talent. They wanted to be famous."

"They're famous now, but they can't read their reviews. Too bad." She was friendly enough; he decided he could ask her the next question. "What was your connection with them?"

"We're a small magazine, but we're widely read by women. They come in and pay to place a personal ad. If they were celebrities or really beautiful, Sean and Paul would pay me a hundred bucks to give them their code numbers. They'd send their pictures and bios to the women. You saw Paul and Sean, the rest you can imagine. Not all women want meaningful relationships, lieutenant."

"Denise, I can't believe someone who's famous and looking for a bedmate would give you her real name when taking out an ad. It might even leave her vulnerable to blackmail."

She shrugged. "I can furnish you with names. It's not just women, lieutenant, men who use out-call and massage services are also dumb enough to pay with credit cards. Famous men. Athletes. Politicians. Maybe their wives don't check the statements. Maybe they unconsciously want to get caught. The Mayflower Madam's cleaned up because with her list of clients, she's untouchable. You find someone with deep pockets, your own pockets become deeper. Right, lieutenant?"

"True enough."

She played with the phone cord for a moment. "You know, a celebrity might have killed them at that. They have money, and most of them have something to hide."

Yablonsky smiled slightly. "You mentioned a list of names?"

"Right." Her chair had wheels, and she flew across the room to her files. When she returned, she had a ream of paper in her hand. Its size surprised him. Evidently, there were a lot of lonely or sex-starved women in New York, famous or otherwise. "And these are just from the first six months of business. If you strike out, come back. I'll have more names for you." She handed the list to him. "Keep it for as long as you want. I have copies."

He stood. "One thing, Denise." She looked at him questioningly. "Most of the women on this are probably not celebrities. How will I know them?"

She winked. "They'll be the ones you've heard of."

Back at his desk, Yablonsky spent an hour separating the names into two stacks: the famous and the nonfamous women in New York.

When he was finished, he surveyed his work. The nonfamous pile dwarfed the celebrity one like a skyscraper towering over a brownstone. In fact, after all this time he had only been able to put three women's names on the celebrity pile.

He checked the list again, wanting to be as certain as possible. He felt like he was reading page after page out of the phone book. He wasn't ignorant; he didn't think he missed anybody. Three names.

A fundraiser for the Metropolitan Museum.

A member of City Council.

A rock star.

He tried to recall what he knew about each of them.

Margaret Ashman was always being written up in magazines like *Town and Country* and *Architectural Digest*. She was a multimillionairess who set up scholarships for the poor, gave large sums to a multitude of charities. She was a doyenne and a pillar of the community. She was also fifty-two years old. He imagined her in bed with Sean or Paul. The image fit.

Marcia Goodman, in her thirties, had been a city council member for the past ten years. She was anorexically thin, not attractive, often the subject of interviews for *Ms.* magazine. Much of her time was spent before women's groups, promoting women's liberation. A secret life, away from the hot glare of the feminist press? It was intriguing.

The last one was not in the league of the other two. She was a rock star, a member of the East Village punk scene. She was supposed to be a wild woman, whose audacious MTV videos had made her infamous in the eyes of the adult world but a heroine to the kids. She was also supposed to be a pretty ballsy woman. Last year he had read in *People* that she and her manager had saved her sister's life in a boating accident at the 79th Street Boat Basin. From that time on, her career had taken off.

Yablonsky felt his first glimmer of excitement. The investigation had not proceeded too badly so far. It obviously made for easier detective work to have fewer names to investigate. Things were looking up.

"Ms. Goodman?"

"Yes?"

"Detective Yablonsky from the Twenty-First Precinct. I'd like to ask you a few questions concerning the deaths of Sean Maysfield and Paul Matson the nights of April 6th and 8th."

A silence. "Who?"

"They were dancers in a club called O'Farrel's. We have reason to believe you might have known them."

"Jesus, detective."

"When did you see them?"

"I never saw either of them," she said quickly. "You probably got my name from that damned magazine. Just because I submitted an ad to *Let's Get Personal* doesn't mean I know Maysfield and Matson."

"Why did you publish an ad then, Ms. Goodman?"

"For company. *Companionship.* You can prove I wrote up an ad, detective, but you can't prove I knew them."

"May I come to your office and ask you some questions?"

"You may not come to my office. Are you nuts, lieutenant? Look, I was worried someone might try to connect my name with theirs. I was somewhere else. Raising funds to preserve landmark buildings the night of Sean's death. A parlor meeting to help the homeless in my district the night Paul was killed. On both nights, I slept over at the hosts' invitation." Click.

"Mrs. Ashman?"

"This is her secretary."

"Is she there? I'm Detective Yablonsky, Twenty-first Precinct."

He heard a voice in the background. "No, Maxine, I'll take the call."

The voice that spoke to Yablonsky was warm and confident, that of a philanthropist. "Yes, detective? Are you calling on account of the police benefit on the 19th?"

He had to be careful with this woman. She had some of the deepest pockets in the city. "No, ma'am. If you'd be kind enough to answer some questions?"

She seemed puzzled. "Regarding what, detective?"

"Regarding the murders of the two dancers last week. We have reason to believe you might have known them."

"Known them? I have to go detective. I'm late for an appointment."

"I would hate to have to subpoena you as a material witness, Mrs. Ashman."

"As a *witness*?" There was a pause. "As you no doubt already know, I'm a married woman, detective."

"Three months ago you submitted an ad to *Let's Get Personal*."

"I really have to run. I know your name, detective. Dare to bring my name in this, and I'll have your two little balls stuffed and displayed in a frame at the Met."

"Mrs. Ashman . . ."

"Detective Yablonsky. I never should have been foolish enough to give my name to that wretched magazine. I assure you I was somewhere else the nights those boys were killed. Whatever nights they were killed."

Click.

He speculated as to what the next brush-off would be like. Women who were famous obviously protected their reputations with the ferocity of cobras. One of the cops from Discovery would check their alibis, but he was fairly certain as to the outcome. Both women were in other places—perhaps in other bedrooms—the nights Paul and Sean were killed, but they were in *other places*.

He checked the list for the rock star's name and number. Suzy Creamcheese. Definitely not in the league of the other two.

"Ms. Creamcheese?"

"Yes."

He gave her his name.

The voice at the other end of the line sounded sleepy. He looked at his watch. Nine P.M. Either it was approaching her bedtime, or she was tired because she had stayed up partying the night before.

"Did you know Paul Matson and Sean Maysfield before they were murdered?"

"It would be pretty hard to know them *after* they were murdered, wouldn't it?"

"Just answer the question. Did you know them?"

The voice at the other end was amused. "Biblically? Or intellectually?"

"You placed an ad in *Let's Get Personal*. Why?"

"If you must know, I was horny, detective."

This interrogation would plainly be different from the others. He wanted to sound as casual about her relationships as she was. "Who did you receive satisfaction from?"

He hoped she wouldn't say The Rolling Stones. "Not the guys you mentioned. That beautiful magazine enabled me to fulfill my fantasies, but it was not Paul Matson or Sean Maysfield who did the filling."

Yablonsky smiled at that. "Were you with anyone on those nights?"

"*Which* nights, detective? Quit trying to trip me up."

"The 6th and 8th of April."

"A few days ago . . . On the 6th I was with my band for

an all-night jam. The other night was spent with Freddie Vaughan, my lyricist. From the newspapers, I have a pretty good idea of what kind of guys they were. Before I hang up on you I want you to know this—I placed the ad because all a woman ends up with in the rock business is either groupies or exploiters. Do I sound like the kind of a woman who pays strippers for sex?"

She did sound like that kind of a woman. After she hung up, he noted her alibis in the margins next to her name. It had been a different kind of interrogation. He would not be seeing her, but he made an asterisk next to her name anyway.

Yablonsky climbed the steps to the office of *Let's Get Personal*. It was late in the evening, but he was welcomed by Denise Levine.

"The last class left over an hour ago, but I decided I might as well wait here for you. You look tired, lieutenant."

"I really appreciate this," Yablonsky said.

"It's nothing. I like to keep late hours, anyway. It's the best time to go over the books if you don't have a date. Maybe I should take out a personal ad." She handed a magazine to him. "When you called and asked if the boys had other ways of making money I immediately thought of this. I should've thought about it when you were here earlier."

"I should've asked you the question earlier," Yablonsky said.

The magazine was called *Fem*. Paul's and Sean's photo spreads were on pages 102-112 and 146-155. Pictures of Paul, then Sean, naked, smiling, in flexed positions, faces artfully turned toward or away from the camera, lying on lush carpeting with their buns sticking up. He tried to connect the handsome faces and the muscular bodies with the corpses he had seen. He read the title again. It was one of the new kinds of magazines, but because of the name he guessed it was published for women rather than gays. He flipped through a few more pages. The crème de la crème of male nude America. His eyes widened as he read the circulation figure printed on the first page: 600,000.

Staring at explicit pictures of naked men was a new experience for him. He was only used to unclothed corpses. He tucked the magazine under his arm. "It's more like a *Penthouse* for women than a *Playboy*."

She nodded. "That's right."

"But it's for women."

"In the battle between the sexes that some still fight, *Fem* fulfills a necessary function. It's the equivalent of all the men's magazines that show pink."

$\triangledown$

Nine

MARTHA BRYANT HAD INSISTED on sending her limousine for him. Yablonsky had tried to be self-effacing and say no, but she had insisted. Now, as he was driven through the tree-lined streets of Beekman Place, he was glad he had given in to temptation. In this neighborhood, the shoofly was nowhere in sight. The townhouses and apartment buildings were muted pastel shades. Each side street was in effect closed off to the rest of the city by East End Avenue, patrolled by the private security force its residents had hired. No mugging, loitering, or soliciting. Still, being a detective, he knew better than to feel safe.

The windows of the limousine were opaque. He watched the people who tried to peek in to identify him look in vain. It was an odd, sensuous feeling. Was he compromising the investigation by having a chauffeur drive him? The limousine had a well-stocked bar, a color TV, plush three-inch carpeting, a burgundy leather interior, and even a bathroom in an enclosed rear compartment. Behind him, the last section of seating folded over into a bed. Yablonsky decided that you could live in this car and have better accommodations than most of the people in the city.

The chauffeur's voice: "A drink, sir?"

"Not while I'm on duty." He had to let them know he intended to hold on to some of his integrity.

"You and me both, sir."

He thought of having had to take the IRT to the West Side to interrogate Denise Levine; now he was sitting pretty, an easy rider.

Beekman Place was on a different level than most of Manhattan. Literally. Its streets consisted of terraces that led to tiny fenced-in parks that you needed a key to enter. The bay windows of the buildings, bordered by ivy, looked across placid water. To the left, linking Queens with Manhattan, was the 59th Street bridge. Being morning, the bridge was not really picturesque, but at nighttime, if you were lucky enough to have a good view, with its strings of lights the bridge resembled a constellation.

The car stopped. Yablonsky waited for the chauffeur to walk around and open his door. It was a rare moment and he wanted it to be done right.

"Ms. Bryant will ring for me when it's time to pick you up, detective."

Detective. Back to reality.

Casually dressed people walked poodles next to manicured lawns that looked well tended. He thought of the hordes of pets he had seen on the West Side, all accompanied by owners who carried pooper scoopers. Here the people walked with unencumbered hands, secure from police interference. From across the street, he smelled the river. He walked closer so he could get a glimpse of it.

He smiled. "I work four blocks away from here, yet except for when there are floaters, I never really get a chance to see it."

The chauffeur also stared at the water. "You and me both."

A doorman escorted him from the building's entrance to a leather-paneled elevator, which stopped on the nineteenth floor. He was not surprised that there seemed to be only one apartment on each floor. By now he had expected as much.

A small sign, *Fem*, was on the door. The door was open. He knocked, then let himself in. He entered a world of oblong whorls of browns and grays. Gilt-edged mirrors, antique lamps: the kind of furniture that used to appear in private clubs.

He heard voices in the next room. He found himself in an area that was as big as most people's apartments. There were desks, couches, files with magazines on top. Lemarck lamps spotlighted several glossy *Fem* covers, framed and hung on the walls as if they were portraits. The bay window had an unfettered view of the water. He told himself that his apartment in Brooklyn was a block away from the beach. Envy was pointless.

Four people were seated around a Fondrel cocktail table. They noted his appearance briefly and kept on talking.

One of the men was speaking. Yablonsky caught a slight accent. "The paintings you chose show excellent taste. You shouldn't worry about them."

The woman said, "Half the joy of buying expensive paintings is worrying about them. Don't deprive me."

The three men laughed. The woman was Martha Bryant. The article Yablonsky had read about her in *Forbes* said that she had acquired majority control of *Fem* only recently. She was still in her mid-thirties, Yablonsky's age. He liked the way she dressed, just an open necked blouse and pleated skirt. No power dressing for her. She smiled at him. "You're detective Yablonsky. I'm Martha Bryant."

The man who was seated closest to her swiveled in his chair. "A detective? That's fascinating."

The man's eyes smiled as he sized up Yablonsky. He looked like he was in his late twenties. His lips twisted slightly, making him even more good looking. He sported an authentic suntan, not the pale imitations that East Siders cultivate in tanning salons. The crease on his brow disappeared when he smiled, contributing to his attractiveness. Yablonsky liked the way he fit into his three-piece suit and custom-made white-on-white shirt. The collar was open, without a tie. He seemed fit and trim. Yablonsky tried to recall the movies he had seen him in.

The man correctly identified Yablonsky's perplexed look. He turned to his friends and laughed. "Everyone thinks they should recognize me. I don't know why. I'm only a diplomat, lieutenant, stationed at Embassy Row. I come from one of those postage-stamp sized banana republics down south."

Yablonsky laughed good-naturedly, along with the others.

The diplomat stood, offering a manicured hand. "I'm Emile Suarez. Martha's neighbor, as well as a friend. I just stopped by to pay a social call. Detective work must be fascinating, lieutenant."

"Not really. Murder investigations are usually tedious affairs. It's not the cops and robbers stuff you see on TV."

"You can say it's boring because you're on the inside. To civilians like me, it sounds pretty exciting."

Yablonsky had had a year's experience in the UN Security Patrol before he became a detective. He looked at the two men who were with Suarez. The one who clutched a briefcase was small, dark, and efficient looking: a bureaucrat. But the other one was something else. A six-foot-two hunk of Latin American beef with arms that were as muscular as Hulk Hogan's, planted on chunky hips and legs. Like the others, he wore a sleek, expensive looking suit, but this was no diplomat.

"This is Rafi," Suarez said, pointing with his chin to the smaller one. "He's been with me since my twenty-first year, when I got into politics." He laughed. "Miguel is a gift from our president to me. His sole function is to guard my body."

"Guard it against whom?"

"Right now we have a guerilla war on our hands. A large emigrant population lives in your country and some of them have become terrorists. They picket our embassy, collect money to support the guerillas, raise hell on the campuses. There've been two bombings in the last three months."

Yablonsky had read the newspapers about bombs being found within the Washington Diplomatic Compound of Suarez's country. He nodded understandingly.

Again the man shook his hand. "You probably want to question Martha. We'll be going. A pleasure meeting you, lieutenant."

He started to leave. "Suarez," Martha Bryant said, as if speaking to a naughty child. "Stay."

"I'd be in the way. I'd like to stay, though. It's up to the lieutenant of course."

All eyes turned to Yablonsky. The detective said, "It's okay with me. I just have to ask a few questions." Suarez sat down again. "Excellent. Now, Miguel, if you would go into the other room and fix us all glasses of port, Detective Yablonsky could begin his interrogation. Port, Miguel. You'll find it on top of the grand piano. the bottle that begins with P." Miguel gave him a look, but got up and headed toward the other room.

They could hear him in the other room, mixing drinks. Suarez played with his hands, spoke softly. "Miguel, speed it up. You're holding up the police department."

Suarez turned to Yablonsky. "Good relations with cops is one of my priorities." He grinned. "We even pay our parking tickets, though of course we don't really have to. That's diplomacy, lieutenant!"

"That's commendable," Yablonsky said. He watched the man eat dried fruit from a silver tray. The bits of fruit that caught between his teeth gleamed like gemstones.

"It is commendable," Martha Bryant said.

Miguel entered, carrying a tray of drinks.

"Miguel, I'm proud of you," Suarez said. "You did everything right."

"Considering it's my job to guard you and not to serve you drinks, I guess I did," Miguel said. He gave Suarez a sarcastic smile, flashing a mouthful of gold teeth. He put the tray on the table.

Yablonsky picked up his drink, and placed it on the table without sipping it. He reached into his side pocket, unfolded the copy of *Fem*, and opened it to Sean's and Paul's photo spreads. "These guys make Arnold Schwarzzeneger look like Woody Allen."

"What do you expect? It was their profession." She turned to Yablonsky. "How may I help you, lieutenant?" Martha Bryant asked.

"When did they pose for these pictures?"

"We usually do a shoot six months before the photos are due to come out. That was last December's issue."

"Did they pose for any other magazines?"

"I don't know, lieutenant. They might have. We used them for a calendar once. One of those silly things where each man represents a different month of the year. Paul was Mr. August, and Sean was Mr. October."

"What were they like to work with? Were you close to them?"

She laughed, took a sip of wine. "Paul and Sean were not on my calendar as lovemates, but I liked them. Everyone did—they were two of our most popular "months." And they liked the business."

"We found a piece of newspaper from *Let's Get Personal* in Paul's hand after he was killed." Yablonsky said. "It might be our first clue. They might have used the magazine to meet women. Did they ever confide to you about who they went out with?"

"That's Denise Levine's magazine. It would be interesting to know what she said about them."

"She said they were celebrity fuckers."

Martha Bryant put down her glass of port. "And so they were, lieutenant. They were always bragging about the type of women they serviced. But they never mentioned anyone specific to me." She paused and leaned toward Yablonsky.

"I suppose Denise gave you a list of names. Tell me what you have, lieutenant. Maybe I can help."

"It's all fascinating," Suarez said. "Those kinds of magazines are not allowed to exist in our country. They promote immorality."

Yablonsky turned back to Martha Bryant. "I don't have much, I'm afraid. Three women celebrities were on the list, but they all had alibis."

"Who are they?"

"Margaret Ashman. Marcia Goodman. Suzy Creamcheese, the rock singer. Do you know them?"

She laughed. "At one time or another, we did interviews with all of them for our guest celebrity spot. Each issue features an interview with a famous woman. We got the idea from *Playboy*." She winked at him. "Maybe we'll interview you for our next issue and you'll be our first man. How about it, lieutenant?"

"I'll have to assess my other offers first," Yablonsky said. "About those women. Would any of them be the type to get mixed up with Paul and Sean?"

She laughed. "Lord, no. Ashman's too classy. Goodman's too smart a politician. And from what I know about Suzy, it's not her scene."

"Why not? I spoke with her on the phone. She didn't strike me as being virginal."

Martha Bryant laughed. "That's Suzy. But she's into punk rock and the East Village. She wouldn't be caught dead at a place like O'Farrel's."

"Then why did all of them place ads in a magazine like *Let's Get Personal*?"

"Are you positive they placed them?"

"We have their credit card statements."

Her mouth twisted. "Levine sure knows how to protect her people's privacy, doesn't she, lieutenant?" She shrugged. "Why do women flock to O'Farrel's? Why do they buy my magazine? They could've been lonely. An estranged marriage. A busy political schedule. A show business career. Maybe it's the only way they have of meeting nice men. Anyway, I thought you said they all had alibis."

"They do." He stood. "You've been a big help."

Suarez grinned boyishly. "Very interesting, while it lasted." Still sitting, he reached out to shake Yablonsky's hand. "You're an impressive man, lieutenant. Stolid, but you do the job. Do you solve most of your cases?"

"When they give me enough time."

He nodded understandingly. "Time is always the factor. May I offer a suggestion?"

Yablonsky gripped the outstretched hand. "Be my guest."

"That's nice of you. From my dealings with the police at the UN, I've learned they're very closemouthed about their work."

"Many of them are."

Suarez leaned back in the chair. "Before I entered politics,

I worked for my country's security forces for two years. I found that it's usually not the criminal who returns to the scene of the crime, but, if he's a good one, the detective."

It was a statement that Yablonsky didn't feel it necessary to respond to. The man was right, but six years as a cop, three of them as a detective, had taught him to guard the ways in which he operated as closely as a country protects its privileged information.

"I hope I was of help," Martha Bryant said.

"Don't worry, you were."

Suarez reached for his briefcase. Yablonsky noticed his camera. "My hobby," he said. "We were looking at some pictures before you came. If you'd be willing to wait a few minutes, I can drop you off, lieutenant."

"No, thanks." He turned to Bryant. "I don't think I'll need that limo of yours, either. I can walk to where I want to go from here."

"Are you sure, lieutenant?"

"Oh yes."

"You know," Suarez said. "Aside from the circumstances, it was nice meeting you. You're sure about that car?"

"I have no need for it."

"Well then, that's it." He turned to Miguel. "The least we can do is show the detective out, Miguel."

Yablonsky went to the rear of the apartment, bringing his evidence bag with him. The place where Sean had fallen was still outlined in chalk. The Medical Examiner's office had scraped blood off the bed and carpeting for samples, then dutifully scrubbed the carpet so meticulously that the blood-stains were barely discernable.

All of Sean's possessions were supposed to be shipped back home to his family, so Yablonsky considered himself lucky that bureaucracy moved so slowly. Everything was still there.

Except for the absence of Sean's body, the cocaine, and the blood pools, the apartment looked unchanged. It was a mess, but intact. The lamp was turned over and lying on the floor, but he flicked it on anyway for extra light. This time he didn't bother to wear gloves or to be careful; he could count on one finger, the middle one, the number of times he had been able to lift a print that had actually helped him.

He went to the closet first, saw once again the racks of designer clothes. All the suits were still there. The cops from Discovery had been honest; the thought cheered him.

He looked through each suit, turning out its pockets, looking for a scrap of paper with a name or address. Nothing.

The area around the stereo was next. The albums were stacked alongside dozens of cassettes. Under Sean's collection of disco music was the more current stuff. Suzy Creamcheese's album was the first of those he pulled up. He stared at the photo. She was bending down, opening up a chest that was labeled *Pandora's Box*. She was about to unleash a whirlwind of troubles on the world; the look in her eyes said she would do so with joy.

The album had been personally autographed, but most of the others in Sean's collection were too. *Depeche Mode. Tom Tom. Club.* Rock stars signed thousands of autographs for fans. She did not have to know Sean to hand him an autograph.

The desk was piled with Sean's correspondence, but none of the letters mentioned celebrities. None of them contained a clue for a possible motive. He leafed through the address book again. Names of some of the dancers at O'Farrel's. A few nonfamous girls. All these boys seemed to be involved in "soft" hooking. Where was Sean's trick book?

It took him an hour to pile the stereo, desk, lamps, and chairs on top of the bed. He then rolled up the carpet. There was nothing there but a bare wood floor. He took out a handkerchief. This was the most exercise he'd had since he'd decided to quit jogging.

Remembering the detective tales of his youth, he opened the refrigerator. Ice trays filled with milky water sometimes concealed diamonds and gold coins, but it was bare inside.

In Paul's apartment, he went through the chest of drawers, bookcases, and shelving; behind the sofa and inside the picture frames. He found copies of *Let's Get Personal* amid the piles of magazines, but none of the ads were circled.

The closets. The writing desk. He fingered through bills and receipts.

The address book he found on the night table contained names of other Matsons, a few girls, a couple of clubs. On one page he saw that Paul had scribbled the names of some L.A. clubs, along with their addresses. Had he written them in recently? Or had he worked in L.A. before coming to New York?

The telephone calls on Paul's answering machine revealed nothing. It was one of those self-erasing tapes and the messages on it went back just a few days. A call from Sean. "It's me. See you at the club."

A couple of women left their numbers, but their voices were not similar to the celebrities he had spoken with on the phone.

A few angry clicks from people who didn't like to talk to machines.

Paul's own message to callers: "If you hear this I'm not here. Please leave your name and number. Like me, I hope you've got nothing to hide."

Yablonsky went over to the stereo and started picking up records: another extensive collection with more autographs. Another album by Suzy Creamcheese. Impulsively, he pulled the album out of its cover. Along with it came the calendar that Paul and Sean had posed for, for *Fem*.

The calendar itself was one of those pop-up kinds: you turned a page, and each month a muscular, handsome male popped out of the picture, slit-eyed and seductively smiling. Glancing at the sleek body of Mr. December, he turned the first page and his eyes widened.

Bring in the New Year with a Bang from Bob, the caption said. This calendar would make the women who purchased it want to get through the year quickly.

Sean had made a wise choice in deciding to represent the month of October. In his photo, he stood before the bare trees of Riverside Park, piles of leaves before him, a rake in his hand. The only thing he wore was a grin. The caption read: *Nothing about Sean ever Falls*.

Yablonsky flipped through the pages slowly and carefully, so as not to stir anything up.

August, Paul's month, was usually hot, so it made sense that he would be photographed at the beach. He was on his belly, looking up at the camera, and smiling sleepily, as if he had just awakened. His buttocks were flecked with sand. The caption read: *Paul can make the Temperature on any Thermometer Rise*.

Beneath it, a short, handwritten note.

> *I'll say.*
> Yours,
> Suzy Creamcheese.

He put the rolled up calendar in his pocket. He picked her album up off the floor. The cover photo showed her playing

Kick the Can with some street kids in a winding, cobblestone alley.

"Liar," he said.

Ten

He PARKED HIS CAR on East 9th Street, under a banner that said: *Rent Strike On. Speculators Beware*. Someone had magic-markered in an additional phrase: *The East Village Tenants' Cooperative*. The red banner flapped in the wind like a high-school cheerleader's pennant.

Children sat on the tenement fire escapes, their legs dangling between the spaces in the iron railings. Storefronts dotted the block: Lazarus's Rehabilitation Center. Latino People's Party. A couple of bodegas.

Salsa music sailed back and forth between the two sides of the street. Congas. Rap music. From out of one of the windows he heard the Stones' "Get Off Of My Cloud."

Near Tompkins Square Park there were people dressed in feather boas and cheap costume jewelry. Hell's Angels wearing black muscle T-shirts, their colors, and tattoos wheeled baby carriages past long-haired hippies with lovebeads and bell bottom pants. On East 6th Street, at the Aztec Bar, a crowd with Mohawk haircuts, safety pins, and razors hanging from black leather jackets stood peacefully in front, studying the list of coming attractions.

Yablonsky cut through Tompkins Square Park and came out on the south side of East 7th. Cobblestone streets. Huge lofts with slogans of one kind or another hanging from the fire escapes. He looked at the posters on the brick wall of the abandoned building on the corner: *Come to the Public Image Gallery. The Alternative Museum. Opening reception. The Dead Kennedy's appearing at the Ritz.*

The telephone poles on East 8th Street were filled with additional advertisements. Yablonsky walked by one that said: *Theatre of the Living Eye. East 4th and Ave. A.* He looked behind him self-consciously. He did not even know if the intradepartmental shoofly was following him. Posters with ads for rock groups were on the walls of the art galleries. *CBGBs: Good Rats. Uncle Son. The Fans. With special guests. Dead Boys.*

He wondered where he might buy tickets. Suzy Creamcheese had told him that her band rehearsed inside a storefront that was midway down the block. Yablonsky could hear a drum beat, a rhythm guitar joining in, then silence.

He walked in. It was a wide-open space, hot, and poorly lit. A skinny, young-looking girl sat on a radiator with her back against the unpainted, peeling wall. The storefront's windows were not opaque, anyone walking by could look in and see the band rehearsing. There were five of them. They stood or sat on cartons, with drum sticks, axes, a miniature keyboard at hand. Another man was standing behind one of the amps, a beer in his hand. "Fuck," he was saying, "It doesn't sound right. Do it again."

The guys tuned their guitars, then ripped out some more notes. The man with the beer leaned forward, his eardrum resting against one of the amps, listening intently. They played barechested, sweat pouring from their arms. Suzy, her back turned toward Yablonsky, didn't sing. She listened to her band.

"Is she good?" Yablonsky shouted above the noise.

"The best. But I'm biased."

"Why?"

"I'm her sister, Karen. She takes care of me." It was only then that Yablonsky noticed that her eyes looked wide and doelike, as if she had been permanently frightened. The result of her boating accident seemed to be one spacy kid.

"I read about what happened last summer. I'm sorry."

"Isn't everyone?" she said. "I'm fully recovered, almost. They'll be finished soon. She'll speak with you then."

"It must be nice having a sister who's famous."

'Oh, yes." She moved back to the radiator.

The progression of chords seemed endless, and to Yablonsky's ear, atonal, an unmelodic drone. It was not like the sixties music he had grown up with. The Airplane. Mike Bloomfield. The band tried to make up for its lack of technical skill with enthusiasm. Yablonsky knew that with this kind of music, one compensated for the other.

The guy with the beer yelled, "Break!" They dropped their guitars and decamped over to a small refrigerator. They brought out beers, sat on the floor with their backs against the wall. Yablonsky drew a few curious stares. They smoked their marijuana, despite his presence.

Suzy Creamcheese, left alone on the bandstand, turned toward him. An eyepatch was draped over her left eye. The dress she wore meandered down her body, conforming to its curves. Under the dress was a floppy pair of pants, patched from top to bottom. The clothes of an outcast . . . A cheap purple scarf hung from her shoulders. Shiny chains, bracelets, pendants, sets of earrings, and bangles. It was not your everyday kind of outfit, but she carried it off. Nothing she wore could detract from her face, which was uncompromisingly alive. She strolled over casually, and Yablonsky decided that her red streak of spray-painted hair was more flattering than garish.

She smiled and put her arm around her sister, bringing her along with an easy, natural gesture that he liked. Whatever else she was, she evidently loved her sister very much.

"Are you the cop I spoke to on the phone earlier?" Her tone was low-pitched. He could not tell if she had a good singing voice from listening to her talk.

"I'm the detective," Yablonsky corrected.

"I don't particularly care about your rank." Her eyes were defiant, but he noticed she clutched her sister tighter. "Are you here to arrest me?"

At the word "arrest," the band members looked up. Yablonsky noticed that they did not stub out joints, but they stopped smoking. Either they respected the law, or it was time for a break between highs.

Suzy Creamcheese turned toward her band. "What a field day for the heat," she said.

They laughed. Her eyepatch took up almost a quarter of her face. She looked like a pirate, but a pretty one. He wanted to learn one more thing about her. "What's your real name?"

"You mean I wasn't born with the name Suzy Creamcheese? Should I be insulted?" She looked at her sister, who nodded solemnly.

Suzy Creamcheese shook her head. "You're wrong. I'll have plenty of time to be insulted after he questions me. Susan Gillian. How'd you know the name was phony?"

He looked at her clothes, jewelry, and hair. "It goes with the rest of the outfit. "Suzy Creamcheese" is the name of a song Frank Zappa recorded with the Mothers of Invention twenty years ago."

She looked him over more carefully than she had before. "You know that?"

He nodded. "You're not a bad detective," she said, and dismissed her sister with an affectionate pat. Her one eye stared at him intently. "Why are you here? Do you plan to clamp the bracelets on, drag me downtown, and grill me? Although I already have enough jewelry, I'm quite willing to be cuffed. Brian here's an amateur photographer. If he snaps the photo, it'll look good for the next album."

What impressed Yablonsky the most was how truly indifferent she seemed to be to whatever he might do.

"You don't mind if I question you about Paul Matson's and Sean Maysfield's murders?"

The band was silent. Her sister shivered, looked uneasy. Suzy stood her ground. "Why should I? In this country, even punk rock stars are assumed innocent until proven guilty."

Yablonsky reached into his pocket, pulled out the calendar, and opened it to where she could read her signature.

"I didn't know you carried that kind of brown-wrapper stuff around, lieutenant. You must enjoy your nights."

"So must have you, before you murdered Sean and Paul."

"I enjoyed Paul. I give people the chance to fulfill their fantasies whenever I'm on stage, so I figured it was about time I fulfilled one of mine."

He edged closer to her, still holding the calendar. "Murder?"

She did not back away, but she looked back to her band and sister, as if for help. "Of course not." She managed a laugh. "I was referring to sex."

"When I spoke with you on the phone you assured me you didn't know Paul or Sean." He handed her the calendar. "It was found in Paul's apartment."

She looked at the calendar intently. She held onto it for a very long time before returning it to him. "I knew Paul slightly." She met his raised eyes directly. "Paul was a fantasy, that's all he was. When we're gigging I work too hard to meet anyone. When I'm not working, all there is to choose from is fans and grabbers. I placed the ad because I was lonely and horny, in that order. Denise Levine furnished me with Paul's name.

"For one hundred dollars," Yablonsky nodded. "She told me. You also told me you didn't know them."

"Jesus, lieutenant, just because I lied about knowing Paul doesn't mean I killed him. Do I look like the kind of girl who'd murder someone?"

The music she played encouraged sex and violence. He answered truthfully. "You might."

She laughed again, but looked frightened. "Look, detective, if you think it'll make you feel more diligent to handcuff and shackle me, drag me to your precinct, and apply the whips and chains, do so."

"What makes you think I'd do any of those things to you?"

"I know your type. But before you bring out the bloodhounds I can save you the trouble. Paul and Sean were murdered on the nights of the 6th and 8th. I know because I read the newspapers. On the night Sean was murdered, I was at home with my sister. All night."

Karen's hands were crossed under her sweater, scratching her arms. But her eyes didn't waver. "She was, lieutenant."

Suzy Creamcheese turned to the guy who had had his ear to the amp. Now he sat with the other members of the band, his hands around an empty beer bottle. "Tell the detective where I was on the night of the 8th, Freddie," she said. "That's the night Paul Matson was murdered."

Freddie met Yablonsky's eyes directly. "With me, in my apartment. We were going over some stuff for the upcoming album."

"What time did you finish?"

"Around twelve. But I spent the night."

Freddie spun the bottle around with his hands. The smile that lit his eyes seemed to grow deeper. "She did, lieutenant."

If she wasn't guilty, at least she could supply him with more information. He realized something. "You knew both of them didn't you?"

She smoothed down the part of her hair that was spray painted. "I went out with them both for about a week each last December. Separately."

"Paul and Sean liked to be seen with celebrities. I believed they also liked to take money from them. How much did they manage to get from you?"

She laughed. "Not much. I have no viable assets, except for my voice, lieutenant."

"People in the music business don't often strike me as being poor."

"That's uptown. Here money comes, money goes." She shrugged, then her good eye winked. "It's the way I live."

"You didn't go out to clubs then?"

"Nope. I don't disagree with you, lieutenant. They probably were experts at living off women, but all they got from me was a few bucks." She straightened, brushed back her hair. Yablonsky thought of a ballet dancer practicing. "Am I free and in the clear?"

"Like a bird," Yablonsky. "Why were you so nervous before?"

"It's not every day that a cop comes to accuse me of murder. How would you act if someone accused you?"

Yablonsky was startled by the question. Save for his current culinary habits, he had never had to deny anything before cops. "I suppose I'd act the same as you," he said.

"So there you are, you confess!"

Her mocking eye became practical. "Are you finished with me?"

"For the moment."

"Good." She headed back toward her group, then whirled abruptly. "You don't know my current A and R man, but he promises to really plug my songs if I sleep with him. Should I?"

"A and R men are a dime a dozen."

She nodded. "I'll keep that in mind."

Her group waited for her, guitars in hand, eager to begin their assault on music again.

"I might have to talk with you again," Yablonsky said.

She was already as far away from him as the room would allow. Without turning around she said, "What a bringdown that will be."

Yablonsky drove uptown, cleverly weaving his way through heavy traffic on Third Avenue. He followed the taxi drivers, plunging through the openings they created.

What little sun there was was now further obscured by rows of buildings with glass exteriors. Yablonsky recalled that criminal slang for a prison was "the glass house."

People streamed into the streets, paying no attention to the traffic lights. As Yablonsky braked to wait for the red light at the intersection of Third and 49th, his right hand played with the radio dial.

Jazz. Classical. An all-news station. Finally, rock.

He had to wait through four songs before one of hers was played. As the discordant guitar chords began, he leaned forward expectantly.

He was disappointed. He had not expected Ella or Billie, but this was not even Madonna. She sang the usual words of sex and violence as if she were bored, in a high voice that was a pale imitation of Janis Joplin's screeches and wails. The article he had read about her before his interrogation said that she, like Joplin, had gotten her start on the West Coast.

He swerved into another lane to make a left. She didn't have much of a voice, but the supposedly stylish women he passed on the corner, compared to her, were as unexciting as the "B" side of a record.

Trucks and buses filled the lane. By the time he reached the bank, the lunch hour was nearly over. He spun through the revolving door and approached Dwyer at his desk. No matter how often Yablonsky saw him, he was always startled by the security garb.

Dwyer looked up, a sandwich in hand. His black-gray hair had thinned. He had put on a little weight. His round, slightly freckled face offered Yablonsky a smile. "So. You haven't been to see me in three months. You must need help with a case."

Yablonsky nodded. "What else?"

"Lunch isn't even half over. How'd you know you'd catch me at my desk?"

"You're always at your desk."

He rubbed his forehead. "I could change."

"Not you."

Dwyer looked at his watch and sighed. "I can give you fifteen minutes. I wish it were more. I really miss the detective work."

"I'll try to come more often. Even when I don't need your help, I mean." Yablonsky looked at the lines before the tellers' windows. "Maybe the bank will be robbed today."

"You're trying to cheer me up." The still-muscular security officer stood, sipped his cup of coffee. When he was on the force, he had had to have at least a dozen cups of coffee a day. Yablonsky observed that he was aging well, then realized that where Dwyer was concerned, he could never be objective. He watched him place the cup back on the desk. "The usual?"

Yablonsky nodded.

"Follow me." He turned, heading toward the rear of the bank. He held the door open. They went down a stairway.

"I bet you had to find parking three blocks away from here," Dwyer said.

"You're still an excellent detective. All the parked cars belonged to the diplomats."

"That figures. But then their pockets always were deeper than mine."

"You really aren't bitter."

For a big man, Dwyer's voice was soft. "You still feel guilty over what happened, and there's no reason for you to. If not for you, I'd have ended up with nothing."

They went down another set of stairs, into the subbasement. Yablonsky wondered about a police force that turned men like Dwyer into chief bank guards. Yablonsky missed him terribly. Just before he was kicked out of the department Dwyer had assured him that one day he would become a fair detective.

Yablonsky was led through a door into a large office that held the main computer linking all the bank's branches. Except for the security guard and the detective, the office was empty.

Strictly speaking, cops were prevented from examining a depositor's checking and credit-card accounts via computer by the right-to-privacy laws, but Yablonsky, like many detectives, had discovered that the process saved a lot of legwork.

"You checking Al Capone's taxes? The Bhagwan? Who is it this time?"

"Suzy Creamcheese. She banks at First Federal in the Village. The guy who runs security there is a friend of yours. I want her file pulled."

"Sure, but who is she?"

"She's a rock star."

"Is that her real name?"

Yablonsky shook his head. "An alias."

"Probably calls herself that because she spreads so easily."

Yablonsky remembered her clothes, the way she looked at him. She probably did.

Dwyer made his call. Fifteen minutes passed. Yablonsky watched Suzy Creamcheese's name and account number appear on the monitor.

Dwyer pivoted around. "What do you wanna know?"

"Credit cards. Checking and savings. Deposit and withdrawals for the last six months."

The computer displayed her Mastercard and Citibank records. Dwyer looked surprised. "What do you know? She's got a gold Mastercard."

Yablonsky wondered if she had worn a sedate, business suit while applying for the card. Probably not. Then again, she might have. Who knew what she might do?

Yablonsky looked for the names of any clubs, restaurants, and hotels she might have visited last December. There were none.

Her savings-bank statement showed a balance of $300. She had $952 in her checking account. No big deposits or withdrawals in December or January. Last March she had cashed a check for $15,000.

"Her monthly checking-account statements," Yablonsky said.

Green numbers filled the screen. A semiannual royalty check from her record company. Fifteen thousand dollars.

Deposited and withdrawn one week later. Gone in a miasma of drugs, booze, and record tapes, no doubt. Her profligacy was almost criminal.

Dwyer shook his head in disapproval. "She's not a saver."

She had met Paul and Sean in late December, after all that money had probably been spent. No viable assets to attract and keep them. She hadn't been lying.

Dwyer looked up at him, his small brown eyes shining. "She a suspect?"

Yablonsky, who had been leaning over, straightened. "Not anymore."

"Those strippers! I bet you thought she killed them!"

Dwyer looked triumphant. Yablonsky shrugged. With all the men she had probably bedded, if she were to sleep with him, comparisons would inevitably follow. "I never really thought that."

Dwyer still knew him better than most people. "You look disappointed that she's not a suspect." He placed a hand on his shoulder and sighed. "I miss being a cop. In a manner of speaking, you're following in my footsteps. Clumsily, though."

Yablonsky said nothing. Dwyer removed the card, took it back to the file cabinet. Dwyer had grown up in one of the poor sections on the North Shore of Long Island, and had been on the force for nearly fifteen years. Yablonsky had heard the stories about him. He had been in shootouts, stakeouts, and had won decorations.

The twenty-four-year-old Yablonsky, on becoming Dwyer's partner, had stared at him with awe. He saw a tall, thin, but well-built guy with close-cropped brown hair and long sideburns, and a chest that was clear of battle ribbons. Dwyer never wore his medals. "They're bullshit. They represent my mistakes. A really good cop should never have to fire his gun."

"That's not what O'Connor says."

Dwyer saw the troubled look on his face. "Fuck him. O'Connor doesn't do anything but sit on his ass all day. He's not a real cop. He's a secretary."

They had worked together for one tour of duty, on the street. Yablonsky as decoy; Dwyer, his backup. Yablonsky felt that the most important thing Dwyer taught him was how to differentiate between the two kinds of criminals, and the appropriate steps to take with each kind.

With the clumsy street hood, all you had to do was follow the obvious trail of clues. If the crime or murder looked like it had been done by a professional, you searched for the little discrepancies that became clues. Motives of the childlike crimes that amateurs committed were myriad. The reason behind a professional killing was almost always money. Dwyer's motto was "Follow the money and you'll find your murderer."

After a two-year tour of duty on the streets, Yablonsky was assigned to UN Security, along with Dwyer. One afternoon, they were patrolling one of the underground UN parking lots. Four men came down by elevator. Dwyer recognized three of them. Delegates from one of the Middle Eastern countries. They seemed to be leading a younger looking man toward their limo. One of them flashed his teeth at Dwyer before he got into the car. "Good afternoon, sergeant."

Two days later one of the newspapers reported that a leader of a dissident group of Middle Eastern students was missing. There was a photo of the student: the boy the men had led to the car that day.

Dwyer showed Yablonsky the article and picture. "I'm going to O'Connor with his. Will you back me up?"

Yablonsky tried to caution Dwyer. "He must already

know about it. You could be risking your career."

Dwyer laughed, then assured him. "I'm the best cop in this department. They can't do a thing to me."

Yablonsky, although ten years younger than Dwyer and not half the cop he was, felt he knew the inner political workings of the department much better than his partner. "They can do more to you than you can ever imagine."

Dwyer was smart enough at least to 'take it' initially to the department. He related what he knew to O'Connor, who at that time was the precinct captain. At the next meeting between them, because it concerned a foreign country, two men from Central Intelligence were there. It had happened in the United States, so an FBI man was also present.

Dwyer focused his attention on Captain O'Connor. "They've probably killed the boy by now. What are you going to do?"

"Nothing," O'Connor said. "Open your mouth and you're off the force."

Dwyer turned to Yablonsky for support. Yablonsky loved Dwyer. He shook his head slightly at him in warning.

The FBI man spoke to Yablonsky. "Did you see any of this?"

Yablonsky shrugged, saying nothing.

"Do I have to go the reporters to see justice done?" Dwyer asked. "Why are you shielding them?"

"They're UN delegates," said one of the men from the CIA. "Because they have diplomatic immunity, it's a messy situation. It works the same way over there for us. Whatever you know, please keep it to yourselves."

Dwyer looked as stubborn, as unafraid as before. "I can't do that."

He turned to Yablonsky. Yablonsky ignored him. Dwyer didn't seem to realize it yet, but he was through. Yablonsky wanted to save at least something for him. "He's six months short of fifteen years. Give him full pension, and I'll be quiet."

"We don't have to buy anything," O'Connor said.

Dwyer stared incredulously at Yablonsky. Yablonsky avoided his eyes, and O'Connor's, focusing on one of the CIA men. He was surprised to hear his voice, sounding steady. "Then I will back him up. We'll go to the reporters. You'd probably be able to keep the lid on if it were just one cop. If there're two of us, you'll never be able to hush it up. He's got six months left before he can retire and vest money towards his pension. Let him keep it."

"He's out, and so are you," O'Connor said.

"Then I'll talk."

Under the deal Yablonsky worked out, procedures against Dwyer were dropped. He was allowed to retire due to "stress." He would receive his full pension when he reached 55. Midway through the negotiations, the department had hedged, but Yablonsky was adamant. Full pension at age 55. Until then, Dwyer would be allowed to work as chief of security in one of the city branches of a South American bank. The bank was patronized by many of the Hispanic diplomats of the UN.

Dwyer, still not comprehending what had happened to him, had surrendered his badge and gone to work. Yablonsky, having had enough of diplomacy, transferred out of the precinct. But his career was allowed to advance like that of any good cop's. Five years later he made detective, first grade, and received his gold shield. They even transferred him back into his old precinct, but under O'Connor he received no assignments that dealt with the UN. A year after his transfer, O'Connor retired, Flood arrived, and Yablonsky was treated like any other detective, allowed to investigate anywhere.

Yablonsky looked at his watch and stood. "Thanks, Kevin. You've been a big help."

Dwyer led him into the hall and up the stairway, then followed him out the revolving door. They stood in the street.

Dwyer stretched out his hand. Except for his profanity-filled lectures, he had always treated Yablonsky formally, as if to emphasize the gulf between their skills. "See you once you find your next suspect."

"Before then," Yablonsky said. He almost wished Dwyer were working alongside him right now. The difficulties of the case would be more than cut in half. But Dwyer was better off as a bank guard, considering the interoffice politics.

"I appreciate what you did for me," Dwyer said. "Even if sometimes I resent it."

"I understand that."

Dwyer pulled away from him. They spoke alongside a man selling hot pretzels. "If you need any more help . . ."

Yablonsky doubted he would. He said, "Of course."

A line of customers began to form around the pretzel vendor. Dwyer followed him into the street. The double-parked cars of UN diplomats who had gone into the bank to attend to business filled East 49th Street, blocking traffic.

Dwyer forced a smile. "Nothing changes, right?"

As Yablonsky walked down East 49th, he sensed that Dwyer still stood there, watching him. He reached his car. The UN limos were now triple-parked, blocking two lanes of traffic. Cars waited in line to squeeze through the single clear lane. Yablonsky pulled out of his space, joining the long line of drivers honking their horns.

Traffic was much lighter on Second Avenue. He made a left, stopping parallel to the phone on the corner. He waved away the approaching meter maid, showing his badge.

All the phones were occupied. There were none across the street. He could have commandeered a phone, saying it was police business. Instead, he waited fifteen minutes until one finally became free.

Flood got right to the point. "Do we have a suspect or not?"

"I don't think she did it," Yablonsky said.

"The media thinks she'd make a great killer. Her name alone makes a great headline. They haven't written anything yet, but they're clamoring."

"Let them clamor. How'd they find out I spoke with her?"

"Not from me. They snoop around. It's their job. Most of them are probably better detectives than half the men on my force." He paused. "No disrespect intended. You sure she didn't do it?"

"She's out of it. Dwyer checked her finances, and nothing suspicious turned up."

"Are there any other leads?"

"None right now."

"This time, I don't want to have to close without a suspect."

"Neither do I," said Yablonsky. "I already have four other cases pending. If I'm still a detective, that is."

"I'm doing my best for you. But watch your diet."

Yablonsky got in his car and drove through the crowded midtown tunnel. Then onto the Brooklyn Queens Expressway until he reached the Belt. He exited at Coney Island Avenue. Home.

Entering his apartment, he turned on the TV, then went into the kitchen and opened a can of tuna. The TV volume was loud. It was one of the quiz shows. It didn't matter what the program was. He liked to listen to the disembodied, impersonal voice.

He munched his sandwich, went back to the living room.
From the window behind the television, he glimpsed the
Atlantic Ocean. It looked rough out there tonight.

What now? Cop shows? Chuck Norris movies on WHT?
Pressing a remote-control switch, he listened to his phone
messages. The first was from his ex-wife. Instinctively he
turned the phone's volume down lower. Possibly to counter
the publicity he had received because of his newest case, she
proudly informed him that her current husband had just
been made chief security officer of *two* Atlantic City casinos
and that they had received a pair of complimentary tickets
to see Diana Ross perform this Saturday night from one of
them.

The next message: a strange, whining voice informed
Yablonsky that he had gotten his home number from Flood.
He was Freddie Vaughan. He would be home all night. He
gave his address and apartment number. Two twenty-four
West 92nd Street, between Columbus and Amsterdam.

There were some angry words, but Yablonsky surmised
that Freddie Vaughan, Suzy Creamcheese's lyricist, had
something to tell him. He sighed, placed his overcoat beside
him on the sofa. Due to the nighttime construction work,
traffic would be heavy on the Belt, so he would have to take
Ocean Parkway into the city. He set his alarm for three hours
thence, then loosened his shirt, pants, and jacket. He
wanted to nap. Justice would have to wait.

The West Side of Manhattan was barely recognizable as one
of the hubs of the city at eleven o'clock on a weeknight.
Occasionally taxis and buses sped by. The traffic lights on
Amsterdam flashed yellow, not green and red as in the
daytime. There were no corner fruit stands, bookstores, and
pet shops on this block. Only bodegas.

A group of teenagers sat on stoops outside a tenement building, listening to loud music. They watched intently as Yablonsky parked his car. As he crossed to the other side, three of them rose and came toward him.

Flood was right, he should always carry a gun. He would listen to him in the future. The tallest of them broke away from the others and approached him. He was Hispanic.

"We know everyone on this block, and you're not from this neighborhood. For people who don't live here, we charge ten dollars to guard your car."

"I'm a cop," Yablonsky said. At least he had remembered to bring his shield. He showed it to them.

The leader gave him a broad, insolent smile. "The offer still stands."

Yablonsky thought rapidly. He could go back to the car and give a distress call, but by the time the bluecoats arrived, this gang would be gone. He could park on another block, but he would still have to come back here to meet Freddie Vaughan. He looked past the boys. The shoofly was not in sight. Except for this gang, there was no one out on the street. There was never a cop around when you needed one. It was extortion, but it was easier to pay up than argue or fight.

He handed the one nearest him ten dollars. The gang leader spoke as if he were a parking lot attendant. "When you coming back?"

There was no reason to lie. Whatever time he returned, his car was completely in their hands. "In about half an hour."

"That means you have a round-trip ticket. We charge twenty dollars in that case."

Yablonsky gave him a look. "Will that mean my car will be safe?"

"We'll look after it like it was mine."

Yablonsky handed over another ten dollars. It hurt, but at least they allowed him to continue walking.

Freddie Vaughan lived on the topmost floor of a cheap tenement building. The apartment was in the rear. Yablonsky stepped through the door into a minuscule, boxy hall and walked past the bathtub in the kitchen. He glimpsed dishes piled up in the sink and on the counters. He found himself in a tiny room with an uneven wooden floor.

Vaughan sat on a bulky chair with ripped upholstery. "My castle," he said. "How do you like it?"

The room was lit with floor lamps. To get any light at all in the daytime, the lamps would have to be turned on. Rear apartments did not see much of the sun.

Song sheets with Freddie Vaughan's name on them covered the wall like wallpaper. A display of gold records was on the wall behind his chair. It looked as if he were framed by borders of gold.

Vaughan smiled, then pointed to one of the golden orbs. "This one may go platinum. I had the misfortune to hook up with a greedy bitch who's been cheating me for years."

"Suzy Creamcheese."

"The one and the same. She believes in an equitable distribution of profits. That's why I'm living in a studio apartment on the worst block on the West Side. With a fire escape for a terrace and neighbors who cha-cha me to sleep every night."

"While she spends money as if it were water," Yablonsky said. "What does that have to do with why you want to see me?"

"It has to do with those strippers' deaths. The night she said she was with me, she wasn't. I mean, she was for a while. We did work on some songs, but she left early. At ten." He paused. "That means she had enough time to commit those murders."

"Why didn't you tell me this before?"

He rested his hands behind his head, his fingers propped against two of the gold records. "She threatened to fire me if I said anything. It's punk rock, lieutenant. Despite the gold records, I'm not famous enough yet to do crossover stuff."

Yablonsky's voice was flat. "You told the reporters I interrogated her. They think she's a suspect."

"I'm glad. That'll pressure you to nab her. Two years ago she and her agent made me sign an agreement that gave her credit as my cowriter. I had to give up three quarters of my rights to the sheet music, otherwise she wouldn't record my stuff. She's done that to a number of songwriters. She's been getting away with murder for years."

She had given Yablonsky a fake alibi. Once again. He did not believe she had committed murder, but she was making it very difficult for him to dismiss her as a suspect. "I'm only concerned with Paul's and Sean's murders," he said. "We already know that she slept with them. Did she ever mention their names to you?"

"No."

"Did you ever see them together? Arguing? Dealing?"

"No."

"How about the band? Did they?"

"She doesn't like guys around her when her sister's there during practice or a gig. She keeps the personal and business sides of her life pretty separate, lieutenant."

"Why is that?" Yablonsky asked.

"You've seen her sister. She's pretty spacy, isn't she? Suzy's protective of her. She loves that kid."

It was the first reasonably decent thing he had heard

anyone say about her. Extortionist. Possible murderer, but also devoted sister. "You've given me nothing that shows she's a murderer. Don't talk again to the reporters. You'll get yourself into trouble if you do."

"Okay, lieutenant. I was so sure she did it, too." He looked disappointed.

"You need sufficient proof of guilt before you can arrest someone, Freddie."

"The way she's bled us all for years, I felt she was capable of it. She lied about where she was that night. Why don't you think she's guilty, lieutenant?"

Yablonsky would be damned if he'd confide in this overworked and underpaid songwriter. "I never said that I think she's innocent, Freddie, only that she doesn't yet appear to be guilty."

Back home, he turned on the answering machine. There were no messages.

He started a beer, but left it half-finished on the cocktail table. Stretching out on the sofa, he fell into a restless sleep.

Two hours later he woke up. He looked around uncertainly for a moment, as if he had expected to awaken in someone else's apartment. The ticking clock had its own rhythm, like the ocean. The street lamp in front of the alleyway glowed. He caught its light through the bottom of the curtain. The familiar furniture shadows on the floor told him where he was.

He poured the remaining beer down the kitchen drain, then went back to the living room. He watched an hour of MTV. Meeting Suzy Creamcheese had reignited his interest in rock, no doubt about it.

He watched a dozen videos before he finally went back to sleep. Two of them had to do with cars and girls and it was hard to tell which one of them the driver was trying to seduce. Three hinted at sex, gently. One, of a guy jumping up and down on stage, said it blatantly. Another dealt with the losses and loves of a transvestite. There was one that showed a crew-cut man trying to prevent a long-haired, Sixtyish kind of rock band from playing by blowing them apart with hand grenades and, as if to emphasize the inevitable triumph of rock, failing every time. He saw one of Suzy Creamcheese's latest hits. The video version showed her hopping from bed to bed, wearing a mask similar to the ones that had been placed over Paul and Sean's heads. The beds were lined up one after the other on a street. A couple of men chased her, wrestled with her briefly, then lost her to the next empty mattress. Musical beds.

Yablonsky pressed the volume switch down. He continued watching the figures in the videos prance, simulate sex acts, work their guitars, electric organs, and drums, in silence. The next video was eleven minutes long, Michael Jackson's "Thriller." He pressed a button on his VCR to record it, then played it back a second time. It was a pleasure to be able to see a video whose storyline could be followed without having to listen to the lyrics.

$\triangledown$

Eleven

THE RECORD SHOP ON East 8th Street was crowded with mohawk-topped and multicolored-haired fans of Suzy Creamcheese. She had sounded friendly enough to him on the phone, though she must have known why he was coming to the East Village to see her. If she told her fans that he intended to arrest her, would they riot?

He entered the shop, brushing by a tough-looking boy with razor blades sticking out of the front of his jacket, dangling earrings, and a scalp that was tattooed to resemble a serpent.

"Please. I'd like to go through," Yablonsky said.

The boy stepped back. "Certainly, sir."

Teenagers were sitting on the floor, smoking pot. The walls of the record shop were covered with albums from the Fifties and Sixties. Blown-up photos of a crew-cut Frankie Avalon and tiny Brenda Lee stared at pictures of Cyndi Lauper and Joan Jett in a kind of showdown.

The only other adult in the place wore an old T-shirt that was spotted with paint and said *Fillmore East*. His hair fell to his shoulders. He had to be the owner.

In this crowd, Yablonsky stood out as if he were the chief suspect in a lineup. The guy said, "You here to buy a record for your son? Or searching for memories?"

"I'm searching for memories." He saw that Suzy Creamcheese was in the rear of the store, facing a pile of albums
and cassettes, signing away. Her latest hit, "I'll Remember
to Forget," rocked the sound system. It was a love ballad.
Yablonsky was surprised and pleased. She still didn't have
much of a voice, but at least she knew something about
phrasing.

She signed one album after another, patting fans on the
back and shoulders. The personal touch. When she saw him
she smiled, pointed to the crowds of fans, and shrugged. He
noticed that her arms were bare and perspiring, but still
heavy with cheap-looking bangles and bracelets. If you plugged her in, she'd probably glow, he thought.

A girl materialized out of the crowd. Her sister. The room
was stifling. Most of the people there wore short-sleeved
shirts and jeans, but she was encased in a long-sleeved
fireman's shirt and a dress that reached to her ankles.
Wasn't she perspiring? She must be cold-blooded, Yablonsky
thought.

"God, it's hot in here," he said.

"Dante's inferno." There was moisture on her lips, and
it clung to her mouth in beads of sweat that looked like
pearls. "You the messenger?" he asked.

"That's what I do." She pushed her way out of the shop
toward the door and Yablonsky followed. "She'll be with you
as soon as she can. You've got to understand how much the
fans love her."

"It must be hard for you."

Her eyes narrowed slightly, but her smile remained.
"What do you mean?"

"Working in this heat."

"Oh. No, I love to do it. Suzy's the best sister a girl could
have. What I do in return is hardly noticeable."

Yablonsky tried to talk above the music. "It's good you're able to help your sister."

She noticed the look of sympathy. She said, "Yes, I know. Despite the accident. Poor me." Turning abruptly, she crossed the street, and sat on the hood of a car. She looked fourteen years old. Yablonsky could see the fans still gathered around the record display.

Ten minutes later, Suzy Creamcheese came out of the shop, accompanied by a small, emaciated boy and a girl with dried-out brown hair who wore wire-rimmed glasses.

She grinned at Yablonsky. "My entourage. Has Karen been entertaining you with anecdotes about me?"

Karen hadn't said a word since they had come outside. She sat looking uncertainly at her sister, waiting to be told what to do.

"She's told me everything," Yablonsky smiled.

"It's all false," she said. Her eye, clear beneath the smear of eye shadow laughed at him. "You see, I'm denying everything already."

"That's the best way to begin an interrogation."

The skinny guy and the girl with the wire-rims were exchanging whispers. Suzy Creamcheese turned, gave them a look. Yablonsky was impressed by the way they froze. The rest of the world might consider her only a troublesome punk-rock star, but to them she was clearly a celebrity worth catering to.

She turned back to him. Now she looked amused. "That's the price I have to pay for fame." Her eye fastened on him as if she were the one doing the interrogating. "Do you think it's worth it?"

Yablonsky didn't know whether he was expected to answer. Karen laughed. "It always is. Those fans in there were *so* full of love for you."

Suzy Creamcheese turned back to her two-person entourage. She wore a long, flowing open man's black jacket on top of a faded polo shirt and somehow managed to look very stylish. Yablonsky had seen skirts like hers in the thrift shops. He watched her eye under its long lashes. "I'd like you to take Karen back home with you, Rob. Wait for me at your apartment. I should be back by one, if detective Kojak here doesn't ravish me, that is."

"What the hell could he possibly want with you?" Rob asked.

"To grill me like a fish," she said.

"But you're innocent," Karen said. She turned to Yablonsky. "She hasn't done anything."

Yablonsky and Suzy Creamcheese crossed the street. He heard Rob say, "Just because she lives in the East Village."

When they almost reached Tompkins Square Park Yablonsky said, "I'm sorry if I embarrassed you in front of your friends."

"Don't be, lieutenant."

"We can't go to the station house. If the reporters see you there with me they'll think you're guilty."

"Then you believe I'm innocent?"

"I don't know what I believe about you."

They stood on the corner of Avenue A and 8th Street, facing each other.

"I think Rob was right," she said. "You admitted to me on the phone that you knew of two other women celebrities who went out with Paul and Sean. I think you're focusing your investigation on me because I'm only a rock star."

"I also told you we later learned that those women told the truth about where they were the nights those strippers were murdered. Unlike you. All *you've* done since I met you is lie to me. The only thing you've said that I agree with is that you're only a rock star. And I wouldn't be so quick to call what you do music."

"If I'm the only suspect you can come up with, I wouldn't be so quick to call what you do detective work."

"Name a place where we can go. I want to grill you like a fish."

"This is police harassment," she said indignantly. "I'm calling my lawyers."

Yablonsky laughed. "Look at yourself. What lawyer would have you as a client? You'd be considered guilty before you entered the courtroom."

She sighed. "That's true enough, I guess. You're right. If it ends up in court I'm a dead woman." She seemed to be lost in thought, assessing the situation. "We can go to the Life Café," she said at last. "And thanks."

It was a rare thing when one of his suspects on a case thanked him for something. He looked at her, puzzled.

"For not taking me to the precinct house." She raised her hand to wave off an approaching fan. The bracelets on her arm jangled noisily. She pointed ruefully at her jewelry. "They'd probably fashion one of these into a metal noose for my neck. I know how cops are. Even you."

"You're wrong," Yablonsky said. "I like you."

They sat across from each other at the rearmost table in the Life Café on East 10th. Yablonsky was surprised. The place had been nicely furnished with cane chairs and tablecloths. Coming here, they had passed an art gallery where empty potato sacks hung on rafters and sold for five hundred dollars apiece. You could buy a full sack of potatoes in any supermarket for less than ten dollars. This café pleased him. They ordered cappuccino and strawberry croissants.

"I hope you sister will be okay," Yablonsky said. "You seemed very concerned about her."

"We're not close to our parents. If I didn't take care of her, she'd end up on the street."

"What happened to her?" Yablonsky asked. "The article I read in *People*, all it said was that the accident happened last July at the 79th Street boat basin. You don't think of people getting injured on boats in Manhattan."

Suzy Creamcheese sipped her coffee. "There was a party. People got high. Somehow Karen got tipsy and managed to fall off Marshall Hunter's boat as another boat was docking alongside. She could've been crushed, but all she got were bruises, scrapes, and a bad scare. The accident traumatized her pretty bad."

"But before that she was normal," Yablonsky said.

"Your typical teenager," she said. "Full of sex, drugs, and rock and roll. The fact that I've managed to become a rock star thrills her. Every kid dreams of that, you know."

"In the early sixties I wished I were Sam Cooke," Yablonsky said. "Even though he was a black guy. Then in sixty-four, I wanted to be the fifth Beatle. In my fantasy, I was up on stage with them all the time, only I didn't play an instrument." He sipped his coffee. "Everybody grows up sooner or later. Now I wish I were on stage with Coltrane."

"He's dead."

"That's why it's just a wish."

She was looking at him contemplatively. "You know, it's hard for me to imagine why you became a cop."

"I enjoy the work. But I'm glad I made detective."

"Why?"

"Less violence," he said. "Are you finishing your croissant?"

"I want it," she said. "It's lunch."

He signaled the waitress for another.

"That's two," she said. "You must be on an expense account."

"Not exactly."

"I imagine your department lets you write off just about

whatever you want. I know when I do my taxes I deduct like mad."

It was hard to imagine her filling out numbers and columns in a disciplined way. "You mentioned Marshall Hunter, your manager. Your sister was on his yacht that weekend?"

"Houseboat, not yacht," she said. She nodded. "Marshall was the only guy on the boat who was sober. Throwing those parties was a necessary part of the music business to him. After he signed me, things really started to move for me. I owe everything to him."

"It's lucky for your sister he was along to save her."

Did she wince? If she had, she recovered quickly. "Yeah, it was pretty lucky."

"Is he still your manager?"

"Not anymore. We went our separate ways. Nothing against Marshall. After a while our goals just became different."

"I see."

The waitress came with his croissant. He bit into it.

"You'll get fat, eating food like that," she said. "Don't you ever eat any good food?"

"Not at the moment." He put down the croissant. "You have nice eyes." He corrected himself. "I mean the one you have."

"Thanks."

He pointed with his chin to her eyepatch. "How did that happen?"

"Another boating accident." Then, laughing, she raised the patch. Yablonsky, prepared for the awful sight, was taken aback. One eye was as good as the other.

"It's a gimmick," she said. She quickly placed the patch back over her eye, looking around the café.

"Don't worry," Yablonsky said. "No one saw you expose

yourself. The eyepatch is supposed to help your image as a rock singer, I bet. I never understood why teenagers enjoyed giving so much of their parents' money to rock stars who only *look* poor. Was the patch your idea?"

She shook her head.

"Marshall was the guy who packaged me. I needed a trademark, something that would make me stand out." She looked at him coyly. "I do stand out, don't I?"

"Like Blackbeard," he said. "Ella and Billie didn't need gimmicks."

"I'm not Ella or Billie, but I enjoy being a celebrity."

He nodded, pushed his coffee cup away. "I saw one of your videos last night, bondage mask and all. Was that your idea? Or Marshall's?"

"It was Marshall's, of course. Why do you want to know?"

"You weren't with Freddie the night Paul was killed."

She nodded. "Freddie's angry at me, but he's still fair. He had to tell you I was with him."

"He did, but you weren't there for the entire night. If you had a motive, you had the time to kill Matson. Don't be foolish enough to use Freddie Vaughan as a shield, Susan. He's not exactly grateful to you for extorting money from him and the other lyricists. Were Sean and Paul also giving you money for some reason? Surprise me. Tell the truth. I can dig for the information if I have to."

She picked up the rest of her croissant, nibbling it casually as she looked at him. "Paul and Sean never gave me a penny. As for the music business, you don't know anything about it. Of course I took money from Freddie and the others. Rock singers and their writers have had arrangements like that for years. Elvis Presley was the first star to do it. He wouldn't record a song unless he shared in the publishing rights. Considering how many records he would sell, he gave his writers a good deal. Most rock singers split the rights these days. Freddie's lying if he told you differently. The problem I have with you as a detective, Yablonsky, is that you use deductive reasoning. If I took money from Vaughan, automatically I extorted money from Paul and Sean."

"You're right," he said grudgingly at last. "But I'm afraid I'll have to hit you with some more of my reasoning. Since you continue to tell lies, you must have reasons to lie. If filling your pockets with someone else's money is such an acceptable business practice, why would someone you've worked with for years be so eager to see you indicted?"

"Vaughan made plenty of money with me, lieutenant. It just goes out of his pocket into freebasing. For a cop, you strike me as being pretty bright. Interrogate him next time, and you'll notice he has an itchy nose. I was with my sister both of those nights. But who would believe that?"

"I like you," Yablonsky said. "But you've seen too many detective shows on TV. Whatever your alibi is, it's still your alibi, you've got to go with it. Besides, there must be some nights you sleep alone."

She shook her head. "My sister would be too unstable to hold up in court. I don't want her involved in it."

"I don't think you killed Paul and Sean, but if you're all I come up with, they may move to indict you."

She looked at him stubbornly. "I'll take my chances. Come on, let's get out of here. I'm glad that at least you don't think I'm capable of murder."

He stood. "So far we have you for extortion, perjury, and, probably, minor drugs. I didn't say I didn't think you were capable of murder. I said that I didn't think you killed Paul and Sean. I can picture you killing someone, if you thought you had a good reason and that a lie would get you out of it."

"Then why are you seeing me? Why did we have coffee together?"

"The usual attraction between a detective and his suspect," he said. "Besides, you're pretty."

"And talented," she said.

"No comment."

As they walked through Tompkins Square Park, they could see that part of the park was filled with flashing police lights, crowds of people, and cops behind wooden barricades. Cops squatted with guns behind the squad cars and stood with rifles behind trees, facing the public bathroom.

On the fringes of the crowd, kids played ghetto blasters and did tricks with skateboards. Yablonsky pushed his way through, Suzy Creamcheese behind him. He reached the ring of cars.

A sergeant behind one of the squad cars seemed to be in charge. Though they were not in the same precinct, Yablonsky knew him. Alex Hauser. The cop alongside him with his gun pointed safely in the air was Sergeant Robbins.

Hauser nodded at Yablonsky. "We were about to make a move on Leroy Smalls in Tompkins. He saw us coming and barricaded himself inside the woman's bathroom with a woman hostage. He swears he's not coming out."

Yablonsky knew Leroy. He was always arresting him when he had worked decoy. "Let me handle it," he said.

"Are you crazy? The motherfucker's armed."

"I know him," Yablonsky insisted. "I can get him to come out without invading the bathroom."

Hauser surrendered his bullhorn to him. They conferred together for a minute. Then Yablonsky spoke into it. "Leroy, it's me. Detective Yablonsky from the old days." Suzy Creamcheese, back with the crowd, stared at him incredulously. He walked partway toward the bathroom. The playground area had been cleared. He moved closer. Leroy peered at him from behind the upright park bench, propped up against the steel door. Muffled sobs came from the woman inside.

Leroy nodded to Yablonsky. "It's all over for me," he said. "And her. Motherfuckers ain't going to send me to jail."

"Let the woman go," Yablonsky said. "Then come out and surrender, Leroy."

"Shit, no."

"How many times have we arrested you?"

"I don't know. About a dozen."

"Have you ever served time in prison before?"

"No."

"Do you think it'll be different now?"

He looked thoughtful. "No," he said slowly. He grinned.

"Then let her go. She's of no use to you. Then come out and let us arrest you."

"That makes sense. You sure I won't end up in no jail?"

"You didn't before."

Smalls stood and motioned the frightened woman outside. She ran toward the ring of squad cars. "They going to shoot me?" Smalls asked.

"Not if you're with me," Yablonsky said.

They sat on a park bench near the corner of East 9th Street, by themselves. The crowd had left. The squad cars were gone. Leroy Smalls had been arrested and taken away.

"The other cops would've shot up everything," Suzy Creamcheese said. "It took you one minute to defuse the situation. I'm impressed."

"They just weren't sure what approach to use," Yablonsky said.

"Tell me what you would have done if he had shot the woman."

"Hauser managed to slip me his gun before I went in, so I guess I would've tried to shoot him."

"Will you get a commendation?"

"Probably."

"What will happen to Smalls?" she asked.

"He'll probably be on the street again by tomorrow. Unfortunately."

Old men were playing chess and checkers around bulky, concrete tables. In East New York, as a boy, Yablonsky had watched old men like this for hours as they played *bocci*. It was not the game that intrigued him so much as their arguments and dramatic gestures. The tension was beginning to go out of him.

"This place reminds me of People's Park in Berkeley," she said. "Flat, no landscape, no trees and hills. The funny thing is that everything else there but the park is full of greenery and mountains."

"You said before that you grew up on the coast." He paused, looking at the patch of red hair. "Happily?"

She shrugged. "At least not unhappily. My parents were so into the sixties they were square. At first I rebelled by being Little Miss Superstraight. Then I discovered the music scene at North Beach. I showed up at my high-school graduation, wearing safety pins and a mohawk."

He laughed. "Were they shocked?"

"They said at last I'd found myself." She shook her head. "Do you know what it's like living in a home where nothing you do shocks your parents because the things they did were so much worse? At least I was exposed to good music. Grace Slick and Janis Joplin were my idols."

He had half expected her to say Mozart and Beethoven. "I

saw Janis Joplin at Woodstock. She was too doped up to be any good, though."

"You were at Woodstock?"

"The year before I went to college."

"I knew you went to college!"

He smiled. "Most detectives do these days."

"I went to Sarah Lawrence." She saw the surprise in his eyes. "Look, detective, the music scene's exciting and it's the easiest way I know to make money. As you said, you don't have to be Ella Fitzgerald or Billie Holiday to be good."

"Do you like the East Village?"

"I like the galleries. The nonconformity. People are more real here than on the West Coast."

"It must be the lack of sunlight," Yablonsky said. "How much longer do you think you'll have here before the developers gentrify it?"

"Not long. Then where will we go? Across the river? What a shame."

He shook his head. "The artists who've been crowded out of Soho and Tribeca are already there." He made an inquiring gesture with his hand. "Were you upset when you heard that Paul and Sean were killed?"

"I'm upset when I hear anyone's been killed, detective."

There was a silence between them. They watched the chessplayers shift their pieces on the table. He took out a cigarette. "Where do we go next?"

She took his hand, gave it a squeeze. "We go to my apartment."

Two hours later he was approaching the precinct house. Climbing the steps, he saw the flock of reporters scurry down to meet him. Their cameramen, lugging equipment, trailed behind. Realizing that he was out of range and therefore safe, he flipped his middle finger.

He had almost made it to the entrance unscathed, but there was Warren Paton from UPI, barring the doorway. At three hundred pounds, he was an unmovable force. Yablonsky slowed.

"Hello, Warren."

"Is there a suspect yet in the double killings?"

"Nothing," Yablonsky said. "The stripper clipper's still on the loose."

"So all the male dancers should look before they leap," Paton said, completing the headline. "I'm going to quote you."

"Quote away," Yablonsky said. "Just don't attribute it to me."

When he reached his desk he sat down. He was confronted by a huge amount of new paperwork.

Smiling, he reached into one of the drawers, clipped a can of Pepsi off the six-pack. It was warm, but he did not have the energy to walk to the gym and get a cold one from the machine. Twice in an hour and a half. The warm Pepsi tasted like champagne.

The clerk who had dropped the load of paper on his desk had been kind enough to organize it for him. There were separate piles for interoffice memos, social obligations and fraternal meetings, speculative newspaper articles about his latest case, all underlined, and a notice of an interdepartmental bowling tourney, to be held at Madison Square Garden Lanes. Yablonsky shook his head. Only cops still bowled these days.

The pile that concerned his caseloads showed a note from Toxicology, pointing out to him that the victim whose body had been found on the 59th Street Bridge had probably been murdered elsewhere. He sighed. He would have to send them a memo, reminding them that the case had been put on hold.

He almost flipped by the next one, a report from Discovery that said *Priority—Matson and Maysfield Murders.* A note had been stapled on: *This turned up two days ago. It might be of possible interest to you.*

It was a photocopy of a parking ticket given for being alongside a fire hydrant on April 6th, the day Sean was murdered, around the corner from the scene of the killing. The on-duty patrolman was Alden Hardis; the time, two in the morning, and it had been made out to Miguel Guzman. Because the ticket was invalidated, he suspected it belonged to someone connected with the UN.

There were not many places to park in the city, although members of the UN delegations had their own designated spots. The patrolmen and meter maids would see the UN delegates parking their cars in front of fire hydrants, hospital areas, no-parking zones. The traffic department sometimes towed their cars, but they could not be impounded. If issued a ticket, the diplomat could pay the ticket if he chose to, or he could rip it up in the cop's face. Some cops solved the dilemma by plastering the UN cars with reams of tickets, but always being sure to leave a space blank or to fill out one part incorrectly so the ticket would not be valid. It was a way of giving the diplomats a message without having to waste a day in court. Usually, a cop gave the perpetrator a chance to move his car first.

Yablonsky folded the ticket, placing it in his topmost pocket. He went back to the web of papers. Yesterday he had read another report that dealt with the UN, from Sergeant Anderson, but that was something else. That report was tucked into his wallet.

Looking up, he saw Flood weaving his way through the rows of desks, exchanging greetings, shaking the hands of his men.

"My most indispensable man," he said to Yablonsky. He flipped his wrist so that Yablonsky could see his watch. "You were supposed to be back over two hours ago. Why so late?"

"It was a lengthy interrogation," Yablonsky answered. When they had reached the apartment, Susan had shrugged out of her clothes with the ease and grace of an elk. Her body had a glow like porcelain. It was curvy, with firm, pale breasts and a slight, sweaty scent from her previous exertions with the band. Yablonsky had not been with a woman in her mid-twenties for years. He wondered aloud if they were all like this. She had laughed and stood on top of her heap of clothes to be kissed. Her arms, outstretched, were ready to take him where he had not been in ages.

Flood leaned against the desk, a pipe in his mouth. "Did you learn anything new?" She was one of the few women Yablonsky had met who offered no apologies for her experience and her enjoyment of the sexual act. Most relationships were based on shared assumptions. With her, nothing was safe to assume. She was not a predictable series of clues or a mystery to be solved. He had no way of knowing, or even guessing, what she might do or say next. He wondered why he found her so attractive.

"She says she was with her sister on the nights Maysfield and Matson were murdered."

"*Both* nights? She doesn't have much of an alibi."

"Most innocent people don't," Yablonsky said, adhering to one of his most strongly held beliefs. "It's usually the murderers who have the good alibis."

"You still don't think she's guilty?"

"Not of murder."

"Then what?"

"I don't know," Yablonsky said. "I'm only concerned with murder."

"If you're only concerned with murder, why are you going to the UN tomorrow? I read your call-in sheet," he said impatiently. "The woman wasn't murdered."

Yablonsky felt the rage build in him. "Almost," he said. She might as well have been. I went over the new report from Sex Crimes. Anderson tracked it down. We know the boy responsible, and we now know the country he's from."

"I thought you were going to drop everything else. You hate dealing with the UN."

"I'm doing Anderson a favor, that's all. He helped me with the floater last month, remember?"

"Fair enough. As a detective, I know you want to discourage violent crime. But my major concern is politics. The reporters I spoke to said you gave them the finger out there. Did you?"

"Of course not."

"You realize how important it is to maintain good relations with the press? It's one of my priorities, if not yours."

"I just gave Warren Paton an interview. Ask him."

Flood took a step back, looked him over critically. "You could end up looking like Warren if you don't watch your appetite. But you can be a fairly good detective. You're diligent. I just wish you were more predictable. You maintain that the rock singer's innocent, but you're not as certain as you usually are when dismissing a suspect. I want you to stay close to her for a while longer."

"I intend to," Yablonsky said.

"I've read a great deal about her since her name turned up." He shook his head disapprovingly. "What a past."

"I don't think it's *that* wild," Yablonsky said. "But I'll keep her under surveillance."

Flood, ready to leave, clapped Yablonsky on the back. "Keep up the good work."

Twelve

YABLONSKY WALKED DOWN A paneled hallway, at the end of which was a mirrored wall that ran the length of the gym. He had known about this health spa for years. Tourists never saw it. It was a place where diplomats, whenever they wanted, could relax in whirlpools and steam baths to lift part of the burden of running the world from their shoulders.

Diplomats lounged around the heated pools or floated on the water like corpulent seals. Some pedaled furiously on stationary bikes or trudged resolutely on treadmills, or did sit-ups on raised exercise boards. Others were pummeled by masseuses. Laughing, chatting, gossiping ambassadors shaved in front of courtesy sinks, patting their faces with scented towels, showering themselves with talc.

Most of the men here were not recognizable to Yablonsky, but some he knew. A man sat on the carpeted floor, lifting his heavily veined legs up and down in a stretching exercise. The chief consulate from the Sultanate of South Yemen. The man often appeared on Ted Koppel's *Nightline*, denouncing America and promising a pan-Islamic victory. Yablonsky knew him from the earlier days. The chief consul had always been polite to him.

"You," the consul said in heavily accented English. "What

151

are you doing here?"

"I'm meeting someone."

"Are you still a cop?"

"I'm a detective now."

The man shook his head in slight disapproval, but he gave Yablonsky a smile. "I guess I should offer my congratulations.'

Alongside the mirrored wall opposite Yablonsky were three men. One, wearing a dark, pinstripe suit, stood on an exercise mat, easily holding a tremendous weight in his hands. Another guy, much smaller, with a furrowed brow, was also completely dressed. The third casually dangled his legs from an exercise horse. Except for a loosely wrapped towel around his waist he was naked. Yablonsky recognized him. Emile Suarez. His body was covered with a mat of jet black hair, and his mouth, the lips dark and sensual, was open and laughing. His pectorals were firm, his stomach tight. Yablonsky still felt that Suarez, now naked and exposed, resembled a movie star.

Miguel, the guy Suarez had ordered to serve them drinks in the apartment, put the huge weight down effortlessly. Probably Miguel Guzman, Yablonsky thought. He took out the ticket and started walking. He would not want to be the patrolman who had to present this man with a ticket, regardless of diplomatic immunity.

Suarez noticed him and was off the horse immediately, approaching him with an outstretched hand. "I hadn't realized that it was you on the phone. How fortunate that we've already met. Do you like our health club?"

"Very nice," Yablonsky said. "It was also nice of you to meet me here."

"Nonsense. It's my understanding that you used to be one of us yourself." He saw that the remark puzzled Yablonsky.

"You used to work UN Security, so in a way you can be considered part of our family." He winked, showed Yablonsky his full set of teeth in a quick smile. "I'm taking a break from vetoing resolutions from the Russians that condemn your country." Taking Yablonsky by the arm, he led him over to padded leather seats. "A little more privacy, lieutenant. Miguel. Rafi."

Suarez straightened for a moment before sitting, giving Yablonsky another glimpse of his trim athlete's body. He crossed his legs and leaned back. There were none of the rolls of belly fat that Yablonsky saw so often in police locker rooms.

"Do you work out, lieutenant?"

"Very rarely," Yablonsky said. "When I was a kid I used to play handball. Now all I do is a lot of legwork."

"Appropriate exercise for a detective. I'm down here at least three times a week."

"You're in much better shape than me," Yablonsky acknowledged.

"I'm not comparing us, lieutenant," Suarez said. "Is that ticket one of my old ones?"

Yablonsky nodded. "We'll get to it later. Three months ago Antonio Mendez, the son of one of your staff members, raped a thirty-four-year-old woman in her bedroom in front of his friends."

"Yes, I remember. A horrid act but, considering the boy's age, understandable. Youthful exuberance. My understanding is he was showing off for his friends."

"The woman has been in intensive therapy since it happened. I want to know what you're going to do about it."

"Why does this concern you?"

"I received the call. What's going to be done about it?"

"The boy will be sent home," Suarez said. He put his hand

up to stop Yablonsky's protests. "Really, lieutenant, as you know, I don't even have to do that. Being in your country encourages a young man's independence. We try to give them some leeway—but you're right of course. We must do something about it, and we will. He'll be gone by next week."

"Thank you," Yablonsky said. He was grateful. Most of them didn't even do that much. "I'd like to bring up something else. On the night of April 6th, your driver, Miguel Guzman, was handed a ticket by Patrolman Hardis."

"It's a silly matter," Suarez said. "A parking ticket. I'm sure everything will be straightened out in a minute. He was parked by a hydrant and he shouldn't have been." He winked at Yablonsky. "Miguel, next time please limit your misdemeanors to speeding and parking in no-standing zones."

"Were you with him?"

"Of course. But why should your department concern itself about a ticket that's probably not even valid? I don't blame you. It can be frustrating dealing with some of these people. Since they can never be prosecuted, they don't respect the law."

"You were out late that night."

"We sometimes are. Why should you care about it?"

"The car was parked around the corner from Sean Maysfield's apartment building at two in the morning. The same night he was murdered."

"I see. So?"

"It's just that we check out a neighborhood where a murder's occurred for anything unusual."

"You want to know how Miguel managed to get a ticket at two in the morning? Knowing Miguel, it's not difficult. Isn't that so, Rafi?" Emile Suarez watched as Yablonsky shifted in the chair awkwardly. Miguel looked stolid, unconcerned.

"You know how grueling our work is, lieutenant. We often go out for coffee late at night."

Yablonsky looked interested.

"There's a Smiler's on that block that stays open twenty-four hours a day. It's about two streets away from the embassy. We're there at least three nights a week. Miguel goes out for coffee and sandwiches. We sit in the car, eating, drinking, and listening to salsa on the radio. So you can see there's nothing unusual about us being there at that time. Ask the store owner."

"It won't be necessary. Do you remember how long you were there on that night?"

"It could've been half an hour. Maybe forty minutes. Next time we're there, I can bet you this—Miguel will not park by a hydrant." He gave Yablonsky a quick grin.

"It's very dry in here, lieutenant. The ventilation's lousy. A drink, Miguel. Champagne for us, coke for the detective. The refrigerator's in the locker room. Straight ahead. Then it's the first door on your left."

Miguel walked off. Suarez looked at Yablonsky and shook his head. "Is there anything more I can help you with, lieutenant?"

"I'll let you know when something else comes up."

Miguel returned, carrying a bottle, glasses, and a can of Diet Cherry Coke. "You've managed to bring it all with you in one trip this time, Miguel. Congratulations," Suarez said.

"I do the best I can," Miguel said. Yablonsky was surprised to hear him respond in unaccented English.

"I know," said Suarez. "That's what's so tragic."

Miguel opened his mouth to show he was laughing. Yablonsky caught a flash of gold teeth.

"I know a dentist on the East Side who takes Blue Cross," Yablonsky said.

"His dental work is fine," Suarez said. "He figures if
there's ever a change for the worse in our country he'll only
have to get himself out. He has his bank roll in his mouth."

"If the price of gold goes up, you'll be a rich man,"
Yablonsky said to Miguel, who was regarding Suarez with
distaste.

"I hope so," he replied.

Suarez stood, put down his wine glass. "Sorry, but I have
to leave you now. You can stay awhile longer, if you like.
Have a sauna. Take a massage." He pointed with his chin
at the sweating, straining diplomats. "They're not deaf, they
know who you are now. Your presence makes them feel more
secure."

"Why are they afraid?"

"Some of them have been threatened by terrorists. I know
we've received threats. Two weeks ago, as a matter of fact,
some of them fired shots into our building. There are small,
immigrant groups of dissidents living here who'd like nothing better than to help topple us. They never will, of course,"
he added quickly. "But with their threats and occasional
actions, they make life interesting. Good-bye, lieutenant.
Don't worry about that young man. Returning to my country
will be punishment enough."

Yablonsky had not been in a health club in years. A
fifteen-minute sauna and massage would do him good. He
decided to stay. "Be careful," he said.

Suarez still faced him. He smiled. His teeth were too good
to cap in gold. "I intend to be. But thanks for the warning."

Yablonsky found himself inside a small, grassy park full of
modern-looking statues, behind the UN complex. Tourists
sat on benches, snapping pictures of the imposing view and
landscape. He cut to the building's side, nodded at the cops

who stood at the entrance way inspecting the bags of the people who were about to enter.

"You're back," one of the cops said to him. "Here for the grand tour?"

Yablonsky smiled. "I've already seen it."

The cop looked through a woman's pocketbook, motioned her ahead. She passed through the open doors. He turned back to Yablonsky. "You miss it here?"

"Not at all." The cop went back to his bags and cameras.

Yablonsky walked down the steps and out the gate, up First Avenue to a phone booth on 44th.

"It's me," he said to Suzy Creamcheese. "How are you?"

"All cleaned up," she said with a laugh. "How's the world's greatest lover?"

"Recuperating. Are you free tonight?"

"I have a band rehearsal at six. I could be free by eight. Meet you at the apartment?"

"Fine," Yablonsky said. "How does nine o'clock sound?"

"Not bad. I'll have time for a shower and makeup. You can take me out for a late dinner. Can't you imagine us at the Four Seasons?"

"I can't imagine *you* there," he said.

"Neither can I," she said, and laughed. "We'll go to a place around here. I'm the hometown celebrity. We'll get good service."

"Who's going to take care of your sister?"

"Be sure not to talk like that around her. A friend. See you."

The proprietor of Smiler's lifted a jar of pickles from a shelf, placing it alongside him on the counter. "You've got to be good at this. Sometimes a bus goes rumbling by and they fall off. It's a skill."

"I can see that," Yablonsky said.

"These days we get the punks from the junior high across the street. They bus them in. Would you believe that all these black kids eat is kosher dill pickles?" He shook his head. "I don't know why. I've never met a Jew with good digestion. Have you?"

"Not too many," Yablonsky confessed. "How often does he come to your place for coffee?"

"Other cops have been here before. You're investigating those murders? I think those boys deserved it."

"How often does the guy come to your place?"

"A couple of times a week. They like my coffee. Everyone does. You sure you won't have a refill?"

"Not while I'm on duty," Yablonsky said. "Does Suarez ever come in and order by himself? Or does he send his men in?"

"Him? Never? His driver comes in, the guy with the gold teeth, and takes out three cups of coffee and pastrami sandwiches."

"So you've never actually seen Suarez then?" If the guy was alert enough to notice gold teeth, he would notice someone like Suarez.

"I know what he looks like. Some evenings he rolls down his window. I can see his face"—he pointed to the store window—"between the tissues and the toilet paper. Scenic view."

"Was his window rolled down that night?"

"Honestly, I don't remember."

"Does he always arrive so late?"

"Yeah, he does. Miguel calls in an order of pastrami and corned beef sandwiches on rye. I make them up, put them in the microwave, and there you are. A nutritious, inexpensive meal."

"Did Miguel call in the night of the 6th? Try to remember."

"They were here that night, so he had to call earlier. If Suarez says he was here at two in the morning, he was."

"Why do you think he comes so late? Most people eat earlier."

The proprietor shrugged. "It's snack food. Some people come even later. This is Manhattan."

"One more question. How long does he usually stay? How long was he here that night?"

"Usually around fifteen minutes. I can't give you a definite time on the other."

"Suarez told me he was here for half an hour on the 6th."

"Then he probably was. It takes time to digest good food."

"Why would he be so definite about the time? Most people can't remember anything they did after a few days."

"He's a diplomat. He's more conscious of time. Anything else?"

"Another question. Do they still come in?"

"They're steadies." They both heard the sounds of rap music, becoming louder. The proprietor turned to his jar of pickles, then faced the doorway. "Lunchtime."

Yablonsky found Patrolman Hardis away from his post, on a bench facing the East River. The sun was out of sight, probably by now over the Hudson.

"A bad place to coop," Yablonsky said. "Too public. I'm glad I was able to reach you."

The patrolman was young, barely out of college. He looked like the kind of guy who had gotten a lot of sand kicked in his face at beaches when he was a kid, but now there was a .44 Magnum strapped to his waist. With his rapier-thin mustache, he looked a few days older.

"What can you tell me about that night?" Yablonsky asked.

"Not much." Hardis looked thoughtful, then shrugged. "The limo was by a hydrant, so I ticketed it."

"Have you ever ticketed him before?"

Hardis laughed. "The guy's a diplomat. Lots of times. Didn't you, when you worked UN patrol?"

Yablonsky shook his head. "I was concerned with their safety. Who did you give the ticket to?"

"That's easy. The guy with gold teeth. Looks like a football player. You don't forget him."

"What was the exact time?"

Hardis looked at the ticket Yablonsky handed him. "If it says two o'clock, then that was the time, detective." They both knew that Sean Maysfield had been killed between two-thirty and three A.M.

"How did they react?" Yablonsky asked.

"Real cool. They didn't protest or try to start a fight like the others do. These diplomats really think they own this city, don't they, lieutenant?"

"They're just trying to do a job," Yablonsky said. "Was Suarez there?"

"The diplomat? He was there."

"How do you know?"

"The partition was open, so I could look in." He hesitated. "To tell you the truth, I couldn't tell if it was Suarez. There was a man in the backseat, lieutenant, but it was too dark to see in clearly."

Yablonsky nodded. Over their heads, a tram began making its way to Roosevelt Island. "He usually travels around with two other guys. How many were there that night?"

"The driver. And the guy in the back."

"Anyone else?"

"Could be. I don't remember."

"Do you know how long they parked there before you ticketed them?"

"I wouldn't know. I came up the street, and there they were."

"Were they eating?"

"There was food. Sandwiches and coffee."

"What did they do after you ticketed them?"

Hardis smiled. "They moved their car away from the hydrant. I guess they thought it was okay to be doubled-parked."

Yablonsky scribbled a note on the parking ticket. "Do you know how long they stayed after you ticketed them?"

"No, sir, I don't. I didn't look back. Anything else? I hope I've helped you."

"When do you go back on duty?" Yablonsky asked.

"In half an hour."

"Enjoy the river."

Karen answered the door. Her eyes were sparkling. "Susan's really excited about your date tonight. She's still busy with her hair."

Was she applying a different shade of spray paint? As for Karen, despite the heat she again wore long-sleeved clothes that covered her body.

"Don't you ever get hot?" he asked her. "I'm sweltering."

"I don't feel the heat, lieutenant," she said. "Come in."

She took his hand. He looked at her wrists. Clean. Stop being a detective, he thought.

They sat on the cheap, Herculeon sofa that he and Susan had slept on yesterday. He remembered countless movies in which the male waited patiently downstairs, to be dazzled by his date when she appeared, beautifully dressed and groomed, completely transformed.

Susan entered, wearing row after row of bracelets and bangles on her arms, a Salvation Army-issue flack jacket, red-tinted hair, and tight jeans that were worn at the knees. Eyepatch too, of course. No assumptions about her, he reminded himself. Her breasts swelled inside her white cotton shirt. She brushed her hair back and pulled at her suspenders.

"You look really nice," he said.

"I know," she said. "Let's go."

He sat with her in the tenth row of the Theatre 80 movie house on Saint Mark's Place. They didn't hold hands. The movie they saw had been released a couple of years ago, *The Jagged Edge*, a thriller. Every time a new character appeared on screen, Susan claimed that he was the primary suspect.

The district attorney, Peter Coyote, sat back in his chair. "I think it was him," Susan whispered.

"You've picked the most unlikely suspect."

"That's why," she said. "Every mystery depends on the detective finding out who the most unlikely suspect is and nailing him."

Glenn Close rode a horse across a grassy plain surrounded by hills and forest. Susan's brow knit with thought. "She might have killed her, too."

"But so far the suspects are all men," he whispered. "That's the most logical thing when it's a woman who's murdered."

"That's why I think she did it." She nodded her head vigorously. "Remember my theory."

Yablonsky smiled. The twist had to be that Glenn Close would get Jeff Bridges off for murder, and he would turn out to be guilty. "I remember," he said.

The murdered wife's ex-lover was interrogated by Glenn Close. "Compared to you, she's an amateur," Susan said to

Yablonsky. "I know how you operate. You make your victims feel at ease by being friendly, then you move in for the kill."

She couldn't be more wrong, he thought. So far his investigation had blazed a trail of clues that had incriminated the innocent. His interrogations had managed to clear his first real suspect. He reached for her hand. "I'm really not that unfriendly," he said. "Who do you suspect now?"

"Everyone," she said.

"Me too."

Traffic moved briskly down Second Avenue. Across the street was the Fillmore East. Sometimes Eddie, Yablonsky's older brother, had taken him there to see rock shows. The street was full of all kinds of restaurants. He and Susan held hands.

"Macrobiotics. Curry. Sushi and sashimi bars. What will it be?" he asked.

"Are you crazy? The Second Avenue Deli. I'm in the mood for a burger."

They sat across from each other in a booth. This was the best delicatessen in New York. Occasionally Yablonsky had been able to wangle a free meal from them.

She poured ketchup on the plump french fries as if it were dressing, then made a face. "Too dry," she said. "Don't tell anyone, but because I'm a neighborhood celebrity and bring them a lot of business, I get my meals comped."

"Your secret's safe with me," he said. He told her about the investigation by Internal Affairs. "As a detective, I don't like the feeling of a cop shadowing me."

She pointed a french fry at him as if it were a pistol. "Serves you right."

"You don't understand the irony of it," he said. "Since being named the investigating detective for this case, I've done nothing but sit in chauffeured limos, luxuriate in health spas, and eat for free. *Everything's* been comped."

"I have the solution. If you don't find a suspect, the good life continues forever."

"I'd like to, but I can't," Yablonsky said. Here it comes, he thought. "I've cleared you as a suspect, but my captain hasn't. I'm supposed to keep you under close surveillance."

She put her hamburger down and stared at him. "I don't see you protesting too much." She paused. "Of course I'm not, either."

Yablonsky was pleased. She might dress in thrift-store rejects, but she was beautiful. He would help her, in spite of herself. "He really thinks you did it, and just about everyone else who's heard about his case thinks so, too. Why won't you tell me what *really* went on between you three?"

"Paul, Sean, and I had sex. You know I'm not a virgin. Since when is sex a crime?"

"When it ends in murder," Yablonsky said. "I know you're not guilty, Susan, but unfortunately every clue I've turned up so far leads to your door."

She shook her head stubbornly and took a big bite out of her hamburger. "I've said all I'm going to. I don't care if you indict me."

"I won't indict you," he said. "The DA will." He paused. "Unless we find someone else, you're the best suspect. If you won't defend yourself, maybe I'm wrong and you did do it, after all."

She met his eyes. "Of course. That's it. I'll go to jail for killing Paul and Sean. They'll put you behind bars for scarfing food while on duty. I bet you'll serve more time than me."

"I think you know who killed them," he said. "Otherwise you wouldn't feel it necessary to lie so much." He picked up his Dr. Brown's. "Good soda."

"Of course I know." She placed the burger on her plate. "Look, detective, take me back to your apartment. Ravish me, interrogate me, and then indict me. I won't discuss it anymore."

"You're out of your mind," Yablonsky said. "They plan on calling you in and indicting you."

"Then it won't do me any good to protest, will it? I must have murdered them."

"They were pretty gruesome murders, Susan."

"I'm capable of it. You said so yourself."

"I guess you did kill them, then," he said. "Please pass the rye bread."

They were not as ready to indict her as he had led her to believe, but she had no way of knowing that. He watched her as she ate her food. Her hands were steady. Incredible. "Good food," she said. "Mind if I have another burger?"

"As long as you don't drown it in ketchup."

Outside, as they walked to his car, she was silent. He tried to make conversation, but she waved him off. She looked at him, trembling slightly, her eyes filling with dislike.

He pointed. "Up ahead. Another block."

"Fine," she said.

They turned the corner. Suddenly he heard loud music. A concert in Tompkins Square Park. A band played guitars and drums on a makeshift stage. In the night under scattered street lamps, hundreds of teenagers slammed themselves against one another, caroming from body to body like crazy, wandering pinballs.

"Hardcore punk," she said. "We'd better go another way to your car."

"Why?"

"They can be violent."

Yablonsky saw skinheads and astroheads reeling as if they were drunk. "I thought they were your fans," he said.

She laughed at that. "What a great detective. I've got a record contract, and they play my stuff on MTV. I'm commercial—I've got nothing to do with these kids."

"It's another world," Yablonsky managed.

"Jail is too, isn't it? That's where you want to put me." She turned to him. "Why?"

"My captain believes you might have had a reason to kill them."

She shuddered. "We're still on that, are we?"

"I'm afraid so."

They reached his car. "Don't talk," she said. "Just drive."

For once, there was no traffic. She looked at him nervously, then stared out the side window. "Put on the air conditioner," she said. He did, and then deliberated played with the radio dial until he reached a new-wave station. They heard one of her songs. She smiled slightly and turned the volume down. "You don't want to hear her," she said. "She's got no talent. A flash in the pan."

Sheepshead Bay. He parked the car across from the boat marina, near Randazzo's. "The best clams in the city," he said as he led her past the boats. They crossed the bridge. She allowed him to put his arm around her. When he kissed her, she leaned weakly against him. "It's the ocean," she said, and shivered. "I'll sleep with you again, that's nothing, but I won't tell you anything."

He entered through the side door, turned on the light. She inspected his apartment. The rows of bookcases were orderly. The kitchen sink was clear of dishes, the dozen or so cassettes neatly stacked on top of the VCR. "I thought it'd look like this," she said.

"Can I get you anything?" he asked.

"Yeah, every copy of that lousy magazine from which you learned my name. I want to burn them all." Her arms hugged her shoulders. "I wish I'd never met you."

"I wish you'd never met me either," Yablonsky said sadly. "It's your sister, isn't it?"

She closed her eyes, nodded. She stared at him, waiting for him to continue.

"I noticed her clothes," he said. He wished he could look at her as gently as he felt. "You can't keep it in forever, Susan. What happened?"

"I can't tell you that yet."

They sat on the couch. She inched away from him, as if rejecting the advances of an unwanted date. He decided that she was not ready for sympathy yet.

"You saw those boats out there," he said. "They reminded you of something, didn't they? Women don't continue to suffer breakdowns a year after an accident unless it was bad. You were also on that boat. I don't think Karen slipped and fell into the water. She wasn't just traumatized, was she?"

"No."

"Marshall Hunter's one of the most famous managers in the rock world. The man who gave you your start?"

"He started my career," she said softly.

"You received a fifteen-thousand-dollar advance from him a year ago to cut a record. Not a large amount for a rock star to receive, but a big sum for new-wave punk, I imagine. Are you that good in bed, Susan?

"You must have been," he went on. "The man you slept with made you a star and then paid you for it. What'd you do for him that you didn't do with me? I care for you, of course, but your voice is not better than any other singer's. You're pretty, but you only stand out because you dress in rags. Most women without talent who want to become stars have to pay the price, but the guy who is the real idolmaker pays money to you. Why?"

"I think you already know," she whispered.

"After you place the ad, Paul and Sean turn up at your door. You're lonely. You go out with them, but you give each of them not only sex, but money too. They know something about you that you don't want anyone else to know. Being blackmailed is a great reason for murder."

"It is, but I didn't mind paying," she said.

"I'll bet you didn't," he said. "How'd they find out about what happened to Karen?"

"I imagine Marshall told them. They moved in the same circles. You care about me, so why are you doing this?"

"You're in danger of being indicted and you don't turn a hair," he said. "Maybe you feel you *deserved* to be blackmailed."

"That's ridiculous."

"Is it?"

"No." Her shoulders slumped. "I do feel that way. It's my fault Karen's the way she is. So far, lieutenant, you've been right about everything. When Marshall invited me on his boat that weekend, I was ecstatic. I knew what to expect, but I figured whatever he wanted, it was worth it. If someone offered you the chance to become police commissioner, you'd take it, wouldn't you?"

"Maybe," Yablonsky said.

"He'd seen me playing the clubs. I assumed he invited Karen along to make me feel more at ease. You see, lieutenant, I hadn't heard *everything* about him. We went out to the harbor, you could see Staten Island and the Verrazano. We fed seagulls. Beautiful. When he summoned me to his stateroom I was almost happy. Up until then, everything I did with men was *my* choice."

"I understand," Yablonsky said. "Go on."

"It was like the yacht scene in *Some Like it Hot*. Soft lights and music. Would I like it to be my voice on the cassette? he asked me. Not only would he let me cut a record, but afterward, he'd make sure it received video and radio play. He'd get me better concert deals. Did I want all this?, he asked. I figured he wanted me to come across." She looked directly at Yablonsky. "I was ready to, you understand?"

"Yes," Yablonsky said.

"Only he didn't want me. I had to get him Karen. I was willing, but he wanted a new version of the casting couch.

"Karen went to him. I wasn't in the room with them. I only know what she told me. After tying her up, he worked her over. You were right, Yablonsky, the clothes she wears mask the scars.

"Marshall hated paying me off. He hated the fact that I had something on him. He might've told Paul and Sean out of spite. They were good looking, charming lowlifes, but I didn't kill them." She hesitated. "I didn't really mind paying the money. The amount wasn't large, and it was worth three hundred a month to keep it quiet. You must hate me."

Yablonsky caught his breath. "No, I don't." But he couldn't look at her. He remembered his conversations with Karen; meeting her for the first time during the rehearsal. It had been warm, but she wore a long-sleeved shirt and a flowery dress that reached her ankles. The camouflage had been inadequate. And three hundred a month. Dwyer had turned up the transactions on the bank computer, but the withdrawals had been so insignificant Yablonsky had assumed the amounts were spending money.

Suzy Creamcheese unclasped her hands and said it for him. "Do you think Karen *likes* to be dependent on me? I did all that to my sister. For fame. My records sell all over

Europe, and I hear they even smuggle my tapes into the Soviet Union." She picked up his hand, held it cautiously. When he did not take it away, she began to manipulate his fingers. "Lousy alibi. A reason for murder. I'm your most logical suspect. However it turns out, I'm guilty of a lot of things."

"You are," he said. "But not of murder. Let's go to bed."

"I don't feel like sleeping with you right now."

"No sex," he said. "Just sleep."

$\triangledown$

Thirteen

DWYER MET HIM OUTSIDE the bank, grooming his wispy mustache with his hand and wearing a superior smile.

"You need me, after all."

"I certainly do," Yablonsky said. "Thanks."

They were in the sub-basement again, Dwyer sipping his ubiquitous cup of coffee, waiting expectantly for Yablonsky to tell him what to do.

Yablonsky's hand rested on one of the computer monitors. He turned it on and the machine hummed. "You used to tell me, 'On a professional hit, follow the money.' I finally have a suspect. I want to see financial transactions for the past six months."

"The rock singer?"

"A UN diplomat. Suarez."

Dwyer shook his head. "This is a Latin American bank. They gave me this job, remember? He's a big shot here. His file is kept upstairs, but I need permission from the manager in order to pull it."

Yablonsky nodded. "But you're chief of security. You can't do this by yourself?"

"Suarez is special access, so I need permission."

He knew this bank was one of the main conduits for Latin

171

American funds. Suarez would be sure to have some of his own people at the bank. "Will Suarez be warned that someone tried to get into his file?" Yablonsky asked.

"Probably. Any inquiry automatically shows up on the computer." Dwyer looked at him questioningly.

"It's my only lead," Yablonsky said. "Tell them you suspect there's been tampering with his financial statements. You heard talk. Someone may be making withdrawals using his code number."

"They may buy that," Dwyer said.

He went upstairs, filled out the required form, and handed it to a teller. He returned with a card that listed Suarez's Mastercard number, the first names of his parents, date of birth, and computer code.

Suarez's code spelled out *football*.

Dwyer punched it into the computer terminal. "He must be a fan," he said.

The numbers appeared on the screen. Yablonsky noted the various transactions on a pad. The withdrawals and deposits were all for five- and six-figure amounts.

"Substantial," Yablonsky said. "But the file doesn't note where the money goes."

"One step at a time," Dwyer said. "Alvin, the transactions have a pattern. The withdrawals and deposits are evenly spaced, twice a month, as if funds were being transferred in regularly from an even bigger source."

"The source isn't named, though," Yablonsky said. "Do you think Suarez is laundering money?"

Dwyer smiled. "A regular laundromat." He handed him the printout. "You'll want a copy for later, won't you—in case they seal it."

Yablonsky nodded. He couldn't be sure, but he felt that things were beginning to coalesce. All because of a parking ticket.

Yablonsky and Dwyer stood before the revolving the door.

"We'll take in a movie some time next week, if you want to, Kevin," Yablonsky said.

Dwyer shook his head. "I'd like to keep the relationship strictly professional. I don't want any part of you if one of these suspects is from the UN." He gave Yablonsky a cold smile. "You see, I learned my survival lessons, after all." He looked directly at Yablonsky, finally glad he was just a bank chief and not a detective. "What'll you do if it is Suarez?"

"I don't know," Yablonsky said. "Probably try to veto it like they do in the Security Council."

He reached Alden Hardis just as he was about to start his tour of duty. The patrolman recognized his voice over the phone right away.

"The detective," he said. "What can I do for you?"

"One quick question. Okay?"

"Take your time."

"When you reached Suarez's car, did any of the men with him seem upset or out of breath?"

"No."

"How did Miguel react when you ticketed him?"

Hardis laughed. "I had to admire the way the guy handled himself. He apologized for being parked at the hydrant, then assured me that if a fire broke out, he'd move his car. I think I heard him complain that the pastrami sandwiches were cold." Yablonsky almost heard the pause. "I got the impression they had been there for a while. You think Suarez had these strippers killed, don't you?"

"I don't have the motive yet. But he was around the night one of them was killed."

"Don't worry about it," Hardis said. "If he did it, they'll never let you go after him."

"I hope not," Yablonsky said. He forced a laugh. "I don't need that kind of trouble."

Flood was in the sub-basement of the precinct house, at the firing range. He shouted to Yablonsky above the roar of the pistols. "If it isn't Wyatt Earp. You're notorious for ducking / the notices for taking practice. What are you doing here?"

They moved to the small, soundproof waiting room. Yablonsky peered at the firing patrolmen. They looked like gunslingers. He had not worn or fired his on-duty revolver since becoming a detective. He resolved to start practicing again next week.

"I hope you've come to bury someone," Flood said. He looked at him meaningfully. "Like the rock singer."

"No burials today, just praise," Yablonsky said. "You can inform your media sources she's been cleared as a suspect."

"They'll want to know why," Flood said. "Me too."

"Plausible motive, but lousy alibi. A professional would have been sure to have a better one."

Flood refused to be impressed. "Maybe she made up a lousy one because she heard about that crazy theory of yours."

"She didn't do it."

"You have anyone else?"

"I may have a suspect," Yablonsky said quickly. "Suarez. A UN diplomat. We should inform the feds." Once they came into it, the case would be over for him.

However, Flood managed to surprise him. "Let's keep it to ourselves awhile longer."

"But shouldn't we tell them?"

"Cautious, aren't you?" Flood said. He sounded impatient. "Murder's not the same as running red lights, and even peddling drugs through their diplomatic pouches. If he's a murderer, I want you to prove it. You've met him before. What's he like?"

"At a health spa, and in an apartment. Good looking. Courteous. Seems like a nice guy."

"He is," Flood said. "I ran into him at a political function once. Looks like an Hispanic George Hamilton, only a little shorter. Someone you don't forget."

"I'll focus the investigation on him, chief."

"Right. You don't look especially happy that you've finally come up with a suspect." Flood paused. "Meeting him was one of the party's highlights. He told some good jokes. Assured me they were a lot dirtier in Spanish. He's good looking and smooth, and you'd think he'd be a lightweight. But he raises the bucks, makes the speeches, and helps his boss in power. He behaves as if, despite terrorists and our occasional interest in him, he knows he's got nothing to worry about."

Fourteen

SUAREZ WALKED IN HIS jungle garden, a U.S. diplomat by his side. The trees were filled with parrots and macaws chatting in Spanish and English.

Chambers smiled. "They sound like the General Assembly, don't they?"

Suarez chuckled, reached for a mango from the South American jungle he had transplanted here. They walked back in, closed the sliding doors to the jungle, and stood in the embassy reception room.

Looking at his watch, Suarez said, "In about five minutes I have to meet with some of your kind ladies who are thinking of building a hospital in my country. If I keep them waiting, I imagine that a lot of people from my country are going to be walking around in poor health."

They took their drinks off a tray and moved toward one of the elevators. "You will back us about the loan to Brazil, then? We think it's best if it's delayed."

"Then delayed it is," Suarez said. "I go against the interests of my own hemisphere, but you have our support. I hope Washington appreciates it."

"We do," Chambers said. Opposite the elevator was a huge portrait of Ramirez. He had held power in Suarez's

177

country for over a dozen years.

Chambers lifted his glass is if in a toast.

"You know, it's too bad he's not more like you," Chambers said. "Maybe someday—"

"Everybody should be more like me," Suarez said. "Some days, even I feel that I should be more like me. Now, please, gentlemen, no more treasonous talk."

"Those terrorists have been rather active lately. Any reason for us to worry?" Chambers asked.

"None," Suarez said. "We've been handling them for years. Would we be giving permission to a group of nuns to enter our country if things were really that bad? After the next offensive, amigos, the only way that left-wing group will be able to enter our country is if they come as tourists."

"Glad to hear it."

He had Miguel escort them to their limousine. He watched from the window as they crossed the street, smiled as he saw Miguel compete with the chauffeur to open the door for the men. He was a slow learner, but Suarez never regretted preventing the death squad from killing him. During the mopping up, when he had focused the camera on Miguel to capture his last moments, Miguel had smiled and said, "Cheese." Suarez smiled. He had had to save him. The man had worked for him for over a year now and was loyal.

Suarez took the elevator down one floor, where the delegation was waiting. Three nuns and a pair of philanthropists. They were seated, eating Lindt chocolate from the lazy Susan, and staring covetously at the jars of coffee beans on the cocktail table.

"Ladies," he said, entering the room. "I can see where your eyes are. The best coffee in the world comes out of my country. Help yourselves."

Their gnarled hands reached tentatively for the jar. He sat

down, gave them his most charming wink. "If Cuba were not communist, I'd have cigars to offer you as well."

They laughed. He glanced at his watch in such a way that they would see. This a busy day. He could give them fifteen minutes. "Sisters, how may I help you? Better, how may we help each other?"

One of them spoke. "We were able to obtain an endowment large enough for that hospital you mentioned."

"But you want something in return."

"Indeed we do. We want to send missionaries to your provincial capitals, but the country is mountainous and difficult to travel through. We want protection. We also want permission to construct a cathedral in Norte."

Suarez felt sorry for these women, but, in a way, he was now negotiating for his and Ramirez's pensions. "If you channel the money through our development fund as before, we'll be happy to have you build the cathedral. May I assume you will use the construction firm we recommend? It's a very good firm. Protection will be automatic."

The woman didn't blink an eye. "Of course."

Suarez seemed pleased. Ramirez's brother-in-law ran the country's largest construction firm. Usually a hospital meant cost overruns, political appointments to the staff, and additional pharmaceutical imports that were legal.

Another nun said, "But why must we channel the funds through this specific agency?"

"Tax purposes." Turning to the philanthropists, he said, "There will be medical scholarships in each of your names. I promise that a wing will be named for each of you." Ramirez, Muchado, and he had children who would normally have used those scholarships.

"When may we leave?"

"Anytime you wish." The government still had to appear

to be capable of doing business. Dismissing the women with his usual politenesses, he took the elevator to the top floor. Castaglia was waiting for him in his office. His next challenge.

Castaglia's eyes followed him as he sat behind his desk. Suarez leaned forward, straightening the photo of Ramirez and himself with their families. He imagined his wife, stirring around their country house, swooping after the lizards, and catching them to the delight of their daughter. She was a beautiful woman, but he was glad she was not here. Eventually he would send for her, but he still intended to live the way he wanted.

Castaglia owned travel franchises and was responsible for selling package tours and gambling junkets to tourists. He received one percent of the net profit for each group he steered to Suarez's country and an additional half percent if they stayed at hotels that were owned by Ramirez. Under Suarez's predecessor Hernandez, business from Castaglia had slacked off badly.

Suarez played with his papers for a few minutes, then looked up. "You don't look well, Hector. Perhaps you should take a vacation."

The man shrugged, reached for a cigarette. "I'm working too hard to go on any vacations. I have four more groups of tourists for you."

Suarez pretended to be examining an imposing-looking document. The pitch for a bigger percentage should come now.

Castaglia folded his hands. "We like working with you. But we feel we're entitled to a bigger percentage of the profits. We want new agreements."

Suarez devoted his attention to another official-looking paper. He hoped he didn't look too bored. He expected Castaglia to say that other governments had approached him.

"Other delegations have contacted us," Castaglia said. "They've made us generous offers. But we don't want to have to end our relationship with you."

"Hector, I advise you to work with the delegation that offers you the biggest percentage. Our other operations have been so successful that we've decided to wind down our activities in tourism."

A sharp intake of breath. "But we like working with you."

"President Ramirez and I have a loftier vision for our country than an economy that is fueled by gambling junkets and secretly-owned government hotels. As a matter of fact, President Ramirez has decided to close two of his three hotels." Hoping the man wouldn't have time to reflect, Suarez went on. "God has been good to us. We've been able to expand our base of operations into so many fields that we can now make money in a more acceptable manner."

As Suarez started to usher Castaglia out of his office, the man gave him a cunning look. "There's no other reason for this?"

As if he were the representative of the most stable country in the hemisphere, Suarez said, "What other reason could there possibly be?"

The next man Rafi brought into his office was an old friend. Suarez had served under him in the army. They embraced, then sat down. Though he had come unexpectedly, Suarez knew why Manfredo was here.

The matter was a delicate one. Under Ramirez, emigration was strictly controlled and the U.S. Immigration Service was unlikely to grant political asylum. Naturally a black market that smuggled aliens into the United States had grown out of this. What hardly anyone knew was that much of the smuggling was done by cohorts of Ramirez. Ban something and its price becomes exorbitant. Illegal aliens entered not only through Mexico, but through Canada and Florida as well. As soon as they hit the ground, many of them were sold to Suarez's countrymen in the United States as factory workers. Manfredo's job was to pick the mules who would bring the aliens into the country and then obtain employment for them.

"Bad news, Emile. Texas border guards interdicted a shipment two days ago. A dozen illegals, carrying three keys."

Suarez laughed. "But this is not bad news at all. You see, we've decided there's no need to continue that type of operation. Grease the appropriate palms so these people can be released. Then, Manfredo, I suppose it's up to me to find you another means of employment. You can now go to sleep with a clear conscience, my friend. At last we're finished with that grimy business." Manfredo left. Suarez plunged back into his work. He went through the papers on his desk, all relatively minor stuff.

Miguel and Rafi entered.

Suarez looked at his watch. "Is it time?" He hesitated. "I just don't see any point to this."

A college student, a leader of one of the dissident immigrant groups, was waiting for them inside the safe house they kept in Washington Heights. He was to disappear.

"Ramirez wants Rafi to take care of this one," Miguel said. "I won't even be there."

"I'm sure that's a disappointment to you," Suarez said.

"Look who's talking. Do you want me to get your camera?" Suarez reached into the bottom desk drawer and brought out the Polaroid. "Ramirez will want proof that the boy's gone, Rafi. So you'd better take it."

Rafi and Miguel exchanged glances. "Of course," Miguel said. "What other reason could there possible be to bring a camera to an execution? Tell the kid not to worry, Rafi. With a Polaroid, he won't be charged for the cost of developing the pictures."

Rafi left, Miguel following. Suarez rode the elevator to his private office. At last the safe phone rang. He waited until the second ring, then picked up.

"Emiliano, is that you?"

"It's me.'"

The tone was warm. "I have some wonderful news for you. Your daughter, Marie, graduates from grade school with highest honors. A future wife for my son, eh? You must be very proud."

Only Suarez would recognize this as a threat. The child had been an accident, but Ramirez knew that Suarez still loved his family. Ramirez wept profusely at movies and brought sweets in his pockets to feed the children of his associates, yet the army officers had nicknamed him the "baby killer" in honor of his littlest victims.

"Are things better or worse?" Suarez asked. "How many guardsmen did they kill last week?"

"We lost nine men in a skirmish two days ago. Three more in an ambush." There was a pause. "The fortunes of war. That's why it's important you hold up your end."

Yet another warning. How much did Ramirez know? It had to be a lot. He suspected that Rafi was a Ramirez plant.

"How are your assistants?" Ramirez asked. "The thing that concerns Rafi?"

"It's being taken care of right now."

"Good. I'm just remembering the old days, before you went to college, Emile. In many ways, it's far easier to acquire power than to maintain it." Ramirez had learned the cardinal rule of power: it is safer to steal small amounts from the many than large amounts from the few.

"More bad news," he continued. "We had some difficulties in Washington. That little radical bomb failed to kill anyone, but it gives the illusion of weakness. I also heard that our bankers had some visitors today."

How did he find out so fast? Rafi. "I'll take care of it, *jefe*."

"I'm sure you will. I don't want to end up like the Shah, Emile. You're the cleanup man. The man who washes our laundry. Remember we may have to close down pretty quickly. He paused. "A question about happier things. Any nice muchachos?"

"A few," Suarez said.

"I'm a romantic," Ramirez said. "Someday I know you'll find Mr. Right."

Ramirez's throat muscles were weak, the result of a slashed larynx during a teenage gang fight. He could only talk clearly for a few minutes at a time.

There was a click. Suarez stared at the now-silent phone. How safe was his position? Ramirez had been his field commander before college. Though just a teenager, Suarez was so handsome, and showed so much enthusiasm and ability for the work, that he stood out. Ramirez had given him his chance and he had responded with loyalty. He had won Ramirez over by tactfully questioning everything he did. Should a pocket of revolutionaries be wiped out? Yes, but a congressional delegation from the U.S. was coming this week. Wait until they left. Put government uniforms on the corpses and accuse the terrorists of killing soldiers.

There would be no more naked extortion. Suarez found better ways to make money for the regime. Make three quarters of the parking spaces in the capital city illegal, then tow and fine the drivers who are forced to park their cars there for lack of space. Build new parking garages to help alleviate the problem. Increase the hourly parking cost. Own the garages.

Newspapers were allowed a small degree of freedom. A stream of unfavorable editorials from an influential newspaper made Ramirez react with fury. Don't eliminate the publisher, Suarez cautioned. Raise the cost of printing his paper astronomically every time something unfavorable appears. He will get the message.

Suarez found Miguel in the recreation room watching TV. "I thought they stopped running *Sesame Street*."

"*Police Woman*," Miguel said. "Angie Dickinson makes me want to cream."

Suarez sat down beside him, flicked the picture off with the remote. "Is Rafi still out?"

"He hasn't come back yet."

"Get me a gin and tonic. You'll find the liquor in the cabinet by the desk. A desk is something you use to lean on while writing. Words are just as effective as your gun."

"Or your lousy Polaroid." Miguel stood. "I know where you keep your booze, boss. You've must've just spoken to Ramirez. Should I bring the bottle?"

"I only want one drink. It's not a crutch." Miguel left, came back. "Thank you." Suarez said. He sipped, put the glass down. "You're a talented man, Miguel. If the assassination business ever slacks off, you'll always be able to find work as a bartender."

"Working for you increases my abilities." He smirked. I've seen it before. One drink only. To keep your courage up. If they asked you to make one of your famous speeches now, I bet you'd weep before the entire UN."

"You don't have much compassion do you? If you hadn't gotten that ticket, I wouldn't be dodging a detective who suspects me of murder."

"You said you wanted me to pull you up close to Smiler's.

Anyway, I thought that detective didn't worry you. Lucky
for you he's from Homicide and not the vice squad. Then
he'd really have some evidence against you, *maricone*."

"He doesn't worry me. It's just that this has to come now,
on top of everything else. And Miguel, I've told you this
before. My sex life is none of your fucking business."

"It's a fucking business all right. If it weren't for your
goddamn sex life, we wouldn't be in this now."

"Shut up." His shoulders sagged. "That's true enough.
The initial mistake was mine. But you're missing the point.
The information had to be protected. As Ramirez says, I'm
the laundromat."

Miguel nodded. "What do you think of the cop?"

"He's a detective, Miguel. Not a cop. There's a difference.
He seems competent but handleable."

"You finished your drink so he must scare you." He
hesitated. "Should I take care of him?"

"Not yet. It's like with drugs, knockoffs, or anything else.
If you want to stop something, you go to the source."

Fifteen

DETECTIVES ANDERSON AND YABLONSKY sat across the table from them. The kitchen they were in had an unobstructed view of the harbor. Yablonsky saw boats passing under the Manhattan and Brooklyn bridges. Across from them, in Brooklyn Heights, were Barge Music and the River Café.

The couple had insisted the interrogation take place in their apartment and not at the precinct. The red-faced woman looked as if she had just attended a funeral. The husband clasped and unclasped his hands, as if only the restraining force of the police prevented him from using them.

Anderson said, "We've raised the matter with a highly placed official from their delegation, Mr. Rizzo. He assures me that the boy will be sent home. He will not be allowed to return here. He will never be able to harass your wife again."

"He didn't harass my wife, detective, he raped her." Rizzo paused. "He confessed to it."

Yablonsky and Anderson exchanged a glance: having the victims find out how little the cops could actually do was always the most difficult part.

The woman nodded slowly, as if in a dream. "You can't touch him."

"In effect we're deporting him, Mrs. Rizzo," Anderson said. "I swear to you he won't be able to come back here."

"Crime and punishment," Rizzo sneered. "Suppose we go to the media? My wife was raped by that son of a bitch, and you tell me that because he's the son of a diplomat he gets away with it. The newspapers'll love that story."

"That's been done before, Mr. Rizzo." Yablonsky spoke as gently as he could. "Unfortunately it's had little effect. They're protected under diplomatic immunity. The young man will be sent back home. That's the best we can do in these cases."

"Some missions don't even agree to do that," Anderson said. His mouth twisted slightly. It was the wrong thing to say.

Rizzo unclasped his hands. "My wife sees a therapist three times a week now. No trial, lieutenant? That bastard followed my wife into our apartment. He was drunk and laughing. If I'd been here, I would've killed him."

"We're sorry," Yablonsky said. "But that's all we can do."

Mrs. Rizzo shook her head. "Letting him go free is an even bigger crime than what he did to me."

Rizzo laughed bitterly. "They get away with murder."

"We're sorry we can't be of any more help," Yablonsky said. "We understand your feelings." He stood.

Rizzo remained in his chair. "You weren't any help, lieutenant."

Outside the door, Anderson put a hand on Yablonsky's shoulder. "Thanks for the backup."

Yablonsky shrugged. He needed a cigarette and had none. Anderson didn't smoke. They stepped into the elevator. "I owed you," Yablonsky said. "Going back to precinct?"

Anderson shook his head. "I've got to go over to the East River and Twenty-Third, establish a crime scene. A floater—just a nice clean case of murder, thank God. No rapes, smuggling, or diplomatic immunity involved."

The elevator reached the ground floor. Anderson was already out the door. "You know, if they kicked out the UN, I bet the crime would be cut by fifty percent." He grinned. "But then we'd also be out of jobs. Maybe we should increase the number of diplomatic missions here. Think of all the overtime."

They sat in the bar and grill around the corner from the precinct. Before the investigation, it had been one of Yablonsky's favorites.

"You pour," Flood said. "Losers always pour."

Yablonsky picked up the pitcher of beer, filled their glasses.

"Poor bastards." Flood put down his mug. "What else can I say? You going to get drunk tonight? There are over one hundred and fifty diplomatic missions, half of them in this precinct. In a way, they make up one of the largest immigrant groups in New York. We're stuck with them."

"I hardly ever get drunk," Yablonsky said. "You know that." Flood smiled. "I'm not much of a homicide detective," Yablonsky continued, "or even that honest a one. It's just that occasionally I'd like to feel that I can stop murderers from murdering and rapists from raping. They're worse than the Mafia."

"Much worse," Flood said. "At least the Mafia works outside the law, for all its corruption. Even before these diplomats come here, they know they're going to be protected by the law. We give them a license to commit crime. What do you expect?"

Yablonsky picked up his mug. "Cancel the license?"

"Then our guys in their countries wouldn't be protected. This stuff's been going on for ages. Originally, diplomats were sent to a country as hostages, to guarantee the country that sent them would keep its word. Look, Yablonsky, I'm the *captain* of this precinct, and the state department ties my hands. But I'm also getting sick and tired of being shit on. Go after Mr. Personality, and if he's guilty, nail him."

"I think he's guilty."

Flood lifted his glass in a toast. "So?"

He met Dwyer in the by-now familiar basement office. They could hear the barred gates opening above them to admit customers to their safe-deposit boxes.

Yesterday Yablonsky had called Dwyer and told him what he needed.

Dwyer wagged his finger like a professor. "I hope you have as much trouble with your future homicides," he said. "That way I'll get to see more of you."

"That's not what you said last time," Yablonsky said. "How come you decided to help?"

"Your wife's left you for a man who's more successful than you. You think you've found love at thirty-six with a punk-rock star. I've never seen a detective deteriorate so quickly."

"I don't think I am."

"That's proof of even further deterioration. Anyway, this case is all you have left. If you lose it, you go down the tubes."

"I'm not going anywhere," Yablonsky insisted. "I'm a detective, first class, and Flood backs me. I figure my position's pretty strong."

Dwyer smiled, reached for his cup of coffee. "That's what I thought when I was the hotshot of the department. You know how that turned out."

"Are you hoping they fire me and I end up as your

assistant in this bank?" He paused. "I can live with that."

"So can I," Dwyer said. "This case has pumped adrenalin in me I didn't know I had. If you want to chase after some UN diplomat, I'll get my kicks vicariously, however it turns out for you."

"Right," Yablonsky said. "I felt the same when I forced them to give you your pension. Show me what you have."

"I was able to get copies of the financial statements of every one of Suarez's associates who deals through this bank." He reached into his coat pocket, pulled out a manila envelope. "Here."

Yablonsky stared at the transactions of a dozen people. Latin American businessmen. Other members of the delegation. A few familiar names. He looked up. "I asked for this stuff yesterday. When did you have the time to get all this?"

Dwyer smiled. "I told you my adrenalin was pumping. Right after you left I traced Suarez's checks back for years. There are more names, but these are the records of the people who bank here." He looked down at the documents, waiting to be complimented.

"Great work," Yablonsky said. His face showed the emotion he felt. He was willing to bet that never before was a detective furnished with critical information by someone who felt so ambivalently about him. He pointed at the dozen names. "You went through all these already, too?"

Dwyer grinned. "Today."

"What'd you find?"

"All the transactions between Suarez and his associates still register on the computer. Except one. Her name was placed under 'special access' this morning. I can't get at her files."

Whoever's account was now inaccessible was the person responsible for the laundering. "Who?' Yablonsky asked.

"Martha Bryant. The publisher. I was surprised Suarez even knew her."

"They're close," Yablonsky said. He punched her code into the monitor. The code registered, but not the account. Yablonsky smiled. "It's her all right. Why would an uptown publisher deal with a guy like Suarez?"

"They're both uptown people," Dwyer remarked. He picked up the records. "I only was able to come up with this—Suarez withdraws money from his account, the identical sum ends up in hers. But there's no record as to what she does with the funds."

"It doesn't matter yet where the money ends up," Yablonsky said. "Only that they use her to get rid of it. Thanks."

Dwyer shook his head. "A UN den of thieves. Even if you don't catch Suarez, glory and a press conference for sure. I guarantee I'll help solve your next case for you, too, Yablonsky."

"If anything comes of this, I swear you'll get more than a mention," Yablonsky said.

Dwyer pulled back in his chair. "That's the least you owe me. You weren't half the cop I was, and you'll never be as good a detective. Visit soon. I enjoyed tutoring you."

Yablonsky reclined against Martha Bryant's plush, modular sofa. He looked around the room appreciatively. He admired her taste. Interrogating wealthy suspects was always more enjoyable than interrogating poor ones.

She looked elegant in her Oscar de la Renta evening gown, with a string of pearls around her neck. She was dressed for a charity ball, not an interrogation, but against a forty-eight thousand-dollar-a-year detective, it was an effective suit of armor.

Yablonsky stabbed out his cigarette. The embers died

inside the conch-shaped ashtray. "As I said on the phone, we've made some progress on the case."

She smiled pleasantly. "And you want to question *me*, lieutenant? Why?"

Yablonsky shook his head politely. "No questions, Ms. Bryant. I'm just here to tell you a few things."

"You don't have to call me Ms., detective. I may be the publisher of *Fem*, but I'm not much of a feminist. You can even open a door for me sometime. I won't bite you."

"I'll open a door for you anytime, Miss Bryant. What I'd like now is for you to open up a few doors for me. We think that you're involved in a laundering operation for Suarez. Why you're washing money for him isn't important. But the fact that you are connects you to the deaths of Sean Maysfield and Paul Matson."

She fingered her pearl necklace. She seemed to be a lot calmer than him. "How?"

Yablonsky reached for his attaché case, took out an old copy of *Fem*. "I asked around for old issues. One of the girls at your office gave it to me."

"That's 'woman,' lieutenant. You don't call Negroes 'boys' anymore, do you?"

"I don't call anybody anything," Yablonsky said. He flipped the magazine open, turned the pages. "Every month you interview a different woman celebrity. In the January issue it was Suzy Creamcheese. Good interview, you wrote it yourself. Pointed questions. I imagine you thoroughly research each of your subjects."

"If I'm interested, I often do the research myself. Go on,—go on lieutenant."

"You did a lot of research for this one. I think you spoke to Marshall Hunter and he told you a few things. Maybe to get back at Susan for having something on him. Your magazine published some photos of Maysfield and Matson at O'Farrel's. I think you were intimately involved with them, and when they bragged they were seeing Susan you told them what you had found out about her from Marshall Hunter. The result was some amateurish blackmail."

Her smile sat on her face, as appropriate a disguise for her as her ten-thousand-dollar string of pearls. "Lieutenant, you're disgusting. I never blackmailed anyone. Why should I? I make more money in one week than Suzy Creamcheese has made in her career."

Yablonsky nodded. "Of course you didn't blackmail anyone. But you have many friends, Miss Bryant. Suarez, for instance, is a good friend of yours. We know his car was in the vicinity of one of the murder scenes. We suspect he's the killer, though we don't yet have a motive. Whatever his reason for killing them, he already knew there would be another suspect. The only way he would know about Susan was by talking to you. Because of her past she wouldn't be in a position to protest too much if our suspicions fell on her."

She nodded thoughtfully, as if Yablonsky were a dinner guest and had just related a fascinating anecdote. "All the pieces fit so snugly, lieutenant. I tell you again, I'm not involved in any murder. Why should a woman of my position help kill a couple of guys who peeled their clothes off for a living?"

"Why should you help kill *anyone*, Miss Bryant? In Paul's and Sean's case, probably because you either owe Suarez something or he has something on you . . . Is there anything you want to tell me?"

She smiled at him warmly, leaned back in her chair. "There are a great many things I'd like to tell you, lieutenant. Here are three of them. You're crazy. If you think I'm laundering any money, find my financial statements. Fuck you, and get out."

Yablonsky rose. "That's four."

It was one o'clock in the morning. He certainly wasn't expecting any phone calls now. He rolled over in bed and picked up the phone.

"Susan?"

"This is Rafael Gomez."

How did they get his number? "Does Suarez want to speak to me?"

"He's much too busy a man to call detectives. Even at night he conducts embassy affairs. Right now he's working on a speech to be read before the General Assembly. He delegated this lesser task to me."

"Maybe he's out wolfing down pastrami sandwiches at Smiler's,"Yablonsky said. "What do you want to tell me?"

"We hear you think you're making progress in solving your strippers' case."

"I come a little closer to solving it each day. Are you calling to warn me?"

Rafael laughed. "Of course not, lieutenant. We were calling to wish you luck."

Sixteen

Dwyer woke up at six-thirty in the morning. The walls of the bedroom of his house were plastered with headlines of the past exploits of the Brooklyn Dodgers. He himself lived in Corona, Queens.

By his bedside was a scrapbook opened to a photo of a smiling, nervous, younger Yablonsky and his not yet ex-wife back from their honeymoon in the wilds of New England. Yablonsky had wanted to visit Italy, his wife had insisted they go skiing at Mount Snow, Vermont. They had spent a week at each spot. It was one of the few marriages Dwyer knew of where the honeymoon had been more expensive than the wedding.

He sat up in bed, stared at himself as he had looked eleven years ago, his arms around the happy couple, behind them. At one of the most important points of their lives, he had been a background figure. Patrolman Hernandez had snapped the photos. Yablonsky had identical pictures. Dwyer knew his ex-partner would still be sleeping. He had always been a late riser.

He rolled out of bed, dropped to the floor, tucked his ankles under the bedframe, and began doing situps. Twenty-five in the morning. Fifty at night. As he stoically went up and down, he faced a yellowing article that showed a disgusted Cal Abrams being tagged out at home to end ignominiously the Giant-Dodger playoff. The article alongside it stated that the Dodger coach who had told Abrams to try for home had been fired.

Failure in any profession usually ended that way. Maybe he ought to shift those articles to a more obscure part of the wall and wake up to a cheerier headline from now on.

He climbed the steps to the kitchen, opened the refrigerator, and took out the leftovers of last night's quiche. He had cooked it according to the recipe and it had come out fluffy and light. Spinach and mushroom. Gourmet food. If Yablonsky had learned to cook like this, he wouldn't be in trouble with the department now.

Half the pie was left. He took a few forkfuls. He loved the taste of cold mushrooms. Inside the refrigerator was a glass of wine and a wedge of honeydew melon. He read yesterday's newspaper while he ate. He seldom had a chance to get to a newspaper on its print day, so he was usually one day behind in the news.

He flicked the radio on to WCBS. The Supremes. Fabian. The Heartones. The Cleftones. Not even Yablonsky knew he was hooked on music from the fifties and sixties.

After washing the breakfast dishes, he slipped into his robe, then went out the back door across the yard to his garage.

Passing his workbench, he turned the radio on. It was always tuned to WCBS. The radio in his house was blasting out Bobbi Freeman's "Do you Wanna Dance?" It was like having stereo.

He hefted the power saw and placed a block of wood inside the brace. It would need a lot of work before it became a sculpture of Jackie Robinson at the plate. The shelves above were already filled with the twenty-four wooden figures of ballplayers he had worked on for the past year. His goal was to create a sculpture of every National League Player who had played in 1955, a decade before expansion had ruined the game. He was undecided whether to do the American League. A compromise would be to carve out scenes from All-Star games, which were usually won by the senior circuit.

He pressed the power saw on, then turned to make the radio volume louder. Two men came through the open door, knives in their hands.

One of them glanced at the power saw. "The perfect weapon for us. He's making our job easier."

Reaching the workbench, the men separated, coming at him from different sides. They appeared to be Hispanic. Dwyer faced the shorter one, extended his arms with the power and moved forward. The man, surprised, backed up. Dwyer feinted with the saw, slipped past him and ran to the door. He'd never make the house in time. The telephone pole by the side of the garage. Climb up and across the roof. If he made it, he could lose them in the alleys. He started forward, then felt a hot flash inside him. His flesh shuddered and he screamed. A kick to the back brought him down. Something was tearing at him. His life was leaking away.

Both men stood over him. One of them reached for the power saw, which had an extension cord. "Finish him off."

The shorter man took a deep breath and smiled. "You see my friend, we keep banker's hours too . . ."

"I'm a cop," he managed. He cupped his hand in front of his mouth. Snot and blood ran down his nose. His hands shook. He looked up. They were coming closer to him. He pushed himself to a sitting position and kicked out. One of them grunted. He rounded the garage corner, heading toward the telephone pole. They were right behind.

$\triangledown$

Seventeen

YABLONSKY PARKED HIS CAR across from Dwyer's home. He had tried to reach him at the bank earlier, then at home. No answer.

In front of the house was Dwyer's '82 Cadillac. Each year he had traded in for a new one, until they had started downsizing them. It was early in the afternoon; Dwyer couldn't be out. Anything he needed or wanted that was more than half a block away he drove to. Walking made him feel like he was pounding a beat.

Climbing the steps, Yablonsky heard loud music. He smiled to himself. Dwyer was perfectly capable of saying "fuck you" to the bank, calling in sick, and spending the day listening to the radio while he cooked.

He knocked on the door. No answer. He pressed the buzzer. Dwyer probably was asleep, but then what was the radio doing on?

He walked through the alleyway. On the outside, Dwyer's home was pure Archie Bunker. Stucco-faced, old-fashioned parlor windows, lace curtains. He smiled uncertainly as he heard music coming from the garage.

The Byrds? Dwyer must be so engrossed with his work, he didn't realize he had tuned in a rock station.

He stopped when he reached the yard. A pool of blood, then a crimson trail that led to the side of the garage.

He cupped his hands to his mouth. "Dwyer?"

No answer. Just the pounding music. He went in through the open garage door. Dwyer's exquisite little figurines faced him from the shelves. He turned the radio off. Yablonsky could hear the one from the house. Martha and the Vandellas. "Come and Get These Memories."

He checked the garage for signs of a struggle. Wooden chips were scattered on the linoleum floor. He saw shoe prints in the sawdust. Dwyer had dodged past his attackers and made it to the yard. Then? His eyes shifted to the power saw at the foot of the garage door.

The streaks of blood led him to the telephone pole. He took a deep breath and climbed. In East New York he and his friends had scurried up these poles to run from roof to roof, but he hadn't been on one since. Dried blood from the handspikes brushed onto his fingers and wrists.

The tarpaper roof had traces of blood on it and pieces of a torn plaid robe. Dwyer's. He picked them up, walked to the roof's edge and peered down. A labyrinth of rooftops and alleyways. Most of the yards were small, neat patches of grass, but some had been allowed to run wild and now sprouted tangled grass and jungle growths of weeds. Blood from the pieces of shirt came off into his hands.

"Dwyer!"

No answer. He climbed down from the pole, went into the garage, and picked up the phone that was alongside the shelves.

"It's me," he said to Flood. "I'm at Dwyer's house. He's missing. There's blood."

"Oh, shit."

The next call he made was to the 109th Precinct in Queens, instructing them to establish a crime scene at

Dwyer's house. Then he drove home. He was supposed to see Susan tonight and he wanted to wash his hands.

"Hello, detective. I was just leaving." Karen smiled briefly at him, twisted her head toward the bedroom. "It's Kojak, honey. On time as usual."

She turned to face him. He noticed that she still wore her oversized clothing. Yablonsky tried not to stare at her ankles, where he was sure the scars began.

Susan came into the room and looked at him critically. "You look as if you've seen Banquo's ghost."

Yablonsky managed a weak smile. "And I feel worse than I look."

She took her sister's hand. "You have a good time." To Yablonsky, she explained. "Rob and Joanie are meeting her downstairs."

"My keepers," Karen said with a smile. Facing Yablonsky, she squeezed Susan's hand. "I'm crazy about this girl. You take good care of her, lieutenant." She left, shutting the door.

Susan came over, wanting to be kissed. Her eyepatch covered much of her face, but that didn't matter to him. Patches of red hair showed brightly from beneath a red bandanna. She wore long, safari-type trousers and a hunter's shirt with the Banana Republic logo. Again she had made the most haphazard apparel seem stylish.

She broke it off, pulled away from him. "I've had better from you, so I'm disappointed. Your heart isn't in this at all. Can I get you a beer?"

"Sure," Yablonsky said. "Do you have a Heineken? One that's really cold?"

She went off to the kitchen. He saw her reach into the refrigerator, emerge with a beer, and smile at him. "You're still interrogating me."

He took the beer from her outstretched hand. "You should be happy I questioned you," he said. "I got you off."

She drank from her cup of iced tea. "I'm grateful for that. Do you have anyone else?"

"A diplomat." He put down the beer mug. "His name's either Emile Suarez or Jesus Christ. I don't really know which, because he thinks he's God."

"You sound frustrated."

He nodded. "I wanted to talk to you about it. I think my ex-partner was killed this morning for giving me some information on him. I know what they're like, Susan. Very polished. Very low-key. But I think they'd run a cattle prod up and down your spine if they thought you'd get in the way...Put on a record. I need to unwind."

She went over to the turntable and began flipping through the records that were underneath. "Ella or Billie?"

"How about one of yours?"

She looked at him warmly. "I thought you said I didn't compare to them."

"You don't," he said. "But who does? I'd say you're almost as good as Joplin."

She put the record on, came to him, and took his hands. "Thanks. I'd say you're almost as good a detective as Maigret."

He listened to the off-key singing and made a face. "It must have been one of your bad days. You sound better on MTV."

"I'm sorry about your friend." She took a sip of his beer. "You don't tell me how to sing, and I won't tell you how to deduce."

Yablonsky took the drink from her hand and put it down on the end table. "I miss him already. Can we make love? Maybe I'm unique. Death and beer don't affect my performance."

She got up, looked at him solemnly. "You're in luck. Do you need to be romanced before I seduce you?" She reached for his hand, gave it a squeeze, and moved to the turntable. She slipped her own album back into the wrapper. He recognized the album she took out. *Sinatra: A Man and his Music.* "It's Sinatra for romance," she said. "And Billie Holiday for the blues."

"And you?" he asked.

"I'm for rebellion," she said, and laughed.

She led him to the bedroom. Afterward, she leaned against his chest. "You can stay if you want."

"Not tonight," he said. "I've got to go home. When can I see you again?"

She circled his right nipple with her finger. "I start a road tour next week. Until then, we can squeeze in a few nights."

"And when you come back?"

"We'll see."

It was the answer he expected. In the darkness he put on his clothes, kissed her, and left.

A light on East 7th Street flickered faintly overhead. A sign warning speculators to beware hung between tenement fire escapes.

There was no one on the FDR Drive. He took up two lanes as he drove under the Brooklyn Bridge to the Battery Tunnel.

The road ahead curved. Ahead of him he could see the Statue of Liberty. In two weeks the Memorial Day festivities would begin. Yablonsky hoped he would be out of town, perhaps accompanying Susan during one of her gigs.

The Belt was also empty. Maybe some steamed bagels at Junior's? He had to get home; he needed a shower and a shave.

Exiting at Sheepshead Bay, he drove past the dimmed lights of the fishing fleet and parked alongside the narrow bridge.

He opened his apartment door and turned on the light. Two men were waiting for him. They smiled at him, as if eager. Before Yablonsky's eyes could adjust to the light, Miguel approached. Threw a right to his head. Rafi, darting behind him, kicked him in the kidneys. Yablonsky went down. More vicious punches to his ribs and the sides of his head. While Rafi pinned his arms to his side, Miguel smashed his elbow into Yablonsky's ear. He hit Yablonsky in the mouth.

"You're killing me," Yablonsky gasped. "I'm a cop."

Foolish, Yablonsky thought. That's why they're beating you. He tried to do something, but couldn't move. Rafi clubbed him in his head with his fist, then rising suddenly, he leaned and Yablonsky received kick after kick to his stomach.

"Please," he groaned. "Enough."

He felt Miguel's hot breath next to him, then sensed him pulling away. Miguel reached the door and took out his gun. He smiled as he pointed it at Yablonsky. "Bang. Bang," he whispered. Then they were gone.

Yablonsky pulled himself over to the closest wall. He sat with his back against it and struggled for breath. Blood leaked out of the side of his mouth. His eyes went to his furnishings. The apartment was still neat and orderly.

He would have felt better if they had wrecked the apartment. The undisturbed orderliness emphasized not the savagery of their assault, but the conviction and calculation behind it.

He might suspect they had murdered Dwyer, but he couldn't be sure. Now they were telling him they were confident enough to beat him up and let him know who his assailants were.

He stared at his bloodied hands, felt his bruised lips and face. In his own home. He wept.

Eighteen

Y ABLONSKY SLOWED AS HE reached the toll, then drove over the Rockaway Bridge. Fishermen were on both sides of the parkway, their lines extended forty feet below to the water. As a boy he used to rest his head against his father's lap on the ride to the family bungalow at the beach. There had always been fishermen when they passed through the toll gates.

Riis Park contained a small nine-hole pitch-and-putt golf course, where the distance between holes, at the most, was sixty to seventy yards. Flood liked to play here on weekends. He was a terrible golfer, but with this course he could lay nine holes twice and still score in the eighties.

If he was displeased at having his weekend game interfered with, he didn't show it. Ready to tee off, he leaned on his seven iron and peered at Yablonsky's bruises. His partner, a deputy fire commissioner, had already driven his ball onto the green.

"You look like you've been playing rough," Flood said. "What's up?"

"I told you over the phone," Yablonsky said. "Last night Suarez had me beaten up. I want you to take me off this case."

207

Flood addressed his golf ball and hit a dribbler that traveled perhaps twenty yards. The deputy fire commissioner walked to the green. Flood motioned Yablonsky to keep pace with him.

"Actually that was not a bad shot," Flood said. "Strategy-wise, I should be on the green in three. Then I three putt for a six. You see, Alvin, I've got it all figured out." A pause. "I'm sorry they beat you up. I'm sorry about Dwyer. Unfortunately, there's nothing we can do to them now. It's your word against theirs."

"I'm a detective," Yablonsky said. "That's got to be worth something."

"Not as much as being a diplomat is I'm afraid." Flood stretched out his club, lining up his shot. "I make it about fifty yards to the green. What do you say?"

"Use your nine iron."

Flood nodded, swiped at the ball, and missed.

"God, you're lousy," Yablonsky said.

"Take a swing at it."

Yablonsky did. Despite his stiffness, he swung easily and chipped it onto the green.

"A lucky shot," Flood said. "I don't blame you for being upset. I promise you the department will line up behind you when it's appropriate."

Yablonsky shook his head. "I don't like violence. I mean it."

The deputy fire commissioner approached Flood. "That's an odd thing to hear from a homicide detective."

"Why?" Flood said. "All a detective does is record acts of violence and try to solve them. He's not like a cop. Yablonsky, I don't want to give this to another detective."

Once again Yablonsky felt himself gripped by a newfound fear. "Let me get back to my other cases."

Although Flood was not in the deputy commissioner's line of fire, he picked his golf ball up anyway. The deputy commissioner shot and made his putt. Flood placed the golf ball on a higher spot on the green, improving his lie. "The reason I want you to stay on this is because unlike most of the detectives in my precinct, you're capable of cheating. That's the only way you'll beat a man like Suarez. Now go back to the office and see what you have. With the overtime, you'll be able to pay for your meals from now on." He turned to the deputy fire commissioner. "He's one of my best men." He was perhaps twenty yards away from the hole. He picked up the ball. "This one's a 'give me.' No need to putt." Before the deputy commissioner could protest, he stepped to the drive-off tee, even though honors belonged to his partner. The ball dribbled out ten yards.

The deputy fire commissioner said to Yablonsky, "Sometimes even cheating doesn't help."

After he reached the precinct, Yablonsky spent two hours going through his paperwork. Sorting out the precinct circulars and forms took an hour and forty-five minutes. Assembling what he had concerning the murders of Paul and Sean took five. A financial statement that implicated no one. A sworn statement from a patrolman indicating he had ticketed a car whose inhabitants were inside eating pastrami sandwiches. If he was able to get patrolman Hardis to perjure himself, he might be able to arrest them for littering. Their government would not be sending them home for that.

During the ride back to his place, he was struck by the huge number of seagulls that had invaded Sheepshead Bay. They were everywhere. Scores were on the roof of Randazzo's. Hundreds perched on the sterns of the fishing ships. He got out of his car. "Is Alfred Hitchcock's studio shooting

Birds II?" he wondered aloud.

Suddenly the boat skippers emptied their leftover barrels of chum into the water. Screeching, the seagulls swooped.

Yablonsky walked across the narrow bridge, trying to avoid the piles of gullshit.

He opened the side door to his apartment. He saw the outline of a man sitting on his sofa. The man rose and stepped forward. Instinctively Yablonsky's hand moved to protect his face.

"Why are you afraid of me?" Dwyer asked.

After Yablonsky recovered from his shock he slipped out a cigarette for himself, handed the pack to Dwyer. "Jesus, I'm glad. I thought they'd killed you."

"They almost did. It's a matter of subterfuge. I kicked the bastards down when they tried to reach the top. Tore my robe so my blood wouldn't leave a trail. Once I reached he alleyways I was safe. They didn't stand a chance."

Dwyer moved stiffly to the couch. "Sit down," he ordered Yablonsky. "What the hell happened to you? You look worse than I do."

"They beat me up. How about you?"

"Lacerations to the back and left arm, but no power saw. I didn't have much time to recuperate . . . I've got something for you." He handed a copy of the financial transactions of Martha Bryant to Yablonsky. "Don't ask me how I got this."

"I won't," Yablonsky said. "How did you?"

"I knew they'd have to show the new head of security at the bank the entire layout, so they'd give him the code to Special Access. He's a retired cop—everyone who does bank security is. I told him what I wanted and why, and he gave it to me."

He made it sound so easy. "Thanks, Dwyer."

Dwyer smiled. They both knew what would come next.

"I suppose I'll have to stay here for a while, but I'm not happy about it."

"Why not?"

"Too much gullshit."

$\triangledown$

Nineteen

Martha Bryant invited him into her living-room office. She wore a floor-length evening gown by Beaumont. Once again, a string of pearls.

Yablonsky seated himself on the modular sofa. The blinds had not been drawn. Through the window he could see cars slowly crawling up the arteries of the 59th Street Bridge. To the right was her desk, typewriter, and stack upon stack of past issues of *Fem*.

She did not yet have reason to lose her smile. "Champagne? Caviar? It's the best beluga there is."

"Neither."

"Now I know you must be involved in serious detective business. This is the first time I've seen you refuse food."

Yablonsky handed her ream after ream of the records of her financial transactions. "Withdrawals from the People's Development Fund, going first to Suarez's account." He handed her another sheaf. "Copies of the complete list of your real estate transactions. I'd say you're the front woman for Ramirez and his government. The amounts withdrawn from the accounts and the cash you used to buy the buildings are the same."

"I didn't flunk math, lieutenant. I can add. Since when is

213

it against the law to buy real estate?"

"Through you, Ramirez probably owns more New York real estate than Donald Trump. It may not be against our laws, but it's against the laws of his country to transfer out such huge sums of money. I suppose to make sure the citizens keep their money back home."

"He's a cautious man. In case he has to go, he doesn't want to end up like Ferdinand and Baby Doc. As for their laws, the last time I heard, military juntas are flexible when it comes to interpreting their constitutions."

She ate the caviar and sipped champagne. Yablonsky looked at the expensive furnishings, the orderly desk, the piles of the sensationalist magazine alongside it. Since the murder of two of the men who had done photo spreads, her magazine's circulation had increased twofold. He had an idea.

"Don't go away," he said. He approached the desk, hoping that what he wanted would be there. The magazines were stacked month by month, with the most recent issue on top. He flipped through. As he looked, he could feel her eyes on him. There it was!

When he returned, she said, "I didn't know you were interested, lieutenant. Would you like a complimentary subscription?"

"I'll take almost anything if it's for free, so why not?" He pointed to the pinup calendar of the months of the year. "I saw it earlier, so I should have guessed."

"Guessed what?"

He turned the calendar's pages. "Muted light. Seductive poses. A real artist must have taken these pictures."

"Thanks," she said, pointing to a corner of one of the pages. "You can see my name right there."

"These photos first led me to you. All the time I assumed

that you must somehow be connected to my case because of the pictures that appeared in your magazine and calendar."

She placed her wineglass on the table that was between them. She was no longer smiling. "Go on."

He tapped the calendar's pages. "It never occurred to me, until now, that the real key might be the pictures you took of them that *didn't* appear in the magazine."

She didn't say anything. He continued. "The *real* photos you took of these men must have been more explicit, much more sensational. I said before you're an artist. The pictures you took of Paul and Sean for your calendar would naturally appeal to a certain market. Curiosity aroused is always satisfied, Miss Bryant, and you were contacted by people who knew how you operated. You sold or gave away the photos that weren't published—that's another reason you run these calendars. Maybe the photos of the men led to contacts of a more personal nature. We already know that Paul and Sean were capable of blackmail. Maybe they chose to try a little of it with the wrong man and he had them killed. Or maybe the person you sent those photos to indulged his fantasies with Paul and Sean and later had them killed because this man is the type who must keep his reputation intact."

"Think of your track record with the UN lieutenant. You're treading on rocky ground."

Yablonsky flipped through a copy of *Fem* until he came to the interview section. "I think you had your subjects thoroughly investigated, and sometimes, when you found out something juicy about them, you'd blackmail them."

"Not me."

"Not alone. You had help."

He called in to Flood. "I never asked you how your golf game went."

"I ended up shooting a ninety-one."

"Not bad," Yablonsky said. "What'd the deputy commissioner shoot?"

"Never mind," Flood said. "What's up? Did Bryant tell you anything?"

"I've got new information," Yablonsky said. "I'm going back to O'Farrel's."

"Good," said Flood. "I guess it's time to make the strippers come clean."

Yablonsky nodded to the cop who was still stationed inside the club.

"Is my pigeon ready for me?" he asked.

"He knows you're coming." The cop pointed with his chin toward the bar. "Will you need any help?"

Yablonsky shook his head. "He should be easy."

Bobbi poured him a beer from the tap. The show had not yet begun. The other bartenders moved freely through the room, polishing tables and cleaning the floor surrounding the bar. Bobbi hung back, standing behind the burnished wood as if it were a barrier that would keep the detective from him.

Yablonsky settled himself comfortably onto a stool. "I told you I'd be back."

Bobbi managed a smile but continued to look at him warily. "So you did."

The detective nodded pleasantly. "Should I question you here or at the precinct?" He pushed his beer away as if ready to leave.

Bobbi polished the bar's surface with a rag. "Suit yourself," he said. "I've got nothing to say to you."

"Let's go downtown, then."

"Fine."

The little hustler resolutely started to move out from behind the bar. Yablonsky raised a hand to stop him. "I'd rather you answer my questions in front of your friends. You let them continue to work here scared shitless, guarded by cops, and all the time you know that probably no one else is going to be murdered. Is that fair to these guys, Bobbi?"

Bobbi shot a smile over to the horde of musclebound men gathered around the stage, staring at him and the over-dressed detective. They looked back at him uncertainly.

"You think I'm protecting someone, don't you?"

"Of course I do," Yablonsky said. "Yourself." He unfolded the calendar from his pocket. "You appeared in this, along with Sean and Paul. You were Mr. March, the third month of the year. You know something."

"What do you think I know, lieutenant?"

"You probably know who murdered Paul and Sean."

The little hustler was white-faced. He turned to his friends, then back to Yablonsky. "You're joking, lieutenant."

Yablonsky tapped his half-empty glass, signaling for another drink. "I never joke about murder."

The hand that poured him the beer shook. "Okay, detective. In the other room . . ."

He led Yablonsky to the dressing quarters and sat down on a director's chair, covering his face with his hands. "Christ, what a mess." He sighed, faced the detective. "I'll tell you what you want to know."

Yablonsky's voice sounded clipped. "Whatever you have to say you'll tell twice. Once here, then at the precinct before my captain and attorneys."

Bobbi's face was drained. "How can you do this to me?"

"It isn't easy," Yablonsky acknowledged. "The diplomat, Suarez. How many times did he see Paul and Sean?"

"I don't know. They never told me."

"But you saw him with them?"

Bobbi nodded. "He lives in a luxury apartment building with a lot of other diplomats. They used the club to arrange dates with us all the time. One weekend I had just completed an out-call to a guy who lives on the same floor as Suarez. I saw the three of them about to enter Suarez's apartment. I hadn't known until then that they were seeing him. They were pretty closemouthed about their dates."

"After you saw Suarez with Paul and Sean, did he ever ask you to trick with them?"

Bobbi laughed. "No. He said he liked me better." His eyes narrowed shrewdly, but he had to go on. "All right. I tricked with him, too, lieutenant. I was one of his favorites. But we were always alone."

"Good, Bobbi. Like Paul and Sean, you posed for more explicit pictures than the calendar?"

"Yes."

"When you were with Suarez, did he ever show them to you?"

Bobbi smiled weakly. "He had copies. He also took some of his own. He's a camera nut." He paused. "Was he afraid he'd be blackmailed over them? Then why am I still alive?"

Yablonsky shook his head. "He wouldn't kill Paul and Sean over some pictures that he could dispose of . . . You're still alive because even though you tricked with him, you didn't learn whatever it was they learned that made him kill them."

"I guess it all makes sense," Bobbi said. He crossed his muscular arms. "You've finished with me, haven't you?"

Yablonsky nodded. "When I first met you, you told me you were willing to help me solve my case."

"And I have, haven't I?" Bobbi smiled. "God, I feel better . . . You won't be back?"

"Except for getting your statement at the precinct you won't ever see me again," Yablonsky assured him.

He rubbed his temples wearily. "At least that's something to be grateful for."

"It is, isn't it?" The doors swung open. The dancers began filing in to change into their costumes for the night show. Yablonsky buttoned the top of his shirt and left.

Denise Levine stood in front of her class and blinked at Yablonsky in amazement.

He leaned against the doorframe. "What are you doing here, lieutenant?" she said in front of the roomful of students. The beginning of an outline had been chalked on the blackboard: *Proper Dating Techniques*.

Yablonsky smiled pleasantly at the fifteen women and three men. If things didn't work out with Susan, he'd know where to go.

"Just a few more questions, Ms. Levine." He paused. "Here, or in the office."

She looked at her watch. "The class ends soon. Give me five minutes, detective."

"Sure," Yablonsky said. He shut the door. Through the windowpane, he could see the students scribble notes. He heard Denise Levine say, "As I said earlier, the best way to meet members of the opposite sex is by 'chance' encounters at museums, boutiques, and health clubs. Of course, for those of you who are shy, there's always my magazine . . ."

He settled into the office chair. She came into the room and closed the door. "Yes, lieutenant?"

Yablonsky casually picked up a copy of the latest issue of *Let's Get Personal* as she eyed him nervously. "I've been a detective for almost five years. I love my job, but occasionally I take the wrong approach. When Susan told me she was being blackmailed by Paul and Sean, I believed her. It's only recently I began putting things together. She gave the money to them, so it was natural for her to assume they were the ones who were blackmailing her. It hadn't occurred to me yet that they were only the bagmen, and that the person behind them was you."

She looked puzzled. "I don't know what you're talking about, lieutenant. I never blackmailed anybody in my life."

"Of course you didn't," Yablonsky said. "The idea wouldn't have occurred to you alone. You had assistance from Martha Bryant. A lot of women celebrities make use of your magazine. If one of them had also been interviewed and investigated by Martha Bryant, you'd inform her. If she had a little dirt on them she'd pass it on to you. You'd arrange for Paul, Sean, and who knows how many other guys to answer the ads, and before you knew it, they'd become your bagmen. I bet you have inside information on half the women celebrities in New York, but I'm not interested in that."

"What are you interested in, detective? You can't prove what you say."

Yablonsky shifted comfortably in his seat and casually lit a cigarette. He smiled at her. It made her angry, as he knew it would. "I don't have to prove it, Denise. Besides, I'm interested in murder, not in a little innovative blackmail. I've wasted a lot of time on a lot of incorrect assumptions. For instance, I thought that the fragment from your magazine I found in Paul's hand was a clue to find the *woman* who had murdered him. You only gave me a list of female suspects, and the fragment was part of an ad that a woman had placed. It hadn't occurred to me yet that Paul wasn't signaling the sex of his killer, but only where the killer could be found. The murderer Paul was trying to lead us to was a

man who placed an ad in your magazine. I think it was
Suarez, and that you were the person who set Paul and Sean
up with him. Do you know why he had them killed?"

"No."

"But he used your magazine as a way to meet men like
Paul and Sean. One of these ads must be his. And now I
have someone who can connect him to them. He laughed
off my suspicions before, but now I have a case."

Her face was white. "I guess you do."

Twenty

SUAREZ GLIDED AMONG THE groups of celebrants. There were about one hundred fifty people in the room: talking, gossiping, waiting on line to shake the Mexican ambassador's hand.

He had just finished explaining to the caterer why his staff could not start packing up food to take home now. They were angry, ready to walk out. He had actually had to assure them that he did not mind them stealing from him, so long as they did so later.

He spotted the emissary from Saudi Arabia. "Hey, the desert sheik himself." He gripped the proffered hand warmly. "No doubt I caught you just before your escape back to Lawrence and his camels. You shouldn't try to hide from me. Not when my country's about to vote approval for financing. I'm a friend, not an enemy."

Rafi approached, a tense look on his face. "I have to speak to you."

"Vaya con Dios." He allowed himself to be led away from the emissary, then turned to Rafi, irritated. "There've been problems all night. What now?"

"That detective is downstairs."

He shook his head, his exasperation complete. "Shake

223

him off." He forced a smile. "Look at me. It took you half an hour to adjust my bowtie and I'm wearing my best tux. I can't be bothered with detectives now."

"Sorry, Emile. I tried. He's still determined to come up."

Suarez made a gesture, as if in disbelief. "All this trouble because of a goddamned parking ticket . . . This is an ambassador's house. There's nothing he can do."

"If there's nothing he can do, then let him come up. If things don't go well, signal us to get the girl."

Suarez nodded. "I'll handle him, but put him through the mill first. A fifteen-minute search for weapons, for instance."

Rafi smiled. "A strip search?"

"Of course not. He's a detective . . . You actually sound eager."

"No way. That's your department."

Yablonsky passed the clusters of tuxedoed diplomats. A waiter pulled up before him, carrying a tray from which he took a glass of champagne. He saw that security men from Suarez's operation bordered the room. Adjusting his collar, he smiled at the people who stared curiously at him.

Suarez was up ahead, the central figure of a small group that included Martha Bryant. He stepped toward Yablonsky with a smile and an outstretched hand. Yablonsky took it. "You've decided to crash my party after all, detective. Well, you're a welcome guest. Would you like some buffet? Martha tells me you're partial to good food. This is LaCaravel. The best."

Yablonsky shook his head slightly. "Not tonight. I came here to talk to you."

"What about?"

"Your murdering Paul and Sean."

Suarez glanced quickly at his cluster of guests. "*Jesus,* lieutenant. I can see I'm going to have to be careful with you." He placed a hand on Yablonsky's shoulder, steering him toward the terrace. "Let's talk out here."

They stepped out onto the terrace. They were high up, and the wind that blew through the summer night was refreshing. Lights from other buildings and the series of bridges lit the sky. To the right, Yablonsky could actually see a small part of the UN.

Suarez faced him, smiling. Yablonsky shut the sliding glass door and waved at Miguel and Rafi, who were standing on the other side. Suarez looked at him, a puzzled expression on his handsome, suntanned face. "I'm sure they thought it was all a joke, but why did you say that out there, lieutenant? Murder's nothing to make jokes about."

"Of course it isn't. I think I told you once I don't carry a gun. I didn't enjoy being probed and searched by Rafi as if I were a passenger on El Al."

A contrite look. "Rafi was acting under my orders, lieutenant. Searches are mandatory now. You know we've had incidents of terrorism. A bomb exploded in our Washington compound just a week ago. What are you really here to see me about?"

"Over two months ago two badly mutilated bodies, complete with bondage masks, were found in East Side apartments. Both men were dancers at a club called O'Farrel's."

A string of Roman candles and cherry bombs went off in the sky above them. Both men looked up. Someone was celebrating an early Memorial Day.

Yablonsky continued. "Why does an important man, in this country as a guest, butcher two marginal people? Is it because these two boys whom he partied with threatened to expose him? I don't think so. Homosexuality's not much of a scandal anymore. Lines of cocaine are left in both apartments. Drugs? Smuggling? Relatively minor offenses that our agencies sometimes help you people cover up—not worth killing over. To satisfy a blood lust, a sex killing? Of course not . . . Blackmail? Sean and Paul would never try to blackmail or extort money from this man because of anything he might have done. They already knew what he was like, respected and feared him. I think these boys were killed because they accidently discovered something, possibly during an intimate moment when this man's guard was down. Laundering a country's finances isn't even that serious, but your country is engaged in fighting a guerilla war. If word of this operation leaked out, people would know how precarious you thought your situation really was. I imagine you also wouldn't want people to know that much of the financial aid we send you finds its way back here as washed cash for real estate to ensure your standard of living if you end up here. So they were killed."

"You think I'm a murderer," Suarez said. "Incredible. Go on, lieutenant. I'm interested in knowing what else you intend to accuse me of."

"Because of your close contacts with Martha Bryant, you even could throw us a suspect. You already knew Paul and Sean were involved in blackmailing Susan and you knew why she was paying. You planned out your murders based on her actions. You watched, learned her habits, and waited for nights when her alibis would be flimsy. In a way, despite your prior experience, you're an amateur, Suarez. People with flimsy motives seldom kill. The acts of murder themselves were executed too well to be 'sex-drug' killings. But of course consciences wouldn't be too strained if we pinned it on Susan. A punk star who sings off-key about sex, drugs, and violence is practically screaming to be blamed for murder. We can't prosecute you because of diplomatic immunity, but you can be forced to leave the country."

"Do you have any proof?"

"My case is more than just speculation, but if you mean do we have anyone who actually can place you at the scenes of the murders, of course not. We do have a witness who can connect you to them, who knows for a fact that you met with them."

"What witness?" Suarez asked. "Did this person see me kill them?"

"Maybe." Yablonsky paused. "No."

"Then I deny it. I like it here. I'm staying."

Yablonsky reached into his coat pocket. "Here are documents that link you to the laundering operation. We also have lists of the buildings your government owns. Your man Miguel. I'd like to do a lab analysis on that pair of shoes he's wearing. I bet they'd show traces of wood chips and sawdust from a man named Dwyer's garage." He pointed to the bruises on his cheek. "Additional evidence. Battery against a detective is a pretty serious crime."

Suarez smiled. "It's too bad punches don't leave fingerprints. And Miguel loses pairs of shoes like other men misplace umbrellas. You know, lieutenant, technically my home is foreign soil and protected. You're not even supposed to be here. May I assume you're about to leave?"

Yablonsky tapped the topmost document. "We can release this information to the newspapers and it would be front-page copy tomorrow. When our witness talks, even if we can't get you for murder, there's drugs and kinky sex. You'll be the most famous noncitizen in this country. Before Ramirez instructs you to return home, that is."

"This is novel, detective. You appear to be blackmailing me. Leave this country—or else I tell. You're a foolish man. You should allow me to bribe you." Suarez gave a small wave of his hand. Miguel and Rafi moved away from the glass doors. "They have various appointments," Suarez said. "Rafi's going to attempt to get the guests started on their way home. Miguel's organizing the catering staff to clean up."

Yablonsky watched Miguel and Rafi make their way through the crowded reception room. He could see Rafi hurrying the diplomats into their evening coats and bidding them a fond farewell. Miguel, however, did not strike him as the type to deal with a domestic staff. Leave the body they were supposed to be guarding? Where were they really doing? He turned back to Suarez. "You mentioned bribery. How much?"

"I told you I enjoyed living here. How does fifty thousand sound?"

"It sounds wonderful," Yablonsky admitted. "But it would mean I'd be rich enough to retire, and I like my work."

"One hundred thousand."

He hesitated. "I don't need it. I have a pension."

Suarez said, "You have the wrong idea about me, lieutenant. I don't believe in committing murder to solve problems. I wouldn't hurt a fly."

"You're not accused of murdering flies."

"So far I haven't been officially accused of murdering anyone. But I certainly don't enjoy having my financial affairs and private life probed into. Don't forget to have some more champagne before you go."

Yablonsky wanted to say something to snap that bland imperturbability. If I were legally allowed to commit murder, I guess I'd be pretty calm on the outside too, he thought. "I'll be back," Yablonsky said. "Since you like it here so much you won't be going anyplace."

The diplomat made a weary, unhappy gesture. "If you say you'll be back, I suppose I'll have to resign myself to it."

Suarez waved to the departing guests. He called to the

emissary from Saudi Arabia, got his attention. The man turned, and Suarez snapped a picture of him with his Nikon.

The man belatedly raised his hand to try to protect his face. "In my religion, taking pictures of people is not permitted."

"Forgive me," Suarez said. "I'm a camera nut, and with your flowing robes you look like an extra from a movie set." He grinned, certain he would be indulged. "I just couldn't resist."

The man looked at him uncomprehendingly for a moment. "Please give me the picture."

Suarez kept the film, excused himself, and went into the room that contained a "safe" phone. He shut and locked the door, placing a call to a pay phone that was two blocks away. Rafi picked up, and Suarez relayed his instructions. He took the elevator to the private garage and squeezed into the front seat of a small sedan that did not have diplomatic license plates. Driving through the park, he made a right and took the Henry Hudson Parkway north. He turned on the radio and slid the window open partway. He found parking two blocks away from the safe house in Washington Heights, folded his evening coat over his arm, and walked.

Miguel and another man from the embassy were in the kitchen. Between them was Denise Levine. Miguel had a firm grip on her arm, and the other man stood behind her. They were about to take her to the car.

She looked at Suarez. He was surprised they hadn't yet gagged her. She was drugged, very pale.

"Why?" she asked. "I don't understand. I called you and told you he had been to see me."

"You also asked what we should do," Suarez said. He turned to Miguel and handed him another camera, his Polaroid.

Miguel grimaced. "Fucking Alan Funt. This isn't Candid Camera, Emile."

"Never mind." He gripped the other man's shoulder. "Miguel doesn't seem to understand Spanish. Take her to New Jersey. No one but the detective knows about her. I don't want her to be found."

"Understood."

"Please," Denise groaned. "I won't say anything."

"Sorry, no." The width of her eyes fascinated him. He borrowed back the Polaroid, focused, and snapped. He thrust the photo into his pocket without looking at it. He watched Miguel take Denise by the arm and lead her out the door and toward the car. She got in. He slipped into his evening coat, reached the sedan, and began the drive to Brooklyn.

Suzy Creamcheese kissed her sister on the cheek. "It's time for my rehearsal. You'll be all right?"

Karen nodded, circled her arm around her sister. "Aren't I always. What time will you be back?"

Susan's eyes darted past her sister. "Jesus," she said. "I forgot my hand mike. Rob, what the hell is happening to me? I think I'll make it an early night. Two hours of rehearsal. Drinks at the Aztec. Maybe we'll drop in at the Mudd Club. Expect me back by two-thirty."

"You're not seeing Al tonight then?" Rob asked.

"Nope. Maybe tomorrow if I'm lucky."

"I don't know how you can date a detective," Karen said.

Susan lifted her eyepatch and winked. "He must be in love with me. He hasn't busted me for anything yet." She raised her hand in a small wave. "Once more into the breach. See you later, guys."

"Come home soon," Karen said.

Susan was already down the stairs. "You know me, so don't count on it."

Outside she began to walk fast. The guys were already there. She thought about the tour. After they got back, if her career didn't pick up she intended to form another band. Of the four members, she would keep only Eddie. He played lead guitar just like Sam Andrews of Big Brother.

When she crossed to the east side of Tompkins a car pulled alongside her. The driver slid down his window. "How can I get to Lincoln Center from here?"

"You're a long way from Lincoln Center," she said and kept on walking. She stood at the intersection of 9th Street and Avenue B. Two men stepped out from around the corner. They pointed knives at her. One of them pointed with his chin to a car that was parked on the other side of the street. "Come with us," he said.

"Is this a robbery? I'm carrying twenty dollars. You can have it."

"Miss, just get in the car."

She hesitated. They came closer, took her by the arms, and forced her in.

Yablonsky finished his Friday night dinner at Izzy and Anthony's.

Izzy leaned toward him. "How was the snapper?"

Yablonsky made a satisfied face. "Delicious."

"Right off the boat, catch of the day."

Yablonsky handed him a five, as a tip. "I happen to know you defrost cases of Mrs. Paul's."

"Detective?"

"Yes?"

"This is the fifth Friday night in a row you've paid for your meal. Have we done anything to displease you?"

A reputation is a hard thing to live down, Yablonsky thought. "No." He grimaced. "I've got to be careful."

Izzy made a gesture of comprehension. "Your eating habits," he said softly. "They're investigating you?"

Yablonsky looked around self-consciously, but none of the diners had looked up. "Of course not," he said. Then loudly, just in case. "Keep the change."

He stepped out, crossed to the parking lot, and was about to get into his car. Suarez and Rafi emerged from its other side, guns in their hands. Yablonsky readied himself to run, but stopped as a man behind him tapped him on the shoulder. "How you doing?"

"Okay," Yablonsky said. He felt the man's gun press into the small of his back. Rafi reached into his inside jacket pocket and took his gun. "What's going on?"

"Quiet," Suarez said. "If you yell, we'll shoot you here. Did you enjoy your dinner? I notice some tarter sauce on your coat collar. You must've had clams."

"Snapper," Yablonsky said.

"Good," Suarez said. "Now get in the car."

Yablonsky felt his stomach grow cold with fear. He didn't move. "I thought you said you never killed anyone."

"I never murder anyone," Suarez said. "People force me to kill them."

"Suppose I back off from the investigation? I'll give you my word."

"You tried to blackmail me," Suarez said. "As if you think I'd enjoy returning to some shit-assed country where indoor plumbing is a goal of the middle class and the national domestic pet is the iguana. I love New York." He pointed with his gun. "Move or we give it to you here."

Yablonsky looked at Suarez, his goddamn camera strapped by his side. If they took him away, at least he'd have more time. He got in. "Where are you taking me?"

"Shut up."

Yablonsky watched Suarez hand his camera to Rafi, then enter his own car and drive away. Rafi sat alongside him, a .9 mm gun resting on his lap. The other man got in the front. Yablonsky's stomach lurched as they pulled out of the parking lot. The car made a right onto Emmons Avenue. This was not happening to him.

The Belt Parkway was practically empty. They passed by tall buildings that seemed to be dressed in shadowy fog.

There were lights ahead. The Verrazano. They moved across. The bridge was outlined by lights and pools of dark water that looked like oil spills. Miguel stared at Susan's eyepatch, her multicolored hair, and faded dress. "Trash," he said.

"You told me you're going to kill me," Susan said. "Why?"

The driver said, "Gag her."

Her arms were already tied; she tried to raise her feet, but was easily overpowered by Miguel. He wrapped a long, narrow towel around her mouth. "No more singing for you."

The driver laughed. "You call what she does singing?" He flung some coins into the basket as the car sped through one of the exact toll lanes. They would pay on their way back. They exited, made a right along a dirt road, and went a mile until they reached a village. Everything had shut down. They climbed a hill, passing areas that were full of marshlands. There were calls of birds, frogs, and crickets. Water lapped against the shore, spray and foam sometimes spilling over to the road alongside.

In front, the driver smiled. "I hear they tried to kill Lucky Luciano around here."

Miguel grunted. "They should have let us do it."

The car went along a narrow path, through tangled scrub and forest. They were descending now. Susan could barely see up ahead. The car stopped. The headlights shone on a swampy, deserted area.

"When I tell you to, get out," Miguel said. "We're going to take a walk."

All four of the car doors were open. Miguel was munching on a salami sandwich, a bottle of Coke in his hand. "I'm really hungry," he said.

The driver said, "Save half for me."

"No way. You should've brought your own." Miguel took another bite out of the salami and rye. "What time you think we'll make it back to New York?"

"It should take us about an hour. Two A.M."

"I hate it here."

"Me too . . . Okay?"

Miguel nodded. "Let's get it over with." Slipping the knife into his pocket, he reached under the seat, pulled up a gun, and pointed it at Susan. "We're going to take that walk."

Susan shook her head violently. Miguel gripped her by her shoulders, lifting her slightly. The driver pulled her out from the other end. Her eyes wide with fear, she still tried to struggle.

The men exchanged understanding glances. Then Miguel yanked her up. His elbow smashed into her neck and she staggered forward. Despite the gag, they heard her cry out. Miguel pressed the gun into her back.

The pointed to a clearing near some trees at the end of the road. "Now walk over there," he said.

Susan felt both men shove her forward. She tried to walk, but couldn't. The driver shifted her weight onto him. They were leading her toward a forested area. Lights from fireflies flickered in the night. She saw the forest more distinctly now, heard her heart pound as she moved closer to the crescent moon above the horizon.

The driver stopped and caught his breath. "How about here?"

Miguel nodded. "Kneel."

She swayed against them as if drunk. Grasping her by the shoulders, Miguel forced her down. Her knees made imprints on the sandy road. They each put a gun against her ears and fired. Her body crumpled to the ground.

"We've got to leave her here," Miguel said. "Suarez wants the body to be found." He bent down, flipped up Susan's eyepatch. "So the left eye's good. What a phony. Suarez can go fuck himself. I won't take a picture of this."

"Then can we go back now?" The man shuddered. "It's spooky out here. I wonder how the others are doing?"

"Killing the detective's a piece of cake. Now, after this, I've got to go back and listen to Suarez ball me out about some petty, bullshit matter."

"I feel sorry for you." He led the way back to the car. When he opened the door he looked displeased. "You didn't save me any of your sandwich."

Miguel smiled. "I will at the next one."

Yablonsky watched the car negotiate the rough side streets of Brooklyn. Rafi sat alongside him, both hands firmly gripping the gun. The car hit a bump.

He could feel the car's speed increasing. Beneath an overhead el he made out the blur of factories, and stockyards filled with trains and buses. When the car stopped for a light, he fell forward slightly. Rafi shifted the gun toward him and settled back in the seat. He ordered Yablonsky to move closer to the other window. Yablonsky obeyed.

Occasionally there would be the muted lights of an open gas station or a twenty-four-hour newsstand. Yablonsky

watched Rafi slide the car window open. His legs felt like
they were paralyzed. In ten years on the force he had never
been in physical danger. He had always seen the results of
murder, but never the actual deed itself. Until now. As a
homicide detective Yablonsky had often asked himself how
one person could kill another. Murder, not death, was the
ultimate human puzzle. After his death, he was sure that
Flood would try to arrest these men for murder and their
government would respond by making them come back
home. He had successfully solved the case, he told himself.
Everything would work out perfectly, except for the matter
of their killing him.

The car was cutting down Rockaway Parkway. Rafi and the
driver were calm. The light they had stopped for changed.
Yablonsky wondered how they would do it, if they were going
to give it to him in the car. If they had to stop and he had to
get out, there'd be pleading. Two quick shots to the head. If he
were able to kill someone, that's how he'd do it. He looked
down at his pale hands, felt the car lurch over the bumpy road.
Part of him longed for a bullet, just to get it over with. His mind
seemed to him to be traveling farther away from him and
reality, but it only went so far and then began to come back.
Something within him came alive, and he began to plan.

He knew where they were taking him. The East New York
auto scrapyard on Flatlands Avenue had been a favorite
Mafia execution spot, a real bone orchard. The area was
poorly lit and secluded. They would kill him there, then
dump his body either in Jamaica Bay or in the surrounding
marshlands of the Wildlife Preserve.

Vinnie Pagano's uncle owned the scrapyard. As kids
Vinnie and Yablonsky had often trekked up Pennsylvania
Avenue to play there. The car slowed, but he felt a twinge of
hope and the beginnings of an idea.

The driver braked. To the right was the rusted shell of Farrel's. Vinnie's uncle used to take them there for lunch. Across the road was a giant baseball field that was called the Five Diamonds, circled by a chain-link fence; opposite that was a now-abandoned bowling alley where Yablonsky's dates had thrown their gutter balls. Rafi nudged him with the .9 mm. "You able to walk?" Yablonsky quietly answered yes. Both men nodded as if in some strange way they were proud of him. He caught his breath as the torrent of fresh night air hit him from the open door, then forced himself to get out of the car. Flatlands Avenue was a mass of pitted tar and huge black ruts in which old rain sat. He slipped on the tar pebbles, got up. Rafi smiled at him. "Good boy," he said. "Let's go."

Yablonsky walked between the two men toward the yard. Usually there were guard dogs patrolling it. Not tonight. He hadn't realized that Suarez had connections to the Mafia, probably through his smuggling operations.

He forced himself to be calm when Rafi slipped the wooden door open. He knew the layout; it never changed. Rusted hulks of cars were to the left of the small oil-stained shack that served as an office. Engines, carburetors, and transmissions littered the area around the shack. Row after row of piled-up tires led to the vast graveyard of cars and trucks. There were no lights. It was dark, but he knew the terrain. That was his hope.

The driver pointed his flashlight at the rows of tires. He held a camera bag. The scrapyard was full of empty cans of oil and gasoline. "God, it stinks here."

Yablonsky knew they'd be suspicious if he didn't plead. "Can't we make a deal?"

"Sure," Rafi said, but he motioned to the driver, who moved to block off any attempt at escape. "Let me have what you've got on you."

Yablonsky promptly emptied his pockets. "I can get more."

"Forty-five dollars," Rafi said. "If it'd been fifty, I'd have let you live."

Yablonsky flinched, but remained where he was. Rafi turned slightly. "He'll be no problem," he said. "It's as good as finished." He eyes shifted to Yablonsky. "Be a good boy, detective, and lead the way. No struggling, and that way it'll be over for you sooner."

Rafi pointed with his gun to where they wanted him to go. The hand holding the flashlight wasn't steady. Behind him, Yablonsky heard the men's breathing. He walked between rows of tires sitting by the auto graveyard. He knew that to the right of them the ground abruptly descended, leading to groves of trees. He stepped to the right. Would they accept the movement? No answering protest. He took another step closer to the bluff's edge, continuing the diagonal pattern. They followed closely behind. Another step. Suddenly he hurtled his body straight down into the darkness. The men gasped. Shot and missed. With the suppressors, the gunshots sounded like thrown pebbles. Yablonsky felt his body crash into the ground, five feet beneath the men. The flashlight was bobbing in his direction.

He crawled through the underbrush, watching the beam of the flashlight follow. He crouched as the men fired at him. Now there were two flashlights. He'd never be able to climb the barbed wire fence. He saw one of the flashlights veer off and fade away in the direction of Flatlands Avenue. They'd expect him to try to reach the entrance. The men called to each other and cursed in Spanish. The other light focused on him momentarily. He worked his way around the grove of trees, then headed toward the rusted cars. He tried to control his gasping breath, but couldn't. He knew that whoever was following him could hear him as he sifted through the tall grass.

Cutting across another rise, he stopped running. The light was coming closer. He stood up, chancing it. More shots. They sounded harmless, like BBs. He forced himself to move forward, knowing where he wanted to go.

Silence. Suddenly Rafi spotted Yablonsky heading toward the rusted car hulks. He squeezed off a shot and missed. Two seconds later the detective was gone, vanishing inside the auto jungle.

Rafi cursed loudly. The driver, Martino, was by the entrance, gun ready, just in case the detective was foolish enough to try to escape through there. How the hell was he going to find him among all these wrecks? He had a light, the detective had none. He had a gun, the detective was unarmed. There was no choice. He'd work his way through the yard methodically, taking one area at a time. Eventually the detective would have to move, and he'd have him.

He reached the spot where the detective had been moments earlier. He moved to one side, shining the light. He was able to hear Yablonsky, perhaps yards away from him, in another row of cars. Breathing heavily, probably looking for a place to hide.

The light revealed scattered piles of rusted doors and cars with open trunks and hoods. He heard a noise and moved in closer, but all he saw were the steel corpses. More noise to the right, then nothing.

Flashlight in one hand, .9 mm in the other, he slowly moved up the rows. Yablonsky would never be able to make it to the barbed wire fence, and soon there'd be daylight. The detective had to know it was only a matter of time before he was found and killed.

Rafi knew the man was desperate. He also knew there was

a chance he might have picked up a tire iron or other weapon along the way. It wouldn't be easy, but in order for Yablonsky to strike at him, he'd have to place himself in Rafi's line of fire.

Suddenly there was movement. Rafi caught a glimpse of Yablonsky making his way through the rows of cars. Rafi cut to the left, then climbed onto a car roof. More noise to the right, then nothing.

He descended and moved in closer. He beamed his light on one car, flashed it over the chassis. He'd bet anything that the detective was in this row, hiding behind or inside one of the cars. Two cars ahead, a slightly opened hood. Rafi's mouth curved in a smile. He definitely heard breathing. The detective was inside the hollow area between the hood and the chassis. There was nowhere he'd be able to run to, and Rafi knew he'd be able to squeeze off at least two shots.

Rafi moved closer. His hands went to the underside of the hood. He opened it. Yablonsky tossed a car battery at his face. The battery was old but full of acid, and it splashed into Rafi's eyes. Dropping his gun, he screamed and fell to the ground.

Yablonsky easily hefted himself out of the car, straining to hear footsteps above Rafi's screams. He didn't hear any. The other man might also be a killer, but he wasn't crazy, Yablonsky thought. He looked at the writhing body and bent down, picking up the gun. Rafi was rubbing his eyes, screaming and crying. Yablonsky took a deep breath, thought about them trying to kill him, and brought his foot into Rafi's nose, face, and groin. The man doubled over, still covering his eyes with his hands.

The detective moved through the rows of autos until he reached the fringes of tall grass near the end of the scrapyard.

Rafi's screams became fainter. It was very dark and he had to move slowly. He could have taken Rafi's flashlight, but didn't want to chance giving the other guy something to shoot at.

He worked his way through the weeds to the rear of the scrapyard. To the left, as he knew there would be, were the rusted parts of the fence, resting loosely in the ground. Pressing his hands against the uneven metal, he pulled it down, then stepped over.

He found himself next to an empty car wash. Slipping the gun into his pocket, he walked out onto Pennsylvania Avenue. The street was empty; there weren't even any gypsy cabs. He walked six blocks, reaching the IRT at the intersection of Livonia.

Yablonsky pushed open the station door, white, disheveled, and still gasping for breath.

"Man, you had a bad day," the token clerk said.

"I did," Yablonsky said. Showing his detective's badge, he walked through the gate alongside the turnstiles. He was alone on the platform. Above him were the skeletons of burned-out buildings. He had gone to high school two blocks away from here.

There was a fifteen-minute wait. A train was coming, but on the other side of the tracks, away from Atlantic Avenue where he had to go to catch the D. He decided to take it anyway. Running downstairs, he forced himself to race through the station and then up the other stairs.

New Lots Avenue, the end of the IRT line. He knew there would be public phones on the platform. He needed to hear Susan's voice. He thanked God he hadn't given Rafi his change. The phone rang. He pictured Susan sleeping, small breasts and tiny, erect nipples visible beneath a scanty nightgown.

On the fifth ring, someone picked up. "Who's there?" Karen asked.

He felt a thrill of relief, then excitement. "It's me, Yablonsky. Sorry I'm calling late."

"Oh, hi. That's okay."

"Can I speak to Susan?"

"Sorry Alvin, but she's out. She missed rehearsals, so she must be partying at some East Village bar. She'll be back late."

$\triangledown$

Twenty-One

YABLONSKY'S WAY TO THE precinct was blocked by hordes of marchers with their fists raised in the air. They wore running shorts, were colorfully dressed, and seemed to be mostly homosexuals.

A cop, his hands braced against one of the wooden barriers, recognized Yablonsky. "Al, you'll never make it through. Over here."

His eyes glided over Yablonsky and showed concern. "The morning after. Rumor had it that you never drank."

"I don't drink, I was beaten up," Yablonsky said matter of factly. "I didn't know a parade was scheduled for today."

"It's Gay Pride Week. They're marching to put an end to all the discrimination. I don't blame them," the cop said.

The marchers chanted, "On, two, three, four. Civil rights or civil war." A contingent of lesbians walked among the men. Groups from gay churches and synagogues held signs. Parents and friends of gays unfurled banners. Food vendors lined both sides of Second Avenue. They were cleaning up.

Twenty minutes went by. The stream of protestors seemed endless. "How much longer?" Yablonsky asked the cop.

"There are thousands of them. They plan on walking until they reach Christopher Street in the Village. Go over to a designated crossing spot if you want to get through."

"That'll take too long. Flood expected me twenty minutes ago."

"A meeting with Noah himself," the cop said, and looked impressed. "Next time they give the exam, I plan on trying to make detective."

Yablonsky knew the patrolman slightly. They ate at the same restaurants. "I thought you liked being a cop."

"No way. There's too much potential for violence." Again he stared at Yablonsky's bruises. "Sorry, detective."

"That's okay. You think you can signal some of them to stop or slow down for a moment so I can get through?"

The cop shook his head. "We can't do it. They'll think we're interfering, and it'll just incite them. Wait."

Yablonsky took a step forward. "I'm going to chance it."

"Good luck, Moses."

It was easier to raise his fist and pretend to be one of the marchers than to fight the tidal wave of traffic. Fist clenched, he made his way through the crowd with surprising ease, but as soon as he stepped onto the sidewalk one of the cheering onlookers approached him, scolding. "Don't quit now, brother."

"I'm too discouraged," Yablonsky said, trying to move away from him.

The man noticed Yablonsky's bruises and smiled. "You must be into some pretty rough stuff."

"The roughest." He avoided the man and followed the parade for two blocks. A photographer snapped a picture of him.

"I'm not gay," Yablonsky said, showing his detective's badge.

"So say they all," the photographer said, and took two more photos of him.

Half a block away from the precinct house, on 46th, Yablonsky made a left and dialed Susan's number from a public phone. "Alvin, she's still out," Karen said.

"Did she at least call?"

"Don't be so worried. She never calls." There was a pause. "She might be with another man." Then Karen hung up.

For once no reporters were waiting on the precinct steps for him. They were all out covering the protest.

Flood was not at his desk, his secretary told him.

"Where is he?"

"He's at *your* desk, waiting for you."

"My God," Flood said as he approached. "You look terrible."

"Thanks." Flood sat with his feet raised on top of Yablonsky's desk. He invited Yablonsky to pull up a chair. Flood was pale but his eyes glittered angrily. "How come you're thirty-five minutes late?"

"I was held up by the gay protest."

"It takes courage to come out of the closet, Yablonsky. Congratulations." Flood paused. "Now tell me about last night."

"Suarez's men took me for a one-way ride. They were unsuccessful."

He inspected Yablonsky critically. "Not entirely." He hesitated. "Any casualties?"

"I might've killed one of them."

"Good," Flood said. "If the FBI steps in, I can justify that. I want you to fill out an arrest form. The usual procedure is that we take it to our embassy. They inform Ramirez, apply pressure, and he sends them back home."

"No newspapers?"

"Only as a last resort, if they fight it."

"I'll sign all the papers in a couple of days," he said. "Right now I'm tired."

Flood looked at him uncomfortably. "Yablonsky, I was wrong to tell you to go after him. His pockets are too deep. All the other cases that you had to put on hold await you. The Feds will take it from here. They'll definitely be able to get him sent back."

"Good," Yablonsky said. "He hates it there."

The phone rang. Even though it was Yablonsky's line, Flood picked up. Yablonsky saw Flood shift his eyes to him. He was listening intently. The nagging fear Yablonsky had had since he'd first tried to call grew.

Flood put down the phone. "Alvin?"

"You don't have to tell me. Susan's dead."

Flood waited for Yablonsky's reaction, but there seemed to be none. He looked pale, but remained silent, waiting. "Her body was discovered near a Staten Island swamp an hour ago."

"Go on," Yablonsky said. "How was she killed?"

"Two shots to the head."

"You don't have to tell me the rest. Information from an anonymous source was given to the newspapers that Paul Matson and Sean Maysfield had been blackmailing her. So she had reason to kill them. Now that she's dead, it's easy for suspicion to once again fall on her, and you'll receive orders to end my investigation. Since she was, after all, a new-wave rock star, she hung out with a rough crowd, and drugs are thought to have played a part in her death. Don't say another word about it, Larry, please . . . Do we still have Denise Levine and is she still interested in talking?"

"We can't find her," Flood said. "At least we can get Suarez for ordering an assault on you. If his man's wounded and still in this country they'll have to accept your word.

What can I say? Our own diplomats in their country would
be vulnerable."

"I understand," Yablonsky said.

"Can I do anything to help, Alvin?"

"No, you can't. Let me get back to work."

"You can take the day off. Tomorrow too, if you need it."

"I prefer to work," Yablonsky said. "I may take tomorrow
off. How many times did they shoot her, captain?"

"Twice."

"The second one to make sure." He moved in behind his
desk. Flood left. He unlocked the bottom file and sighed as
he looked at all the other murders that awaited him.

The phone rang. "Hi, Yablonsky. Bob Anders from the
Post. You were the investigating detective on the case in
which Suzy Creamcheese was a murder suspect. Do you
have anything to say about her own murder? Is it true that
drugs are suspected to have played a part?"

"I don't know," Yablonsky said and hung up.

Another call. "You know who this is don't you?"

"Bill Goldman of the *News*?" Yablonsky asked.

"Your recall is as good as ever. Can you give me a
statement about you know what?"

"Not at this time," Yablonsky said. He began to organize
the information that he had available for each pending case.
Again the phone rang. "Is this detective Yablonsky?" Emile
Suarez asked.

"It's me," Yablonsky said.

"I've just heard the news about Susan. Do I have to tell you
how shocked I am, detective? I know how this must be affecting
you, and I called because I wanted to offer my sympathies."

"Thanks," Yablonsky said. He spoke again only when he
was sure he was in control. "Did you enjoy murdering
Susan? Did you ejaculate?"

"You are a very sick man, lieutenant. I feel sorry for you."

"I remember you're a camera buff," Yablonsky said. "This time, did you use your little polaroid?"

"I think you actually enjoy this line of questioning, lieutenant, so you must be sick." He paused. "If it'll be helpful to you, according to the news reports I've heard she might've been killed for any number of reasons. But it was probably drugs." There was a silence. Yablonsky knew why Suarez had called. Killing wasn't enough, not where power was concerned. What Suarez wanted was the pleasure of having it known he had gotten away with the murder. Suarez spoke again. "Regardless of who murdered Susan, is there anything you can do about it?"

"Probably not, my investigation's over." He paused. "How's Rafi?"

"It's funny you should ask about him, detective. Rafi unfortunately had an accident. He's blind. I'm sorry to hear that about your investigation. Actually, you're a very good detective. Anytime you want to transfer back to your old UN post, let me know. I'll write you a recommendation."

"If I decide to take you up on it, can I call you?" Yablonsky asked.

"Call anytime," Suarez said, and hung up the phone.

Yablonsky went back to his files. Dorrie Stevens, seven years old, found inside one of the subway tunnels near 42nd Street. The usual suspects in the area would have to be rounded up. Mental-clinic patients would have to be checked. So would the Sex Crimes files. Possibly, a plainclothesman could be stationed at Grand Central to try to find out things.

He turned pages. Billie and Mavis Green's bodies, discovered in a Toyota on the FDR Drive. Once again, his modus operandi would be easy. Scour the area for derelicts. Speak to the inhabitants of apartment buildings whose windows overlooked the scene of the crime. Often in these cases people did witness something but were afraid to come forward.

He looked through the rest of his files. Not one of these murders showed carefully planning and skillful execution. He wondered which was worse. Getting caught and then serving practically no time at all, or being allowed to commit murder because of diplomatic immunity. Even in an imperfect world, there was no contest . . . A body had been discovered in a pothole on East 63rd. Question the people who lived on the block. Interrogate the shopping-bag people who slept on that particular street.

The procession of funeral cars rode out to the sprawling cemetery in Greenpoint, Queens. Though Suzy Creamcheese's family lived in San Francisco, she had not wanted to be buried there. She had confided to Yablonsky that a week after her producer informed her that her second record had sold over three hundred thousand, she had made the arrangements. He had thought of Joplin, Allman, Sid Vicious, and all the other self-destructive rock stars. Was she planning to die young? he had asked. Of course not. It was only that she did not want Karen to be burdened by any of it whenever it should occur.

Yablonsky moved behind the crowd of mourners to the spot where she would be interred.

"She has a fine view of the East Village from here. It would have pleased her," Bob Anders of the *Post* said to him with a wink.

"I know you work for the *Post*, but show some tact for once, Bob." Yablonsky walked away. He watched as the casket was lowered by ropes into the round. A priest said that life was a strange and awesome melody. Until now, Yablonsky hadn't known she was Irish Catholic. He looked past the cemetery towards Manhattan. There was the real bone orchard.

He tried to move closer to Karen, but she was surrounded by reporters, photographers, and Susan's friends from the lower East Side.

After the funeral he was able to approach her. She stood away from the crowed, shielded by Rob and Joanie.

"Karen, I'm sorry," he started to say.

"Don't be," Karen said. "She wasn't much of a sister, and she deserved what she got." She turned to Rob and Joanie, who had their arms around her. The dress she wore touched the ground, and her arms glittered with bracelets. She spoke to Yablonsky. "An agent's already talking to me, trying to convince me to cut a video."

"I hope it's not Marshall Hunter," Yablonsky said.

She did not react the way he had expected. There was a shrug, then she allowed Rob and Joanie to lead her back to the waiting cameras and newspeople. Yablonsky got in his car with Bob Anders and drove back with him to the city.

Twenty-Two

BOBBI THREW HIS BASEBALL glove underneath the bench and cursed. "You swore I'd seen the last of you, detective."

"I lied," Yablonsky said.

They were standing behind a screened fence on a baseball field in Central Park. Across from them, people waiting in line to get into the Delacorte Theatre had spread out blankets and picnic baskets. Vendors were moving from group to group, selling Sangria, chilled bottles of champagne, and six-packs of beer.

"They're performing *Twelfth Night* this season," Yablonsky said. "I didn't read too many good reviews about the production."

"Goddammit lieutenant, you promised you wouldn't see me."

"I had to see you, Bobbi," Yablonsky said. "You're the final weapon in my case."

"The newspapers said the investigation's over."

"Yellow journalism," Yablonsky said. "You can help me get the guy who murdered your friends."

"I wasn't that close to them," Bobbi said. Yablonsky watched as the batter took the third strike. Bobbi started to move toward the bench, where his glove was. The name

O'Farrel's had been stenciled on the back of his T-shirt. The team they were playing against was from another club, a woman's joint over on Lexington Avenue.

Yablonsky placed a hand on Bobbi's shoulder to restrain him. One of Bobbi's mates approached. Yablonsky knew him. Maurice. He did an act with birds and a magician's costume at the club. "Can we have him back, lieutenant? He's our center fielder."

"He's caught his last fly ball today. Find someone else."

Yablonsky pointed to a shade tree that was near the first-base line. Bobbi followed. The lead-off hitter for the women's team swung at the ball, hitting a grass cutter through the infield for a single. She rounded first, thought better of it, and returned to the base.

"Christ," Bobbi said. "They'll score another five runs this inning. Do you know how humiliating it is for us to lose to a women's team?" He paused. "If I refuse, I suppose you'll pin a plainclothesman to the back of my ass each night, or a decoy who'll bust me for soliciting."

"The decoy hadn't occurred to me," Yablonsky said. "But it's a good idea."

"No, it isn't. Get on with it, lieutenant."

"When was the last time you saw Suarez?"

"A month ago. I usually see him twice a month. You want me to sleep with him, don't you?" He hesitated. "I'm afraid of him now."

"You said you were his favorite."

The next woman up sent a line drive screaming over the third baseman's head. The teammate scored from first. The left fielder, a man with bulging muscles and a V-shaped frame, bobbled the ball. The woman pulled into second with a double.

"Ten to two," Bobbi groaned. "They must've practiced

overtime for this. Why is it important to you that I sleep with Suarez?" Bobbi's hand groomed his long lashes. "Not that he's a bad fuck."

"You don't have to sleep with him," Yablonsky said. "I want you to give him a call and set up a date for Thursday night. He'll be giving a speech at a UNICEF Fund Raiser. Make the date for ten o'clock, but show up half an hour early."

"Suppose he says no."

"Use your masculine charm."

Bobbi nodded understandingly. "You want to take pictures of us in bed together and then blackmail him. His bodyguards are all over the building. You'll never be able to get in to do it."

They watched as the next woman up swung and missed. She took another pitch, then popped up. "One down, two to go," Yablonsky said. "No, Bobbi. Every time you or some other young man sees him, he takes pictures. I want you to get inside his bedroom before his arrives and find those pictures you, Paul and Sean posed for. Then I'll blackmail him."

"Suarez'll want them back badly," Bobbi said. "Suppose I keep them for myself?"

"He's not the kind of man who'll let you blackmail him," Yablonsky reminded him.

"Maybe not," Bobbi said. He paused. "Then why would he let you?"

"I'm a detective."

At nine-twenty on Thursday night Bobbi strolled through the lobby of Suarez's building. He was wearing a dark, conservative business suit, his hair slicked back. The concierge put down the phone and looked at him knowingly.

"Mr. Suarez isn't in now, but you can go up. You're expected."

The elevator ride took a full minute; Suarez lived in an apartment with a good view. Bobbi glanced nervously up at the mirror in the corner. It distorted his face. He was tempted to get off at another floor and leave the building. He peered into the mirror and slicked down a few strands of hair.

Miguel and a man he didn't know were waiting for him outside Suarez's apartment, in the hall.

"Where's Rafi?" Bobbi asked, his voice friendly.

"Resting his eyes," Miguel said. "You're early."

Bobbi said in an easy, relaxed way, "He likes me to be here early so I can freshen up. You know that."

Miguel looked at him with contempt. "We know a lot of things." He pointed to the briefcase that was tucked under Bobbi's arm. "You'll have to show us what's inside."

Bobbi smiled. "My best photos, full spread." He began slipping back the clasps. "Suarez loves to see them. I'm proud to show them to you."

"Never mind." He gave Bobbi a disgusted look.

Bobbi strode past him, into the reception area. "*Maricone*," Miguel said.

Bobbi went into the living room and sat on one of the Chinese chairs. He turned the chair so that two men would not be able to see him. His face was white. He stared at his watch. Twenty to ten.

"I thought you needed to freshen up," Miguel said.

"I walked partway up the stairs for the exercise," Bobbi said. "I have to catch my breath."

"I hope you catch AIDS," the other man said. "Both of you."

Bobbi was silent. He watched the seconds on his watch tick by helplessly. He wanted no part of this.

"Get the fuck out of this room," Miguel said. "You stink it up just be being here. If you're not out in three seconds I swear I'll put that little prick of yours through a wringer."

Bobbi stood, headed for Suarez's bedroom. "Make sure the door's closed," he heard Miguel say.

He opened the door. His suit was drenched. He fell into Suarez's large club chair and sat. Suarez's bedroom faced southeast. There was a view of Roosevelt Island and beyond that the grimy factories of Queens. Yet because the apartment was high up, the polluted East River looked clean and placid; the buildings, just another set of soon-to-be-gentrified homes.

He sat for another five minutes, then at last forced himself to stand. The room was furnished with faded Oriental rugs, oversized upholstered chairs, antique lamps, and a lacquered Art Deco dresser with an oval mirror on top. The first time Bobbi had been here he'd fallen in love with the place. Suarez slept on a king-sized bed, with silk sheets and an almost transparent silver-flecked cover.

Five to ten. He pulled open the bottom dresser drawer. The photos were under Suarez's underwear and socks. Silently opening the door, Bobbi moved through the hall, away from the men. The elevator that was reserved for Suarez's private use was next to the library, near the second bathroom. He pressed the button. The door opened and he got in.

Outside, he leaned against the guard rail. He looked up at the building, pinpointing Suarez's terrace, and then at Roosevelt Island, not believing he had gotten away with it.

He crossed the street. Posters said there was a sale on at Bloomingdale's. He'd have to go there before he left New York.

East 64th. He enjoyed looking at Manhattan women in the summer. They looked like perspiring packages waiting to be unwrapped. Of course he also loved looking at men. It was too bad so few of them wore dresses.

East 61st Street. He was grabbed from behind. A hand grasped his neck and snapped his head back. "We want the case, motherfucker," one of the members of a wolf pack yelled.

They threw him to the ground, taking off with the briefcase. Bobbi got up, trying to keep sight of them as they expertly weaved through the York Avenue traffic.

He'd never catch them. He patted the envelope of photos that were in his inside pocket with relief and continued walking.

The bedroom door was slightly ajar. Suarez entered, loosening his bowtie and top shirt button. Things had not gone well at the fundraiser. They were two hundred thousand short of their goal. He had a headache.

Where was Bobbi? "It's me," Suarez said. "Come out. I won't hurt you. I'm a friend, remember?"

He opened the bathroom door, but there was no sign of the little hustler. Christ, his head hurt. "Why is everyone breaking my balls today?" he said aloud.

It was puzzling. Miguel and Hector had assured him when he came in that Bobbi was inside here waiting for him, but obviously he wasn't here. A sudden thought occurred to him. He went to the closet and opened it, slipped out a manila envelope. No, the money was still there.

"Bobbi, are you hiding under the bed? You're supposed to be on top of it. Let's go!"

His eyes went to his Nikon resting and ready on the night table.

Another idea came to him. He threw open the bottom drawer of the dresser. "Oh, shit, Bobbi," he said, sinking down on the bed. "Not you too."

He remained on the bed, trying to collect his thoughts. The pictures were gone. He had to be calm now, and patient. Panicking would be the most destructive thing he could do now. He'd had no idea that the little hustler was tied in to Yablonsky. He was surprised; the detective had outsmarted him. Bobbi had ripped him off, stolen not only the photos of Paul and Sean but all the others as well.

Perhaps Bobbi was working for himself and was not tied in to Yablonsky. Paul and Sean had obviously had ideas, too. He'd brought them up to the apartment together one day and dropped his attaché case on the bed before going to the bathroom to freshen up. Even though he had finished his shower, he had stepped out, keeping the water running. The water temperature he had caught was perfect, and he wanted to maintain it for when they were finished.

When he came into the room, there were Paul and Sean, with the attaché case open, leafing through his papers.

They looked up at him, embarrassed. "It was open," Sean said. "We were just curious."

"I understand," Suarez smiled. "Of course." He paused. Then calmly. "Look through the rest of them. Satisfy your curiosity."

The attaché case was promptly closed. Paul handed it to him. "What's in here must be very private and valuable to you. We're sorry."

Suarez casually dropped the attaché case on the bed by Sean's crossed legs. "Nothing important. You're welcome to look again."

They vehemently shook their heads. After a moment Paul said, "There were lots of interesting-looking figures. You must be involved in something very big."

"Affairs of state," Suarez said. "Now both of you lie down."

He had had them killed as soon as the best opportunities had presented themselves. He could not be sure of what they had actually seen, but he couldn't risk letting them live. They had made no attempt to extort money from him, but if word got out that the government was laundering money, people would know how precarious the situation was: that even Ramirez was preparing for the worst.

His suntanned face stared back at him from the oval mirror. Somehow Yablonsky had threatened or convinced Bobbi to steal those photos for him. Diplomatic immunity counted for nothing when you were dealing with the dishonesty of the police force.

He went into the living room. Miguel and Hector, Rafi's replacement, were lounging on sofas, drinking and smoking. Miguel's feet were sprawled over the cocktail table, his shoes still on.

"I've told you a million times not to sit that way," Suarez said. His employees exchanged glances. Miguel's socks were a brightly colored tropical green. They reminded Suarez of iguanas.

Miguel took off his shoes, pulling at his socks until they were up around his knees, the way soccer players wore them. He offered Suarez a cigarette. "You've finished early."

"I thought I'd surprise you," Suarez said. "Tell me, Miguel. Were you a good host to my guest?"

Miguel smiled. "I was a perfect gentleman."

"Didn't say anything to make him nervous and leave?"

"You know me," said Miguel.

"I know you," Suarez said. "Bobbi's left, but not before stealing all the pictures, Miguel. That means trouble for me."

"I'm sorry," Miguel said. "But you were the one who insisted on snapping them. I always wondered why you had to take them."

"Just for the record, Miguel, how do you think he was able sneak by you so easily?"

"He might've tried the elevator down the hall while we were in the living room. We heard the shower going and thought he was getting ready for you." He paused. "If I meet up with that kid you'll have another photo opportunity. Will that satisfy you?"

Suarez sat down. "I'm afraid it won't. That won't solve our problem."

"The one *you* created. Mr. fucking Scavullo."

"You don't seem capable of focusing on particulars," Suarez said. "Forget Bobbi. He's gone. The detective has the photos now."

"Jesus Christ," Miguel said. "Denise Levine . . . all your Latin American subjects. The complete album."

"I brought you with me to this country to help me, Miguel. I'm your boss, remember? One more insult and you'll be back in the Third World. Understand?"

There was silence. "You're the boss, boss. So tell me what to do."

"I want to work with Hector on this. You've already let me down once. You're lucky I know you're my man, not Ramirez's.

Yablonsky was working on the Dorrie Stevens murder on Friday morning, when again the phone rang. He had just requested two decoys from the Plainclothes Division. With a lot of time and a little luck, the case was solvable.

He had decided to let all his incoming calls ring at least eight times before picking up.

"So you're there after all," Suarez said. "This is the third time I've tried to reach you, detective."

"Sorry, but I've been busy," Yablonsky said. "What can you possibly want?"

"My photos. The ones you ordered Bobbi to steal."

"If you feel you've got probable cause then arrest me."
Yablonsky said. "Being a detective gives me a certain kind
of immunity, too. As I told you earlier. The investigation's
over. So why this call?"

"You know damn well why, detective."

"Not as friendly as you were before, are you?" said
Yablonsky.

"Or as diplomatic."

"Never mind. Just tell me when we can talk."

Yablonsky opened his desk, took out the manila envelope
and spread the pictures out before him. "This is not like
most family albums I've seen, but there are a lot of good
shots." He took out a picture of a frightened young woman.
His voice lowered. "Denise Levine." He looked at a few of
the others. "Your scorecard from Latin America. Where's
Susan? She in a special place?"

"Miguel told me she wasn't a very interesting-looking
corpse," Suarez said. There was a pause. "He was referring
to the newspaper photos of her of course. Now come on. Tell
me what you want."

Yablonsky flipped through the photos as if they were a
deck of cards. "Paul. Sean. Bobbi and others. You're in some
of them. Did anyone ever tell you you look like Fernando
Lamas? We can link you to the murdered boys directly now."

"Promiscuous sex. Drugs. Prostitution. Those boys were
asking to be killed by someone," Suarez said. "Forget about
them."

"You're innocent of that too?"

"As the day I was born. Stop playing games, lieutenant. I
know you want to meet with me."

Yablonsky hesitated, but it came out as calmly as he
wanted it to. "I'd like to do other things to you besides meet

with you. There's a Kodak place right on this block. They'll make up any amount of copies I want in less than twenty-four hours."

"We'll discuss that at our meeting," Suarez said.

"Your place. Tomorrow. At two in the afternoon," Yablonsky said. "Formal wear isn't necessary. You'll have to promise to keep the security council out of it. I'm talking about Miguel."

"He'll behave."

"Maybe later I can make a deal with your friend Martha Bryant for a photo spread, but I don't want her there tomorrow. By the way, I won't have the pictures with me. Got that?"

"I've got that," Suarez said.

Twenty-Three

As SUAREZ SHOWERED, HE rotated the portable nozzle over his buttocks. His lower back ached today. He decided to call his chiropractor for an appointment. Since he felt optimistic, he'd make it for next week, sure he would still be in the country. He adjusted the shower head. Suarez liked the spray to be strong. It reminded him of the days he'd spent in his country at the beach.

Dripping wet, he stepped out of the tub. He dried off, then covered his body with talcum powder, patted it down, and gave a final buff with the towel. He wore casual clothes: flared pants and an open-necked white shirt. The clock said it was one-thirty. He had slept through the night and past noon, while no doubt the lieutenant had been up since early morning, immersed in exhaustive detective work. That meant the advantage was his.

In the office he reviewed the notes his secretary had recorded at the last meeting of the General Assembly. Then the other things. There was a meeting next Tuesday with a record producer who wanted to unload twenty thousand bootleg cassette tapes. He wondered whether they would have time to distribute them. That would have to be canceled. Attaché case in hand, he examined a communication that had come to him in secret code. His eyes widened slightly. Ramirez had been pressured by the United States to raid cocaine manufacturing plants in the countryside. While doing so, the troops had been ambushed by insurgents. Eight killed, three wounded. Disheartening news.

He had a quick lunch, washed it down with iced coffee, then hurried back to his office for a meeting with Miguel and Hector.

"What time did he say he'd be here?" Hector asked.

"Two," Suarez said. "Want to bet he'll be on time?"

"Something's up," Miguel said. "He's been beaten up and almost killed. Why'd he want to meet with you here?"

"Because he has the upper hand now," Suarez said. "He feels he has every advantage and wants to meet with me in my home. It's a power move."

"Suppose he won't give them up?" Miguel asked.

Suarez shrugged. "I can't predict the future. But I know you like the Yankees, Miguel. They'll be in town next week. Let's go to the Tuesday-night game. Box seats."

Miguel smiled. "I'll call in the order."

"Good," Suarez said. He rose, and the men followed. Stepping into the living room, he watched as Miguel and Hector arranged chairs by the window. He opened his attaché case, placed his gun alongside him on the chair, and sat down.

Yablonsky walked up the block past all the embassies. He did not look foreign, so the doormen did not nod to him.

Diplomats' cars were all over the place: beside fire hydrants, double-parked on both sides of the street. He watched as a driver turned into the block. Seeing she couldn't squeeze between the cars, the woman tried to back out, but another car was now behind her, and the driver in this one wouldn't reverse. Moving forward, the woman scraped a car with diplomatic license plates.

Out of the car came the diplomat, furious. "Where did you learn how to drive?"

Yablonsky moved across the street and showed his badge. "I witnessed the whole thing. She was trying to park and your car collided with hers. Take down my badge number, miss. Tell the patrolman who answers to contact me when he makes out his report. I'll back you up."

The woman looked up at him. "That's how it happened. Thank you, detective."

"Fuck you very much, detective," the diplomat said.

Yablonsky crossed back. The inhabitants of the block were out: carrying packages, walking poodles and chows. A delivery boy pedaled by on his bike, balancing a Sicilian pizza on the basket. A view of the East River showed tugboats and scows circling the island. He entered the apartment building.

"Good afternoon, detective," Suarez said, and he motioned with his hand. "Please sit here." He inspected Yablonsky's face closely. "You must be working hard. You're a diligent man."

They faced each other on the terrace, a table between them. Miguel and Hector had met him outside the apartment, but they were not here now.

Suarez said, "I was really very sorry when I heard about Susan. Rock stars can get involved with some pretty destructive types, lieutenant."

"So it seems."

Suarez reached for a jar of honey and spread some of it on slices of apples. "A delicacy in my country. Tell me, detective. Have you decided to bring my pictures back to me after all? It's outrageous, making me pay for my own photographs."

Yablonsky shook his head. "I didn't mention money."

"I thought that's why you wanted to meet. To discuss the amount of money I'm to pay you to get my photos back."

"I'll give you the photos for free. Even the extra copies I made up last night. Right now everything is in a safe place with reliable people."

"You're a generous man, Detective Yablonsky." He paused. "When will you give them to me?"

"You've got to agree to let this country prosecute you for murder," Yablonsky said. "Then you get them."

Suarez spread more honey onto the apples. "You keep on insisting that I killed some people, but you can't prove it."

"I can prove that Rafi tried to kill me," said Yablonsky.

"He's no longer in the country. Rafi was always a little crazy, though. Any action he might've taken against you was without my orders. I'm not responsible for him."

"You're responsible for killing Paul and Sean."

"You have the pictures showing I made love to them. What would I want to kill them for? The political dissidents from my own country that you saw in the other photos won't be much trouble for me either, detective. It's difficult for Ramirez to prosecute me when he was the one who gave the orders."

"I can see you believe in planning out your alibis before you commit your murders. What about Susan? I just want to know if you personally witnessed your men kill her."

"I knew you would blame me for the death of that woman. I don't believe it was drugs, lieutenant. Terrorists did this. They have their own sources of information here, as do we. They might have learned things about your case. They're perfectly capable of murdering all those people to make you suspect that our government did it."

"By the number of buildings your friends are buying for

you over here, I figure the terrorists know they'll be in power soon anyway. Why would they do this?"

"To further discredit us. To make us look like a pack of animals. Why'd you agree to this meeting, detective? I'll tell you why we agreed to it. We want to do business with you. If by threatening to publish the pictures if I don't waive immunity you think you'll increase our offer, then you've succeeded. I'll raise the price."

"How much will you pay me?"

"Anything up to a quarter of a million." Suarez smiled. "You can retire early now. You don't have to oversee the disposal of dead bodies anymore. You've won the lottery."

"If those photos are made public, they'll put Ramirez in an embarrassing situation," Yablonsky said. "You'll be sent back to your country. Your operations here will have to end. Ramirez will welcome you with open arms . . . around your neck."

"I know what kind of man he is, lieutenant. What do you think I should do?"

"Waive your immunity. Let us prosecute you for murder."

Suarez gave him a tight smile. "Quite a choice. The baby killer or an American prison."

"At least you'll be safe from Ramirez. Give up your immunity, Suarez."

"I won't let myself be prosecuted for murder," Suarez said.

"Then we'll give those photos to the *New York Post* and let them run them on page six for a month. I'll mail copies to Ramirez myself."

Suarez moved from behind the table. "Sorry, detective. Your deal offers me little advantage."

"You mean you won't waive immunity?" Yablonsky added hurriedly, "You won't be able to run from Ramirez. As long as he retains control of his government, his intelligence services will get you. Or he might kill your family in retaliation."

"You've deduced that I'm gay, lieutenant. Ramirez forced me to marry because of my political position. I never wanted to. I can think of worse things than being a bachelor again. Spending time in an American prison, for instance. Go after me, lieutenant. Homosexuality and nude photos aren't that much of a scandal these days. As for Ramirez, I'll take my chances with him. I have some photos of him that you weren't able to steal. We go back a long way. I think he'll let me live."

"You're about to become the first UN casualty."

Suarez shrugged. "There're a lot worse things in life than being infamous for a while. Compared to some of these delegates I've been an angel." He extended a hand to Yablonsky, who refused to take it, glimpsing a gun resting on the chair. "Goodbye, detective," Suarez said.

"See you in the newspapers."

$\bigtriangledown$

Twenty-Four

AT 2:05 IN THE morning Suarez awakened. Under the covers he was wearing jeans and a pullover sweater. He quickly turned off the alarm clock. He went into the bathroom to splash water on his face. There was a small refrigerator in his bedroom. He ate and drank quickly, then walked into the hall, taking the rear elevator down to the basement. He passed the laundry room, climbed a flight of stairs, opened the door, and stepped out on to the street.

The embassy was four blocks away. He entered from behind the building, using the delivery entrance. He had the key. He climbed the two flights of stairs to his office. Again he went into the bathroom to splash water on his face. The attaché case he took from his floor safe contained the rest of the papers for the real estate transactions and two hundred thousand dollars that he was supposed to have had laundered. The photos he had of Ramirez were back home.

Outside he reached into his pocket and pulled out a cap. Though it was summer, it was cold. Except for the bag people the streets were deserted. On Third Avenue a Child's Restaurant was open. Across from that, a twenty-four-hour Korean fruit-and-vegetable stand.

He walked across to the stand so he would be in the light.

He stood for five minutes. Then his hand shot up. "Taxi."

Getting in, he spoke to the driver behind the plate glass. "Take me to Kennedy Airport."

$\triangledown$

Twenty-Five

ONE-THIRTY A.M.

Miguel walked out the embassy door and onto the street.

He refused to use the pay phones at either end of the corner. The phone two blocks away was probably safe. He let the phone ring. At last Montoya picked up. He was a minor member of the delegation. Like many of their people, he lived in the same apartment building as Suarez.

"You know who this is?"

Miguel could sense the man shake off his sleep and become alert.

"Meet me in front of your building. You've got fifteen minutes."

Earlier, Miguel had managed to find parking alongside the Mission to Chile. He got in the limousine. The drive to Suarez's apartment building would take ten minutes.

He pressed down on the gas, made a left at the corner onto First Avenue. Two hours ago Ramirez had called with his instructions. Miguel imagined the look on Suarez's face when he and Montoya came for him. Both men would be grim. "You're to be killed," Miguel would say. Then he'd lift up the camera Ramirez had jokingly suggested he bring for the occasion. "Get the picture?" He had been feeding information to Ramirez about Suarez for months now. At ten o'clock this evening Miguel had given Ramirez a recitation of everything that had happened. Ramirez had said, "Too bad. I liked Emiliano. Quick and painless. Lose the body."

He drove through East 49th, made a left onto Third Avenue, and another left onto East 47th. Montoya was in front of the building. In the darkness, and with his build and clothing, he looked just like Suarez.

Miguel pulled alongside the curb, keeping the motor running. The man came over, motioned for Miguel to roll down the window.

"What's up?"

"The situation's become too serious," Miguel said. "I'm acting under Ramirez's orders."

The man nodded, walked to the other side of the car, and got in. "Why not go in and take him now?"

"We're bringing him to the house in Washington Heights. We've got to prepare a few things first." He swung out, away from the curb. "We'll be back for him by three."

"I never liked him. Too handsome and sure of himself."

"Congratulations, you're being promoted. Ramirez wants you to head the delegation."

The man nodded. "He'll call?"

"Nothing will be announced until the shit hits the fan. That way we'll know exactly what it is we have to refute."

"Things sure went wrong, didn't they?"

Miguel grunted. "Blame it on Alan Funt and his goddamned camera."

Miguel slowed down for the red light but did not stop. He was already halfway into the intersection when a small remote-controlled bomb under the car's chassis exploded.

Twenty-Six

THE LUNCH CROWD WAITING for a table at Ratner's spilled out the door and into the street.

Inside, Yablonsky studied his menu. "They have the best vegetable soup in town," he said. "Guaranteed to improve your golf game."

"I shot a nine on a sixty-yard hole the other day," Flood said. "I'm thinking of giving up."

"Maybe Internal Affairs should launch an investigation into the golf course," Yablonsky said. But Flood was preoccupied, staring out the window, trying to guard his car from the overzealous meter maids on Delancey Street.

He turned back to Yablonsky. "It doesn't matter anymore if you're a police captain. They'll tow your car to the 55th Street Station. One hundred twenty-five dollars or they keep it forever. The ironic thing of course is that with my wife's connections I could have been the Deputy Commissioner of Traffic." He paused. "I've been conferring with the Feds. They'd like to hear you recite your story again. You were at your home with Dwyer the night those two men were blown up."

"The entire night. Dwyer will swear to it."

"He's already sworn to it. I remember that Dwyer was in

273

demolition in Korea. He knows how to make a bomb."

"He was with me that night," Yablonsky said. "We had nothing to do with it."

"You've both got ironclad alibis, haven't you?"

"I guess we have." Yablonsky paused. "Two vegetable soups. We should also order the blintzes."

"I thought you said the soup was a meal in itself. You always told me as a detective you're suspicious of people with ironclad alibis."

"I'll take whatever I don't eat back with me," Yablonsky said. "*I'm* suspicious of them. But you don't have to be. You're not a detective."

"Who do you think killed those men then?"

Yablonsky buttered two onion rolls, handed one to Flood. "Terrorists."

Flood looked at him unhappily. "Still sticking to that? You know, if the Feds were right and Miguel and Montoya were going to kill Suarez that night, whoever exploded that bomb probably saved Suarez's life."

"That's my guess, too."

"If the bomb was intended for Suarez, that means another man was killed by mistake. I wonder if the men who exploded the bomb can live with that."

"I think they can," Yablonsky said. "My understanding from the newspapers was that Montoya was going to replace Suarez in the delegation. He'd probably have been worse."

"Replacements usually are," Flood said. "The bomb's really shaken everyone up. I mean, on the streets of New York. This is not Lebanon."

"The news and TV reports say it happened at an intersection during early morning. If it was, in fact, run by remote control, the terrorists were able to see that no one else was around. No other people were injured."

"Considerate terrorists," Flood said.

Yablonsky didn't answer. Flood ate his onion roll. "Ramirez's government is furious," he said. "My backchannel sources tell me they want you prosecuted. If we take no action they threaten to go to the newspapers with their suspicions about you."

Yablonsky reached for an ashtray. No matter what he *had* done on that night, he realized the Feds and Ramirez would assume he'd exploded that bomb. "I won't let myself be prosecuted," he said, enjoying using the same words that Suarez had used earlier. The man had been responsible for four deaths in this city. Six if you wanted to be ironic and include Miguel and Montoya. Yablonsky didn't know what had happened to Suarez—but wherever he was he wasn't happy. He was probably in fear of his life. In a world where UN delegations in effect received licenses to commit crimes, he knew he'd have to be satisfied with that. "Tell your backchannel sources that if any action is taken against me, I'll go to the newspapers with those pictures I have of Suarez and half the male strippers of New York. I also have photos of his Latin American victims. Word's already leaked out about his real estate transactions. The photos will make it worse. For Ramirez. And the UN."

Flood sipped his glass of water and smiled. "It's nice to have deep pockets, isn't it?"

"I also want the investigation by Internal Affairs ended. If those photos start circulating, the Feds will inevitably be drawn into the picture too. That'll be embarrassing for them because it will become obvious that they know what goes on concerning the UN."

"I'll tell them," Flood said. "A lot of our people despise these delegates. I bet they'll let you get away with it."

A muzak version of one of Susan's tamer songs filled the

restaurant. Flood looked at Yablonsky and tried not to smile. "It's not Sinatra."

Yablonsky nodded. Since Susan's death her music was being played more frequently than before. He'd have to get used to that. He imagined himself a month from now. Turning on the TV and catching glimpses of her on MTV as if she were still alive.

Despite her mediocre talent, she'd become a cult figure for sure. Yablonsky was certain where her career would go. "The movie version of her songs will be better," he said. "They'll probably use a different singer."

"Maybe." Flood's eyes narrowed. "Will you accept a warning from me?"

"Keep out of classy, expensive restaurants," Yablonsky said.

"Right. Your stomach will be the ruination of you, despite your abilities. You don't see me coming to places like this, do you? You don't see me endangering my career over comped checks and free food. I usually eat at the precinct. Cold sandwiches and warm Coke."

The waiter came over. A smile lit his face. "The usual, captain?"

If you have enjoyed this book and would like to receive details of other Walker mystery titles, please write to:

Mystery Editor
Walker and Company
720 Fifth Avenue
New York, NY 10019